Unconditional

An Alessi Brother Novel

Sonia Stanizzo

Contents

To My Readers
Thank You!

Chapter One

ALYSSA

Rain pours hard and fast as I glance up at the dark sky from the doorway of *The Temple*, a strip club I work at. Sheets of water obscures my vision of the New York City street. Should I go inside and wait out the rain? I'm sure if I did, my manager would ask me to either work the bar or do another dance set. My ankle is throbbing after rolling it during my routine. I need to get home as soon as possible to ice it. With a ten AM audition for a musical tomorrow morning, I can't afford to have an injury.

Hovering at the doorway, waiting for the rain to subside, a couple of men brush past me to enter the club. I don't miss the way their gazes travel over my body. I'm wearing an oversized black t-shirt, black stockings, and biker boots. My dark brown hair is in loose waves down my back, and with my stage makeup, I can tell they think I'm a stripper from the club. Their sleezy grins tell me they're hoping I'll come back inside and give them a lap dance. I'm not that kind of dancer. I don't strip, and I definitely don't give lap dances. My sets are classy, well-choreographed dance routines. Not that there's anything wrong with stripping. A girl needs to make money. I just prefer to make mine with my clothes on.

"Keep moving," I tell them before they can make lewd remarks. I know the type. Men who've had far too many drinks and think they're Adonis and us mortal women will fall at their feet begging for their attention. I don't fall at no man's feet.

Turning my attention back to the stormy sky, I sigh with indecision. Do I wait it out or go back inside? The longer I stand at the doorway, the longer I'm putting weight on my ankle. I need to be physically fit for tomorrow. The thought of another audition and another rejection sits heavily on my chest. How many more can I take?

I shake off the melancholy. I have bigger things to worry about right now, like making my way home without getting saturated. With a dubious glance at the sky, I sigh. There's no chance I'll get out of here dry.

Making up my mind, I toss my dance bag over my shoulder, tuck my makeup kit under my arm, and with my free hand, flick open my umbrella and step out onto the street. Within seconds, a gust of chilly wind whips the umbrella inside out. I try to shake it back into place with no luck. Water is stinging my face and plastering my t-shirt to my body.

As I fumble with the umbrella, the makeup kit drops onto the ground. With rain trickling into my eyes and wind blowing hair into my face, I can't see, and I trip over the makeup kit. At lightning speed, the ground rushes up to my face. My arms flay about as I make one last attempt at steadying myself. It doesn't work. All I can do is hold out my hands to save myself from face-planting the concrete.

With a thud, I hit the ground hard, knocking the breath from my lungs. In a state of shock, I push myself up and sit in a puddle. Looking at my hands, I hiss at the stinging skin ripped off my palms. The backs of my eyes prickle with tears. "Motherfucker."

"Hey, are you okay?" a deep voice says from behind me.

My face heats with embarrassment that people around me have witnessed my fall. A man squats next to me, and I swipe at the water from my eyes. Is it rain or tears? Maybe a combination of both. I turn my face away so he doesn't see how mortified I am.

"So much for falling at no man's feet," I mumble under my breath.

"What did you say?"

Crap! I didn't mean for him to hear.

"I'm fine, thanks," I answer his first question. Scrambling to my feet, I wince as I put weight on my injured ankle. Shit! It feels worse than before.

"Careful." The man tentatively places a hand on my elbow, like he's asking permission to touch me. I don't shrug him off—now that the embarrassment is wearing off, I'm grateful for the support. "You're hurt. Let's get you out of the rain."

Dropping his hand, he picks up my bag and makeup kit. The no-good umbrella is nowhere to be seen. He then guides me as I hobble to an awning over a closed tobacco store. In the dim light shining from the window, I take my first look at the good Samaritan.

My breath catches in my lungs. Dark, wet hair clings to his forehead. Damp, spikey lashes frame hazel eyes. Stubble covers a strong, square jawline. His saturated white, wet shirt clings to impressive muscles, defining his huge physique. He looks hot as hell while I must look like a drowned rat.

My rescuer is none other than Hayden Alessi. Part owner of the world's most successful fashion house, Alessi Fashion, and my best friend Harper's brother-in-law. I briefly met him once at Harper and Finn's wedding and saw him from the distance in the club over a year ago. He has a face that can't be forgotten.

Standing so close under the small shelter, I breathe in his citrusy cologne mixed with the rain. Heat coils in my belly. I may be embarrassed and aching in certain body parts, but there's nothing wrong with my eyes. Rubbing my hand along my arm, fire shoots through my palms. I bite my lip through the pain.

"You've hurt your hand. Can I see?" he asks.

At my nod, he places my bag and makeup kit on the ground. He takes my hands into his large ones and leans down to get a better look. His lush hair falls forward, and if he weren't holding my hands, I'd like to run my fingers through his dark locks.

"Does it sting?" He tilts his head back to look at me, and I get caught in his beautiful eyes. When seconds pass and I don't respond, he frowns and scans my head. "Did you hit your head when you fell?"

Snapping out of my trance, I say, "No, I didn't hit my head. My palms only sting a little." Not letting go of my hands, he does another scan of my head, probably looking for lumps and bruises just to be sure.

"You need to clean the grit from your palms as soon as possible, Alyssa. You don't want this to get infected." He lets go of my hands and I immediately miss the warmth.

"You know who I am?"

He shuffles back a step like he's realized he's standing too close. "We met at Finn and Harper's wedding."

"Yes, I remember. I'm surprised you do." After the introduction, he took off so fast, I thought he had an emergency to get to. For the rest of the night, to my disappointment, he never came near me or looked at me again.

"How could I forget?" His voice deepens to just above a whisper, sending tingles up and down my spine. For a beat, our eyes hold. Breaking the connection, he clears his throat, looks at his feet, then up the street before looking at me again. "You were so busy running around after the bride you were hard to miss."

Right...of course. Being the dutiful maid of honor kept me in the spotlight too. I'm not that memorable. Just like in auditions. Story of my freaking life. "It was such a beautiful day."

"Yes, beautiful." His gaze flicks over my face.

For some reason, I'm thinking he doesn't mean the wedding. Surely, he's not talking about me. A horn from a nearby car blasts through my thoughts, and he glances away.

The rain tapping on the awning eases. A weak, pale glow from the moon is shining through the parting clouds. As much as I'd like to stay here with Hayden a little longer, I need to get to the subway. I hate catching it so late. "I should head home. Thank you for helping me, Hayden."

Instead of moving aside, we stare at each other. I get caught in his eyes. When his gaze drops to my lips, my breath catches in my chest. Like I'm being pulled to him—hoping for something I have no right to because I hardly know the man—I step closer. Pain shoots through my ankle. I groan as it gives way from under me. Damn it! What a way to ruin the moment.

Hayden holds my elbows to steady me. "You've hurt yourself. Let me check your ankle."

I don't care about my ankle; I want to go back to the *moment*. Was it a *moment*? Or was I imagining things under the mask of the silvery moonlight? Whatever it was, it made my libido spike to the heavens. Well, until my damn ankle messed it up.

Hayden squats, and his gaze travels over my legs. Unfortunately, not in an I-want-to-remove-your-pants-and-get-it-on kind of way.

He looks up at me. "How well do you deal with blood?"

"Blood?" With a quick glance at my leg, I see a bloody gash on my knee through a tear in my tights. I sway, and Hayden springs up and grasps me by the forearms before I land on my ass again.

"I'm guessing from the color draining from your face, you don't do too well with blood." He chuckles softly. "Between your banged-up knee and swollen ankle, I'm surprised you're still standing. You better sit down before you face-plant the ground again."

"I didn't face-plant the ground." I hold up my skinned palms. "My hands saved me." All jokes aside, my ankle is hurting like a mother-fucker. I really need to get home and get off my feet. "I have to go. Thanks again for your help." I limp around him and hiss through my teeth.

"I'll give you a ride," he offers.

"That's okay, the subway isn't far."

He shakes his head. "You can't catch the train in your condition. You're soaking wet, you'll either freeze to death or expire from blood loss." His full, kissable lips twitch to the side. Lips I wish I was kissing right now.

"I'd hate for that to happen." I smile back while imagining what his lips would taste like. Oh God, what is wrong with me? I'm wet, bleeding, in pain, and yet, I'm lusting over Hayden Alessi. A kind man who is just trying to help me in my time of need.

"My car is parked a few feet away. If you hold on to me, do you think you can walk to it? If not, I can carry you."

Have I just stepped into a romantic comedy? The term 'swept off your feet' is well-known, but do men carry women these days? None of the guys I've dated would ever suggest such a thing. Probably because they were half the size of Hayden with the muscle density of a toddler. Hayden's broad chest and muscular arms tells me he wouldn't have a problem whisking me off my feet. As romantic as that looks in my head, I can't let him do that.

"I can walk," I say.

Picking up the dance bag, he adjusts the strap over his shoulder. Next, he picks up the makeup kit and tucks it under his arm. Reaching out his free arm, he says, "I'll hold you around the waist and hold you up so you can lean on me for support. Will that work for you, Twinkle Toes?"

I cock an eyebrow. "Twinkle Toes?"

"You're a dancer. It suits you." A teasing smile crosses his face. Oh, it's so sexy, I feel it down to my toes.

I make a face like I don't like it. Deep down I can't help the joy filling my heart that he's given me a nickname. "At the moment, my toes are far from twinkling." I grimace.

His face drops. "Come on, let's get you home."

Shuffling against his side, I place my arm around his solid back. Muscles ripple under my palm when he moves. He slides an arm around my waist, resting his hand on my hip. With the side of my torso pressed against his, a wave of heat washes over me.

"Are you ready?" Hayden asks. His Adam's apple bobs as he swallows hard. Is he feeling an attraction too?

Not trusting myself to speak, I nod my head.

"We'll take it slow. Let me know if you need to stop."

Again, I nod. If I open my mouth to speak, I'd only make incoherent sounds. The feeling of our bodies pressing together has caused my brain to short-circuit.

We take tentative steps with no mishaps, and I hobble to the car, late night wanderers bypassing us on the way. I love the way Hayden's warm body feels against mine. His heat burning off the wet chill.

Too soon, we're standing at his black Bentley. I wish the walk had been longer so Hayden could keep holding me. To my disappointment, he lets me go and leans me up against the car so he can open the passenger side door, then he helps me slide onto the soft, leather seats.

Hayden jogs around the front of the car, opens the door, and settles into the driver's seat. Reaching into the backseat, he pulls out a navy sweatshirt and hands it to me. "Here, put this on."

"You're wet and must be cold too. I can't take it from you." I try to give it back to him. His large hands cover the tops of mine, stopping me.

"I'm fine. I don't want you to freeze to death."

"Thank you." I slide the soft, warm sweatshirt over my body, getting surrounded by his manly scent.

"Better?"

"Yes. Thanks."

"Where am I taking you?" he asks.

I give Hayden my address, and he pulls onto the street.

"You danced at *The Temple* tonight?" The lights on the dashboard reflect on his face as he concentrates on driving.

"Yes, but I just dance, I don't strip if that's what you're asking," I say in case he doesn't remember the time he watched me dance when he came into the club with his brothers. "Not that there's anything wrong with stripping." I get a little snappy. I'm tired of judgemental people.

For a second, he takes his hands off the wheel, holding them up like he's surrendering. "Hey, it was just a question."

"Sorry. When I tell people I dance at a strip club, most automatically judge. No one should pass judgment on how people have to make a living."

"Agree. I've seen you dance, you're very talented. I'd say your talent is wasted at a place like The Temple."

So, he remembers. "Don't I know it."

He turns his head to give me a quick look before he flicks his attention back onto the road. "You don't want to work there?"

"You've seen the club. What do you think?" Although the club is supposed to be stripping and lap dances only, the ladies frequently take customers into a private room for a more 'personal' lap dance for extra cash.

"So why are you working there?"

Good question. Why *am* I? "I moved from Paris to New York four years ago, determined to make it on my own. I needed money fast, and The Temple was hiring." I'm still surprised they agreed to let me keep my clothes on. Although, what I wear leaves little to the imagination.

"Why New York?" He takes the corner and then stops at a red light.

"I grew up here, and I have big dreams of making it onto Broadway." Is it actually my dream, or am I trying to live up to my family's expectations? Either way, I have something to prove, and I will not fail.

Looking over at me, he says, "By your tone, I'm guessing it hasn't worked out for you yet."

I lean my elbow on the window and drop my head on my fist. "No, not really. Sometimes I wonder if it ever will. I've landed in the ensemble a couple of times, which was great. But my dream is a principal role." That's the only thing my parents will consider successful. "How long do I keep trying?"

"For as long as it feels right."

"How do I know if it feels right?"

He turns toward me and looks straight into my eyes. Soft wings flutter in my chest. "If it makes you happy. When you feel that's the only thing you want to do deep in your gut."

At the moment, with Hayden looking at me that way, my gut's telling me I want this man. This is crazy! I don't even know him.

The light changes to green, and Hayden turns away and starts driving. Before I can think about what craziness is coming over me, he pulls up in front of my building. A run-down townhouse I used to share with Harper. Now that she's married to Hayden's brother Finn, I haven't looked for another roommate. No one can replace my best friend.

Unbuckling, I twist in the seat to face Hayden. "Thanks again for your help. I really appreciate it." I want to ask him in...for what? Coffee... To chat... Sex?

I mentally slap my forehead. He did a good deed for me, and all I'm thinking about is wanting to take his clothes off. It's only been three weeks since I last had sex. That was with a guy I'd been seeing for several months. The relationship ended when he wanted to invite other women into the bed. I haven't been without sex long enough for me to be feeling this tight ball of lust.

"No problem. I'll grab your bags and help you inside," he says.

Great. He solved my dilemma of asking him in. Although, I have to keep things PG. Why though? *Just because he's looked at your lips and stared into your eyes doesn't mean he wants the same thing. That's why.* Maybe I did knock my head when I fell. That would explain my wandering thoughts. But it doesn't explain the way my body is reacting to him.

So I don't sound like a totally hopeless case, I say, "It's not far. I'll be fine." I don't want to put him out or put myself closer to temptation.

He unbuckles his seatbelt and gives me a dubious look. "Yeah, right."

He gets out of the car, collects my bags from the backseat, and jogs around to the passenger side, helping me from the seat. Standing next to me, he holds onto me much like he did earlier.

"Are you okay with walking? I can carry you if that's easier."

Again, the offer to carry me. Not only is he freaking gorgeous, but he's also caring and sweet. I imagine him sweeping me off my feet like I weigh no more than a feather, kicking open my front door, so impatient to get me to my bedroom where he'd place me on the bed ever so gently. What wasn't so gentle was the way he'd devour my body and— Oh God! What is happening to me?

"Twinkle Toes, are you okay to walk?" he asks again. Oh, how I'm loving that name.

"Yes, I can walk."

"Hold on to me like you did earlier." He slides a hand around my waist. Just an innocent touch is giving me not-so-innocent thoughts.

Slowly, we walk up the cracked, concrete path leading to the building. Once inside we carefully climb the rickety, timber stairs. Stopping at my door, I dig out the key from my bag hanging over Hayden's shoulder and unlock the door.

"Thanks again for your help," I say. "You've been so kind. I have to tell Harper her brother-in-law is a knight in shining armor."

He chuckles. "I couldn't let you sit injured in a puddle of water."

"Well, I appreciate it. I don't know what I would have done without you."

His arm is still around my waist. The side of my body is still pressed against him. It's like we don't want to let each other go.

His gaze, once again, drops to my lips. I swallow hard. "Would you like to...arhhh...come in?"

"Sure. I'll bring your bags in."

We step into the apartment, and I hobble to the sofa. My apartment isn't much. It's small and run-down. If it were up to my parents, they'd buy me something in SoHo Manhattan. They hate that I'm 'roughing it' as they liked to call my living arrangements. I liked to call it character building. If I'm going to be a struggling artist, I may as well live like one.

"You can place the bags over there." I point to a corner of the living room.

Hayden releases me so he can put the bags down. Immediately, I miss having him so close. Maybe I should sway on my feet so he can catch me? I mentally slap my forehead. I need to stop watching so many rom-com movies.

Taking it easy, I sit on the sofa and prop my leg on the scarred timber coffee table and take a better look at my knee. I bite my bottom lip as a chill runs over my skin. Blood has dried over a good-sized abrasion.

"You need to get dry. Where are your towels?" he asks.

I point to a door. "The bathroom's through there. Towels are on a shelf."

When he disappears to get them, I scan the room for anything I don't want Hayden to see. I'm not the tidiest person, and it's not uncommon to find a bra tossed on a piece of furniture. Thankfully, the area is clear of any underwear.

Hayden reappears holding two blue towels and hands me one of them. He uses the other to scrub his damp hair, messing it up into sexy spikes. He's just as wet as I am, but at least I'm wearing a dry sweater. *Hayden's dry sweater.*

"You must be freezing. Here, take this." I remove his sweatshirt and pass it to him.

He takes it but doesn't put it on. Placing it on the arm of the sofa, he says, "I'm okay. Can I get you something dry to put on?"

"No, that's okay. I'll jump into a hot shower to warm up."

"I'll come with you."

We both suck in a surprised gasp. Our eyes lock. My heart pounds hard against my ribs.

Hayden clears his throat and averts his gaze. "I mean, I can help you get to the bathroom. I'll give you privacy once you're inside."

Of course, he's only trying to help again. Nothing more. I mask my disappointment with a playful grin. "I'll probably need help undressing. And in case I fall, can you stand in the shower with me?"

"I... Arrhh..." He swallows hard.

I laugh softly. "I'm kidding." Or am I? I won't deny the thought is appealing. I just needed to say something to lighten up the situation.

He gives me an unsure chuckle and can't quite look me in the eyes. I wonder if he's thinking about it too.

I dab the towel carefully over my tights, avoiding my injured knee. "You need ice on your ankle and a patch on your knee." He points toward the adjoining kitchenette. "Do you have an icepack in the freezer?"

"I'm a dancer. There's always an icepack in my freezer. I'll get it." I stand without putting pressure on my ankle.

Stepping in front of me, he places his hands on my elbows. We're so close I have to tilt my head back to look into his eyes. With our chests almost touching, the heat from his body sizzles toward me, burning off any lingering chill.

A flash of desire lights up in his eyes. Is he going to kiss me? I lean a little closer to test whether he'll follow through. All too soon, the look disappears and he shakes his head like he's clearing away his thoughts.

Guiding me to sit back on the sofa, he says, "I'll get the icepack. Prop your foot on the coffee table and rest. Do you have a first aid kit?"

"On top of the fridge."

He heads into the kitchenette. With a sigh of frustration, I sink into the sofa, tilt my head back, and stare at the ceiling. Am I imagining the attraction between us? The looks Hayden has given me are enough to melt my panties off. Something is holding him back. But what?

Before I can think too much about it, he's back with the icepack and first aid kit. Hayden kneels in front of me and assesses my leg. "I need to take your boots off. I'll be as gentle as possible. Are you ready?"

I nod. My body tenses, waiting for the jolt of pain.

He unfastens the thick, black laces from my boot. I'm always wearing ballet and tap shoes or stripper heels; biker boots make me feel badass. They also go with the black cargo pants I usually favor.

Hayden opens the boot as wide as it can go. "Tell me if I'm hurting you." Slowly, he slips it off my foot.

My body relaxes when the pain doesn't hit. He's so gentle. "You're not," I say.

After removing the other boot, he wraps the icepack around my ankle.

I hiss.

"Did I hurt you?" His gaze flicks up at me with concern.

I shake my head. "It's cold."

"It's an icepack, it's supposed to be cold." He grins. That smile hits me straight in the chest.

I roll my eyes. "Ha-ha."

Pointing to my ankle, he says, "It's swollen and bruised. You should have someone look at it in case you've done some serious damage."

"It's fine. I've done worse. It will be back to normal in a day or two." I hope. I have dance classes, work, and of course auditions I need to get back to as soon as possible.

Next, he looks at my knee through the frayed edges of my tights. "I need to get the grit out of the wound, or it might get infected."

"That's okay. I can manage." He's done so much for me already; he shouldn't have to clean me up too.

"Relax. I can get to it better than you can." He unzips the first aid kit, removing saline spray, antiseptic wipes, and a bandage, placing them next to me on the sofa.

Relax! How can I relax with him kneeling between my legs? What would happen if I let them fall apart? Would he look? Touch?

Why am I feeling like a horny teenager? I need to get a grip. He's here to help me. Nothing more. I plaster on a smile and say, "Thank you."

"It...arhh...might be easier to clean and bandage your knee if you take your...arhh, tights off."

Did his face flush pink? Oh, how adorable. He doesn't look like a man who'd be embarrassed taking off women's clothes. In fact, he looks like a man who'd enjoy tearing them off with his teeth.

"You can cover yourself with the towel if that makes you more comfortable," he suggested.

I tug at my oversized t-shirt that acts like a short dress. It's not long enough to avoid flashing Hayden my goods when my tights are off. Not that I'd care. But if he flushed bright pink at the suggestion of taking my tights off, what would he do if I flashed him my lady parts? I can't do that to him.

Taking Hayden's advice, I drape the towel over my lap. With awkward movements, I shuffle to get my hands under my t-shirt and to the waistband of the tights. The movement puts pressure on my ankle, and I whimper. Shit! That's not a good sign. If that slight movement is causing pain, maybe I've done more damage than I thought.

At the sound of my discomfort, Hayden places a gentle hand on my knee, stopping me from moving again. "Don't move. Let me help you."

Help me? The only way he can help me is to take the tights off of me himself. *Oh boy!*

"If you prop yourself up onto your hands, I can slide the tights down your legs for you," he continues, unaware of the heat fanning my insides.

I sit in silence as steamy fantasies play out in my mind. First, he'd remove my tights, then slide his hands up the inside of my thighs until he reaches my—

"Alyssa?"

I snap out of my daydream. "Yes?" What did he say?

"Is it okay?" His deep voice washes over me.

"Huh?" My brain is still filled with the remnants of my fantasy.

"Is it okay if I take your tights off?"

"Yes!" I reply, sounding a little eager. In a more subdued tone, I say, "That would be helpful. Thank you." His lips quirk into a grin, causing my stomach to somersault.

Propping myself onto my hands, careful of the scrapes on my palms, I lift my butt off the sofa. On his knees, Hayden shuffles closer. My heart accelerates. My arms grow weak, and not because of my weight. With a feather-light touch, Hayden's hands skim slowly along my thighs, disappearing underneath my shirt. My eyes drift closed for a beat. Are my fantasies coming to life? I suck in a breath as he reaches the top of my legs.

"Did I hurt you?" He raises his gaze to me. Desire shoots from his eyes, replacing the adorable, embarrassed expression from moments ago. This man is far from adorable. He is pure sex on a stick. And the way he's looking at me is making me burn.

I'm so caught up in his gaze, I can't form any words, so I merely shake my head no.

Trailing his hands to my waist, his eyes remain locked with mine. At the waistband of my tights, he pauses for a beat before sliding his fingers under the elastic. The backs of his fingers brush along my skin, leaving a trail of fire.

I bite my bottom lip to stop myself from making any inappropriate sounds. The gesture makes his eyes zero in on my mouth, looking like he wants to devour it. I haven't imagined the way he looks at me. This man wants me as much as I want him.

As much as I love the way he's staring at me, my arms are fatiguing from holding myself up in an awkward position. "Are you having trouble removing my tights?"

He shuffles on his knees. "Just trying not to hurt you."

Yeah, right. I know an I-want-to-jump-your-bones look when I see one. I inwardly smile at his lie.

His nimble fingers slide the fabric down my stomach. As he hits lower on my hips, they snag onto my G-string. He pauses and drops his head forward like what he's doing is exhausting. Like he's losing a fight he's inwardly battling. When he raises his head, his jaw is clenched, his chest heaving. Does he want to touch me more intimately as badly as I want him to? With each hard swallow, his Adam's apple bobs. For a second, his eyes squeeze shut.

"On or off?" he asks, his voice deep and husky, barely above a whisper.

On or off? He's already taking my tights off— Oh! He's not talking about my tights. He wants to know if I want my panties on or off. A pool of desire floods to those panties. I've been fantasizing about this since he first touched me. Now that I know we're on the same page, can I go through with it? Can I let a man who I only know of through my best friend, a man who is practically a stranger, touch me sexually? Will I let this lead to sex?

From the moment he helped me from the ground, my body has reacted to him like I've been familiar with him for years. Which is ridiculous. How can that be? This has never happened to me before.

With his fingers still hooked in my panties, I know he's waiting for an answer. I'm not usually a one-night-stand kind of girl, nor do I need to have a deep and meaningful relationship. Sometimes I have needs. Buy me a drink and take me out to dinner, and if sparks fly, I'd be up for some dancing under the sheets. Hayden's giving off more than sparks. I'm getting zapped by lightning bolts.

When I don't respond, because my tongue is stuck to the roof of my mouth, he asks again, this time through gritted teeth. "On or off?"

"Off," I whisper. "Definitely off."

Hayden blows out a long breath. "Thank fuck."

He takes his sweet damn time pulling the tights and panties to my knees, taking extra care with pulling them over my wound. I want to scream with frustration at how slow he's moving.

My gaze is drawn to his damp shirt stretching across his broad chest, and my fingers itch to pop open the buttons. He doesn't give me the time to follow through because his hands are on my thighs, causing my legs to roll open and my nipples to poke through the fabric of my t-shirt into hard twin peaks, giving him the suck-me signal.

His palms glide up my legs, and once again, disappear under my oversized t-shirt. I squirm on the seat, my sex throbbing with need.

"I shouldn't be doing this," he says as a hand floats over my sex, sliding down to the center of my slit.

At his touch, my hips buck off the sofa, pressing me firmer against his hand. A finger enters me. I moan. Oh, this feels so good. I need more. But there's something niggling at the back of my mind. What is it? My brain has short-circuited with his fingers doing all these wonderful things.

Oh...he said he shouldn't be doing this. "Why?" I'm almost too scared to ask in case it makes him pull out of me. I lift my hips a little so he knows I want more.

With a growl, he says, "Fuck what I said." Keeping one hand busy between my legs, he braces the other hand on the back of the sofa, next to my head, diving into a kiss. His lips are demanding, and I open to him.

All thoughts of not normally being a one-night-stand kind of girl disappear. The kiss, me riding his hand, solidifies that sometimes in life you have to live a little. Take the bull by its horns—or in this case, Hayden by the waist—and take what you want.

He breaks the kiss to run his tongue along the curve of my neck and over my racing pulse, giving me a moment to catch my breath. I run my hands over the muscley plane of his back to his ass and back up again. The man is impressively built. What's even more impressive is his enormous erection prodding against my thigh. His jeans are an annoying barrier between us. He skims his mouth from my neck to my breasts, and I suck in a gasp as he draws a nipple into his mouth, his hand massaging my other breast in a slow, circular motion.

He pulls back to say, "I want to see you naked. Top off. Now!"

Gone is the blushing man from earlier. I love the take-charge side of Hayden. It's so sexy. A quiver shimmers down my spine, and I gladly do as I'm told. Yanking off my top, I toss it on the floor. I hadn't bothered with a bra; my B-cup breasts need little restraining. Once I'm completely naked and exposed to him, his gaze travels over my body with appreciation.

Staring at my heaving chest for a beat, he then cups my breasts in his firm hands, flicking his thumbs over my hardened nipples. "You're gorgeous. Perfect."

He looks quite enamored by my itty-bitty titties. A lot of guys don't pay them much attention. I guess they're not impressed by their size. Hayden's looking at them like they're the best thing he's ever seen.

When he closes his mouth on them, he devours them like they're the best thing he's ever tasted. My head falls back on the sofa, and I moan my pleasure, hooking my good leg around his waist and pulling him closer. I want to give him the hint that he can take things further. Not that I'm not enjoying him worshiping my chest, but with the way my body is coiled up so tight, I'm not sure how long I'm going to last.

Leaning forward, I reach between our bodies and unzip his jeans. My hands shake as I slide them into his underwear, taking hold of his hard, hot cock. With a firm grip, I squeeze and slowly stroke.

Hayden tosses his head back and groans, "Fuck, that feels good."

I encourage him to pump in my hand, and his hips thrust forward. Being naked with my sex on display and his dick in my hand, I want this man inside me now! I shift my butt closer to the edge of the sofa. It's not easy to get myself in the perfect position with one leg propped up on the coffee table, but I'll make it work even if it kills me.

Hayden notices my predicament. "Let me take you to bed so I can kiss every inch of you and fuck you properly."

Oh. My insides quiver. No one has ever been so forward with me like this before. I freaking love it! His bossiness and take-charge attitude makes me wet. I quickly nod my agreement, and he helps me from the sofa.

Standing naked against him, while he's fully clothed, I search for my t-shirt to cover up. *Remember you're taking the bull by its horns—or more like Hayden by whatever body part you can hold onto.* Preferably what's between his legs. Forgetting about the t-shirt, I press myself against him and wrap my arm around his waist.

Hayden dips at the knees. "Fuck, Alyssa, you're killing me," he says on a strangled sigh. "If it weren't for your ankle, I'd fuck you where you stand." This time my legs do give out. Hayden throws his arms around my waist to support me. "Where's your bedroom?"

The apartment is tiny, yet my room feels like it's a mile away. I point to my door. Hayden whisks me off my feet, and with two long strides, he's in my room. He carefully lays me on the bed and straightens, looking at me with so much desire my belly flutters at the thought of what's to come.

"Are you sure you want to do this?" he asks.

At the moment I want nothing more. "Yes, I want this."

"Your leg?"

"I can barely feel it." It's true. Adrenaline has taken over. It might hurt like a bitch in the morning, but it will be worth it.

He stands at the side of the bed, and I watch him unbutton his shirt. Tanned skin with a light dusting of dark hair on his chest peeks from the parted fabric. With his shirt slightly open, his jeans unzipped, I've never seen a man this sexy in my life. I can't wait to see more.

Before Hayden joins me on the bed, a cell phone rings from the living room. It isn't my ringtone, so it must be Hayden's.

He stiffens. "I need to get that. It might be my—"

"Oh God. Please don't say wife." Earlier, he said he shouldn't be doing this. Is it because he's married?

His lips curl into a smile. "I'm not married. It might be my daughter. She's staying at Finn and Harper's tonight. I'll be right back." With that, he rushes from the room.

I blow out a relieved breath. Of course he doesn't have a wife. I knew that. Harper has mentioned it. For a second, my brain had malfunctioned.

While he's in the living room, I take the time to finger-comb my damp hair, cup a hand over my mouth to smell my breath, and check to see if the laser treatment I've been paying a fortune on is keeping downstairs hair-free. Should I get under the covers or stay on top?

Do I have condoms? Crap! I haven't bought any in a long time. Twisting to my side, I open the nightstand drawer and scatter the few items inside around. I find a box at the back of the drawer and open it. Thank God it's not empty. Should I take one out and leave it on the bed? Will one be enough?

Christ! Why am I so nervous?

After a few more moments of fidgeting, I hear the front door open and close. What the...

"Hayden! Is everything okay?" I'm met with silence. "Hayden!" I call again.

Nothing.

Getting out of bed, I reach for the fluffy robe on the chair in the corner of the room and slip it on, tightening the belt around my waist. Using the walls as a crutch, I hobble to the living room.

"Hayden?" I glance around the room and into the kitchenette.

My shoulders sag.

Hayden is gone.

Chapter Two

HAYDEN

As I drive away from Alyssa's apartment, I shake my head with shame. I'm an asshole for not telling her I was leaving. It would have taken less than a minute to let her know I had to go to my daughter. I'm sure she would have understood. Instead, I left her naked on the bed, aroused and waiting for me to return. I couldn't go back and finish what we started. Because I don't do this. I don't fuck around. Thankfully, the phone call snapped me out of my daze.

Alyssa had mesmerized me. Sucked me into a haze of lust and wanting. Something that hasn't happened in years. Something I don't *allow* to happen. So, I panicked and ran. Not because the call was urgent. Harper had called to tell me Lily had a bad dream and was asking for me. She insisted Lily was okay, she'd settled her and not to hurry, but I used the distraction as an excuse to flee. *Like a scared fucking asshole.*

I was terrified of going back into the bedroom. What if I got caught up again, making a huge mistake? There is a reason I don't do shit like that—sleep with random women or women at all. For the last eight years, my hand had worked perfectly well when I needed the release. And I've never given into temptation, no matter how beautiful the woman. Until Alyssa. From the moment I put my hands on her, I knew I wanted her more than anything.

No, that's a lie. I've wanted her from the moment I first saw her dance. A night over a year ago when Finn convinced me to spend my free night from Lily and go with him to The Temple. I watched Alyssa dance, enthralled by the way her body moved. The way she got caught up in the music, looking as if she'd forgotten there was a room full of people watching her.

I've been back three times since. I'm rarely alone at night or I'd probably go back more often. Tonight, like the times before, I sat in a dark corner of the club, waiting for her to come on the stage. She never knows I'm there. I don't want her to know. Because I'm not there for a strip show or a drink. I'm there to see Alyssa.

In the car ride to Alyssa's apartment, I'd acted like I didn't know she'd been working tonight. God, what kind of sick fuck does that make me? After what happened between us, I can't go back to The Temple. Keeping away from temptation is for the best.

Shoving my fingers through my hair, I blow out a long breath. Tonight, I'd let my guard down. I don't do relationships, and I'm not interested in one-night stands anymore. Speaking from experience, they can change your life in an instant. I'm focusing on raising Lily and not letting any distractions get in the way. Especially a woman in an oversized AC/DC t-shirt, combat boots, and a face and body to die for.

Arriving at Finn and Harper's house, I knock on the door.

A few seconds later, Harper answers. "You didn't have to rush. She's okay."

"Where is she?" I ask as I step inside.

"In the kitchen with Finn, having hot chocolate."

Following Harper, I find Lily sitting at the breakfast bar, sipping from a red mug. Finn paces the room, rocking his one-month-old daughter, Avery, in his arms. The baby's the reason Lily wanted a sleepover, to spend time with her cousin.

When Lily sees me, her eyes light up. "Daddy!" At eight years old, Lily thinks she's too old to call me Daddy. Most days, she calls me Dad. But sometimes Daddy slips out, and I love hearing it. She's growing up too fast. I want to hold onto these moments forever.

"Hey, Lily Pily." I whisk her off the stool and prop her on my hip. Another sign of her growing up is that she's getting a little heavy and big to be held like this, but I'll hold her for as long as possible. "Everything okay?"

Her soft arms wrap around my neck. "Yep," she says with a slight crease between her eyebrows.

"Aunt Harper said you woke up because you had a bad dream. Do you want to tell me about it?" I rub soothing circles on her back.

"I can't remember it."

"Why are you dressed like that? Have you been out?" Finn rakes his gaze over me. "It's two AM. Shouldn't you be in bed?"

I put Lily back on the stool. Folding my arms across my chest, I reply, "Couldn't sleep."

"Couldn't sleep or couldn't *sleep*?" Finn wiggles his eyebrows with mirth as he bounces Avery in his arms.

Finn is onto me. I'm still going to try to get him off the scent. "I went for a drive." What I do in my own time is none of his business.

"Must have been a good *drive*." Finn points to my chest. I look down. In my haste to hightail it out of Alyssa's apartment, I'd mismatched the buttons of my shirt. Shit! I quickly adjust them.

"Anyone we know?" Harper whispers with a smile, trying not to let Lily overhear the conversation. Thankfully, she's flipping through a book, showing no interest in what we're saying.

"No," I lie. There's no point denying I've been with a woman, but I don't have to tell them who I was with. I don't know how Harper would feel about me leaving her best friend in bed without an explanation. Although, if they're close, Alyssa might tell Harper what an asshole I am. I'll deal with that when or if it happens.

"Damn, I hope we didn't disturb you before you finished. That would suck, considering how long it's been since...you know..." Finn glances at Lily. "You read a book." He gives me a cocky grin. I want to wipe the smug smile off his face. It's times like these I wish I wasn't so close to my brothers. We know too much about each other's personal lives.

I scowl at Finn.

"I take it that the book didn't have a happy ending?" Finn snickers.

"This book has a happy ending, Dad. You can read this one." Lily slides the book on the counter toward me. So much for her not listening.

"Thanks, Lily Pily." I throw Finn a filthy look. It only makes him grin harder.

"Lily, let's take Avery to the nursery. You can help me change her diaper before we put her back to bed." Harper lifts the sleepy baby from Finn's arms.

It's surreal seeing my younger brother with a kid of his own. Not so long ago, after a terrible breakup, he'd sworn off relationships forever, and now he's a husband and a father. It suits him.

Lily slides off the stool and holds onto Harper's free hand, following her from the room.

As soon as the girls disappear, Finn turns to me with a huge, shit-eating grin. "Man, I'm sorry we interrupted your night."

"Your joyful expression says otherwise," I say derisively and perch onto the stool Lily vacated.

Finn scratches the stubble on his chin. "I didn't get the name of the woman you were with."

"You know perfectly well, asshole, that I didn't give it to you."

Finn chuckles, not taking offense at the name-calling. "So, who is she?"

My lips are sealed tight.

Slapping his hand on the counter, he laughs. "It *is* someone we know!"

"I didn't say—"

"It's written on your face. I know you too well. How long have you been seeing her? Is it serious? How have you hidden this from us?"

Squirming in my seat, not comfortable with the interrogation, I grumble, "What's with the twenty fucking questions?"

"I'm curious." Finn shrugs a shoulder.

"Well, it's none of your damn business." Since when has Finn become a gossip?

"Come on, man. Give me something. All I talk about these days are dirty diapers, baby bottles, and feeding schedules. I haven't slept in weeks."

"And you're loving every second." I've never seen Finn so happy.

Finn's longer-than-normal hair hangs over his forehead, dark circles smudge under his eyes, and it looks like he hasn't shaved in days, but his face lights up with pride. "Yeah, my baby and baby momma are awesome."

"I should let you get back to them." And hopefully stop him from asking questions. I rise from the chair to get ready to leave.

Finn holds up a hand. "Not so fast. You're not getting away that easily. Does this mean you're putting yourself first for once and living a little?"

"What's that supposed to mean?"

Finn leans his hip on the counter and crosses his ankles. "Since having Lily, you live like a monk. You don't go out—"

"I go out."

Finn shakes his head. "Work doesn't count, and a lot of the time, you work from home. When was the last time you went out with buddies for a drink?"

I scratch the back of my neck. "I have Lily to think about. Now that you have Avery, you should understand that all you want to do is put her needs first. Keep her safe. You'll do anything to protect her."

"I get that. I'd die for Avery." Finn rubs a hand over his chest. His baby girl has buried herself in his heart. "But you need some time for yourself. This woman you're seeing—"

"I'm not seeing her," I interrupt. "It was just..." A mistake. Something I should never have let happen. Yet those moments together—touching her...tasting her—I can't get it out of my mind.

"You picked up a woman for a one-night stand?" Finn's eyes widen. He knows how I feel about them, and the reason I'd never have one again.

If it hadn't been for Harper's call, I would have gone against my rule. Would I have come to my senses and stopped before it was too late? The way Alyssa felt under my hands, the way my body responded to her... I'm not so sure.

"It was a mistake." I prop myself back on the stool and drop my head in my hands. "I don't know what I was thinking." I'd been thinking how much I wanted her.

Finn pushes away from the counter. "There's nothing wrong with having needs. God, you've gone eight years without sex! It's okay to let off steam occasionally. Even if it's only for a night."

"The last time I needed to 'let off steam' it changed my life forever."

Finn points at the door the girls left through. "And Lily is amazing. I bet you can't imagine life without her."

Yes, Lily *is* amazing. She's the best and hardest thing in my life. The first two years raising a baby on my own had not been easy. Yet every time she smiled, laughed, and held my hand, my heart melted more and more with love, and I'd remember how lucky I was to have her.

"Lily is a blessing, but I can't risk going through it again," I say.

"Okay, I get you're worried about sleeping with a stranger, but it doesn't mean you can't have a lasting relationship."

"A relationship is the last thing on my mind. Between work and Lily, I have no time."

Finn shakes his head. "Make time. Maybe you'll stop walking around like you have a stick up your ass and smile once in a while."

I throw Finn a fuck-you look. "I'm happy with my life the way it is."

"Yeah, it looks like it," Finn says, sarcasm dripping from the words. "Good luck having to deal with blue balls for the rest of your life." He chuckles.

"You have blue balls?" Our heads turn toward the kitchen's entrance to find Harper and Lily. Lily's eyes light up with excitement. "Can I play with them?"

⸻ ◆ ⸻

At home, I tuck Lily into her bed. She snuggles with a blue penguin stuffed toy—which is missing an eye—that she'd gotten as a baby. As

I brush her sandy-brown hair from her face, her eyelids blink heavily over her deep brown eyes. She resembles her mother. It always causes my heart to ache that a person could be so callous and not want anything to do with their daughter. How had she looked into her newborn's face then tossed her aside? Like she meant nothing more than trash?

At first, I'd assumed she'd been going through postpartum depression. I'd offered her the best care and treatment available. Soon I learned she wanted freedom over the responsibility of raising a child.

Hopefully, I'm providing enough love for two parents, and Lily won't feel like she's missing something. One day soon, I know I'm going to have to explain to Lily why her mother left her. I've been putting it off, not wanting to break her heart.

"Daddy?" Lily says around a wide yawn. "Are you mad at me?"

I sit on the edge of her bed. "Why would I be mad at you?"

She tucks the penguin under her chin. "Because I bugged you to let me sleep over at Aunt Harper and Uncle Finn's house and you had to pick me up."

"I'm not mad." I brush her hair away from her face.

"Can I do it again another night?" Her voice slurs with fatigue.

I kiss her forehead. "Sure."

Lily smiles. "I love Avery. Can I have a baby sister or brother?"

Her words hit me hard in the chest. I can give her almost everything she could ever need. A baby sister or brother isn't an option.

Chapter Three

━━━◆○◆━━━

ALYSSA

The next morning, I drag myself out of bed. My ankle is still throbbing, and I can't put my full weight on it. Carefully, I hobble into the kitchenette. My body's aching like it's been hit by a truck.

I turn on the coffee machine and sit on a stool as I wait for the brew to percolate. I need an extra-large, extra-strong cup. I hadn't had more than two hours of sleep. After Hayden left, I'd cleaned and bandaged the wound on my knee and went to bed. I'd tossed and turned for the rest of the night, worried about what happened.

Why had Hayden left so suddenly? The phone call must have been something serious. It would explain why he didn't say goodbye. Was it something to do with his daughter? I'd wanted to call Harper to find out if she knew anything, but I didn't want to disturb her in case she was asleep or busy with the baby.

When my coffee is ready, I pour it into a mug and carry it to the sofa. I prop my leg on a pillow on the coffee table.

Maybe I should call Harper to see if everything is okay. But then I'll have to explain how I know he'd gotten a call in the middle of the night. So what? We're both adults. We can see or do what we want with who we want. So, why do I feel I need to keep this to myself? Is it because it's her brother-in-law and I don't want her to make a big deal about it? If something is wrong, I'm sure Harper will tell me.

With my decision not to call Harper settled, I drink my coffee and let the hot brew do its magic. When I feel ready to interact with people, I pick up my phone and call my agent to tell him I'll be out of action for at least two weeks. I had hoped that this injury was just a little twinge that would feel better after a few hours and an icepack. Unfortunately, that's not the case. I can feel some damage, and I need to rest it. Like I expected, my agent isn't happy I'm missing an audition and tries convincing me to strap my ankle and see how it goes. But I'm not risking causing more damage.

After ending the call, I toss the phone on the sofa. Have I ruined a good chance of finally making it on Broadway? I sigh. Oh well, there isn't anything I can do about it now. Even if I strap my ankle and take pain killers, I can't dance in this condition. Hopefully, my ankle will heal soon and there'll be another opportunity. I also have to remember to call the club once they open today to tell them I won't be able to dance for a couple of weeks.

All that's left for me to do is relax. When was the last time I sat home all day with nothing to do? If I'm not at auditions, I'm at the dance studio training to keep up my fitness and skills or working at The Temple. It looks like a day of binge-watching shows on Netflix. Reaching for the remote control on the arm of the sofa, I accidentally bump it onto the floor.

"Damn it." I shuffle to the edge of the sofa to pick it up.

From underneath the sofa something gold catches my eye. Getting to my knees, I pull out a Rolex watch. Wow! This is an expensive piece of jewelry that definitely doesn't belong to me. The only person it could belong to is Hayden. Flipping it over in my hand, I check the clasp. It's loose and doesn't lock into place properly. That would explain why it had fallen off his wrist.

I have to give it back to him. But how? I don't know his phone number or where he lives. I could call his office to tell him I have it and also find out if he's okay with whatever emergency had him running out of the apartment last night.

Reaching for my phone, I google the number for Alessi Fashion. When the receptionist answers, I ask to speak with Hayden but am told he isn't in the office at the moment.

If my ankle wasn't such a mess, I'd go to Alessi's and drop it off, but it's too big of an effort. When he realizes it's missing, maybe he'll figure out it could be at my apartment and come back to get it.

I hate having such an expensive piece of jewelry in my possession and don't want it here any longer than necessary. I need to contact Harper and get her to pass on a message to Hayden. If she's curious why he was here...well, I'll just tell her the truth. No big deal.

I call Harper.

"Hey, Alyssa," she answers on a yawn.

"Oh, sorry. Were you sleeping?"

"Sleep? What is sleep?" I hear Harper yawn again. "What's up?"

"If this is a bad time, I can call back later."

"With a baby, there's never a good time. You have my attention for approximately five minutes, I need to nurse Avery soon, so speak."

"Okay, okay. I need a favor."

"Sure, what is it?" she asks.

"I need you to pass on a message to Hayden."

Harper is quiet for a second. "As in my brother-in-law Hayden?"

I pick at a frayed thread on the sofa. "Yes, your brother-in-law."

"What message could you possibly have for Hayden?"

"I...arrhh...have his watch."

Another second of silence. "You have his watch?"

"Yes. It looks expensive. I need to get it back to him. Can you call him and tell him I have it? I'll be home all day if he wants to drop by to pick it up."

"Wait...wait...wait... I'm confused. Although it might be baby brain. Why do you have his watch? When did you see him *to* have his watch?"

I could lie and tell her I found it as we passed each other on the street. Or think of any other way I could have it, yet I can't lie to my best friend. "He...arrhh...dropped it in my apartment last night."

"Why was he in your apartment?" She gasps. "Oh my God. You're the woman Hayden was with last night! He was going to have sex with you?"

Here I am trying to keep what happened private and Hayden has told them. "We weren't... We were just..."

Harper scoffs. "Oh, please. His shirt buttons were all over the place. You're seeing Hayden, and I'm just finding out about this now? I thought we were best friends. We tell each other everything." I hear her sniffle.

"Are you crying?"

"No... Just a little. I swear my hormones are all over the place. I'm crying over coffee commercials!"

I giggle. "The one with the dog running home is sweet."

"I know, right? I break down every time I see it— Hey! I know what you're doing. You're trying to change the subject."

Damn it. She's onto me. Then something hits me. Harper mentioned something about his shirt. Did she see him after he left my apartment? "Did you or Finn call Hayden last night?"

"Yes. If I'd known what he was up to, maybe I would have waited a little longer to make the call. It wasn't urgent. I even said so on the phone."

I rub my temple. "So, nothing serious happened?"

"His daughter had a bad dream and wanted her dad. I told him he didn't have to rush over, because after the dream had worn off, she was happy and helping me with Avery."

The breath knocks out of my lungs. "When he left me in my bedroom to answer the phone, he ran out of my apartment without saying a word to me. I thought it was urgent. He was just using the phone call as an excuse to leave."

"Tell me you're joking." Harper's tone turns serious.

"I wish I was."

"I'm going to kill him. How could he do that to you?"

"It's nothing. Don't worry about it," I say through a tight jaw.

"It's not nothing. I'm coming over. I'll bring ice-cream."

I shake my head. "No. You have too much going on with Avery. I'm fine. It's nothing."

"Give me time to feed Avery—I hear whimpering—and I'll be right there."

"Harper, it's not necessary—"

She interrupts me. "I'll leave Avery with Finn and be there soon." With that, she ends the call.

As I wait for Harper to arrive, I sit on the sofa, boiling with anger, wishing I had two functioning feet to pace out my frustration. The call hadn't been urgent. Nothing serious happened. He used the call as an excuse to run out on me. *Coward!* Underneath that Mr. Nice Guy persona is a big fat jerk. One I had lost sleep with worry over. I'm such an idiot. Well, I'm never giving him the opportunity to mess with me again.

An hour later, there's a knock on the door. I shuffle onto my feet and limp to let Harper in. She barrels in with a tub of Ben and Jerry's super fudge chunk. She places the ice-cream on the coffee table and heads into the kitchenette to grab spoons. On her way back into the living room, she notices me hobbling to the sofa.

Harper covers her mouth with her hand. "Oh my God. What did you do to your leg?"

I'm wearing another oversized t-shirt. My wounds are too sensitive for pants or tights. In the light of the day, my leg looks banged-up. With abrasions, bruises, bandages, and a swollen ankle, it doesn't look good.

"I had a little fall at the front of The Temple after my shift last night." I sit back on the sofa, prop up my ankle and cover it with an icepack.

Harper takes the seat next to me. "Are you okay?"

"It looks worse than it is. I'll be fine in a couple of weeks." I hope.

"Can I get you anything? Tea? Water?" she asks with concern.

I point to the container on the coffee table. "The ice-cream is enough."

Gathering the container and spoons, Harper passes me one then flips open the lid. We both scoop chocolate goodness into our mouths.

"Mmmm. This is delicious. I'm glad you made the trip over. Although, I hate that you've had to leave Avery on my account."

Harper drops her head on the back of the sofa. "Finn can manage while I'm gone." She sighs heavily. "I'm so tired. Can I sleep here for an hour or twenty?"

I giggle. "Stay as long as you like. Your old room is free if you want to lie down."

Turning her head toward me, she groans, "Don't tempt me. I love her so much, but God, it's nice to have some time alone."

I point at myself. "Arrhh. You're not alone. I'm here."

She waves dismissively. "You don't count. So, tell me," she says as she sits up, "how long have you been seeing Hayden?"

"Last night was the first night."

"How did he end up in your apartment?"

Taking a deep breath, I explain about the fall, Hayden stopping to help me, and how he drove me home.

Harper looks at me expectantly, like she's waiting for more. When I don't say anything else, she says, "That doesn't explain how his shirt buttons were mismatched and how far you got."

I roll my eyes. "There's nothing much more to tell. There was this fierce attraction—well, that's what I thought, but with the way Hayden sprinted out of here, it wasn't mutual." It was humiliating that he needed to rush away from me so fast.

"That was a shitty thing to do."

I couldn't agree more. I pick up the watch laying on the coffee table. "Can you or Finn give this back to Hayden? I don't want him back here."

Taking it from me, she says, "You don't want to do it yourself to give him a piece of your mind?"

"No. I won't waste my breath."

"Are you sure?"

"Yes. I never want to see him again."

Chapter Four

HAYDEN

In my office, I'm working through the budget report for our lead designer, Juliette Monet's summer line when Harper barges into the room. I glance past her, expecting to see Finn and Avery. When I don't see them, I ask, "Is everything okay?"

Her thunderous expression tells me there's something wrong. So does the way she marches to my desks and smacks something onto the timber surface.

"Lose something?" she asks.

When she snatches her hand away, my gold watch glints under the light. I'd been looking for it all morning. "Where did you find this?"

Harper rests her hands on her hips. "I didn't. I got a call from Alyssa asking me to give it back to you."

Shit! I must have dropped it in Alyssa's apartment. And judging by the death glare Harper is throwing my way, she knows I ran out on her friend without an explanation or a goodbye. "Harper, let me explain—"

She slaps her palms on top of the desk and leans forward. "What's there to explain? I already know you led Alyssa on then disappeared without saying a word. How could you?"

I know I fucked up. In the moment, I panicked. I feel like absolute shit. "I'm sorry I ran out on her. It was a shitty thing to do. But I never meant for things to go as far as they did."

Harper pushes away from the desk. "So, that's your excuse? That doesn't justify leaving her like you did."

"Who left who?" Lucas strolls into the office.

Fuck. Why did he have to come in here now? I don't need the whole family knowing my business.

"None of your damn business," I snap.

Lucas holds up his hands. "Woah. What's up with you?"

Harper glares at me while she says to Lucas, "Your brother is hopefully feeling guilty about treating my best friend like crap."

Lucas props a shoulder on the wall. "What did he do?"

"What part of 'none of your business' don't you understand?" To change the subject, I turn the conversation toward work. "I noticed you didn't include the photography costs in Juliette's budget. Why not?"

"I've been busy," Lucas says without an explanation. Lucas is the head photographer at Alessi Fashion. Photography is his art, and he sometimes has a more laid-back attitude toward the business.

"I need it by no later than four o'clock this afternoon."

Lucas straightens from the wall and salutes. "No problem, boss."

He's just as much the boss as I am. Finn, Lucas, and myself took over Alessi Fashion after our father retired, and we built the company up to be one of the biggest and most prestigious fashion houses in the world.

"So, what did he do?" Lucas asks, grinning at Harper.

Before Harper speaks, I point to the door. "Get out and stop sticking your nose where it doesn't belong."

"Okay, geez. Don't get your panties in a twist," he says and ambles out of the office.

"Scared to tell Lucas what a jerk you are?" Harper crosses her arms over her chest.

Christ, she isn't letting this go. I blow out a breath and push myself from the chair. Walking to the window, I stare out over Central Park. "I'm sorry I ran out on Alyssa. I panicked."

"Why?" she says, coming over to stand next to me.

"I don't do one-night stands. Not since Lily was born." I turn toward Harper.

Harper's face softens. "I know. I understand. You've had to raise Lily on your own. It's difficult. If I didn't have Finn, I don't know what I'd do. But what you did—"

"Was a fucked-up move. I know. I'm sorry. Am I forgiven?" I give her a hopeful smile.

"I'm not the one you need to apologize to." The heat in her words have died down.

I rub the back of my neck. "Should I talk to her and explain?"

Harper shrugs. "She said she never wanted to see you again."

I wince. "She's that pissed?"

"How would you feel?" Harper pulls a face.

Probably like crap. "If you give me her number, I can call to apologize, so technically she's not seeing me."

Harper thinks for a beat. "I can't give you her number without her permission. But I'll text her and ask."

Pulling a phone from her bag, she taps out a message. A few seconds later, it beeps with a reply. As Harper reads Alyssa's text, her eyes widen with mirth. She bites her bottom lip, and I suspect she's trying to stop herself from laughing.

"What did she say?"

"Umm...she said she doesn't want me to give you her number." A giggle escapes from her lips.

I frown, not believing that's what's written. "What did she really say?"

"I told you." Harper grins.

"Give me that!" I snatch the phone from Harper's hand.

She reaches for it, but I swing my body away from her. "Hey!" she yells.

I hold the phone up out of her reach and read the message.

You can tell Hayden that no, he can't have my number. He can stick his apology where the sun don't shine, because I know you're the one who's probably making him feel like shit for being such a sneaky jerk. You can also tell him he missed out on the best sex he would ever have in his life. Now he'll never know!

I hand the phone back to Harper. "I hate that I've hurt her."

Harper tucks the phone in her bag. "She'll calm down soon, and hopefully, one day we can all laugh about this."

I raise an eyebrow, not believing a word of what Harper said.

"I said 'one day,' not tomorrow or the day after. It will be a day *far* into the future. Now, I have to get back to Avery, she's due to be nursed." I watch her cup her breasts as if weighing them and smile like she's about to do the most wonderful thing in the world. "See you later." She waves and sails from the room.

I sink into the chair, resting my head back. That's what raising a baby should be like. A mother excited to feed her baby, be with her baby, *raise* her baby. It was doubly perfect because she was doing it with a man she loved, who was just as excited about parenthood.

I missed out on that. Missed out on the loving partner to start a family with. I had no one to turn to when things got tough.

But I'm not the one I'm concerned about. Lily is the one who missed out on so much. Missed out on a mother's love. It is up to me to give her the best life I can. I can't let anything, or *anyone*, get in the way of that.

Chapter Five

<hr>

ALYSSA

For two days, I've been sitting in my tiny apartment doing nothing but going stir-crazy. I'm not used to so much down-time. I've always kept busy and active, and I don't think I can take much more.

The swelling and bruising in my ankle has lessened, and I'm able to walk around without too much discomfort. However, standing for long periods of time or attempting any dance moves causes shooting pain in my ankle, so I know I can't work yet.

I could catch a cab to Harper's house and have cuddle time with Avery. But what if I run into Hayden? I haven't in the year that she's been married, but knowing my luck, it would happen. I'm still too annoyed about his flash-and-dash to be in the same room with him. I meant it when I said I didn't want to see him again.

I make my way into the kitchen and go about making myself a turkey sandwich for lunch. As I sit at the counter, ready to eat, my phone rings, and my old ballet teacher's name flashes on the screen. I was sixteen when my family moved to Paris and I last took one of her classes, but in the years since, we've kept in touch. Although, with my busy schedule and her teaching, time has flown by between catch-ups.

"Hi, Miss Lucia," I answer. Even though I'm no longer a student, and we are friends, I've never felt comfortable calling her by only her first name.

"*Ciao*, Alyssa. How are you, *bella*?" Even after living in America for over forty years, Miss Lucia still has a strong Italian accent.

"Better now that I'm talking to you. I've missed you."

Miss Lucia's dance studio was my second home. When I lived in New York City as a kid, I spent more time there than I did at my house. Every afternoon after school, I donned my pointe shoes and practiced until I got every pirouette, arabesque, grand jete, and chasse perfect. I bawled my eyes out for weeks when we moved away, and I never found a school I loved as much.

"I've missed you too," she says. "What have you been up to these days? How's the job at The Temple? I've been meaning to come and watch you perform."

That would be a sight to see—Miss Lucia at a strip club. In her late sixties, she holds herself like the elite ballet dancer she was in her twenties. Head high, back straight, and a walk that makes her look like she's gliding across a room. She's too classy for a place like The Temple.

"Work is good. I don't draw in the crowds like the strippers, but I still get good tips."

"Well, I'm sure you're wonderful. I can't wait to watch you." Miss Lucia is always my biggest cheerleader. With no judgement. It would be nice if my parents were more like her. "The reason I'm calling is to ask a favor of you if you have the time in your busy schedule."

"Sure, what is it?"

"One of my teachers has gone on maternity leave, and I need to fill her position for a few months. She thought she'd be able to work until the end of the month, but she's had some complications with the pregnancy and her doctor prescribed immediate rest. I've also cut back on classes—"

"Are you okay?" I stiffen with concern. It's not like Miss Lucia to cut back on classes. She's a machine.

"*Si, si*. I'm fine. Nothing to worry about. But I'm not as young as I used to be."

"You're not old. And you'll be dancing forever." Because that's the way it's meant to be. Sure, it's impossible, but I have to keep her like that in my mind. She was the best part of my childhood. When my parents were demanding I dance to be the best, Miss Lucia told me to always dance from the heart.

She chuckles. "Tell that to my arthritic bones. Long days at the studio aren't as easy as they were when I was young. It's got me thinking about selling the studio."

"Are you serious?" Oh, that's a dagger to the heart.

"It's just a thought. Nothing concrete. Anyway, I'm calling to ask if you're interested and have time to cover ballet lessons a few afternoons a week?"

Any other time I'd do anything to help her out. I wish I could now. "I would love to say yes, but unfortunately, I've injured my ankle and don't know when I can dance again."

"Oh no. How serious?"

"I've sprained it. I need to keep off it. Possibly even get some treatment."

"I'm sorry to hear that. What can I do? I know an amazing physiotherapist who has magical hands. I'll send you her number."

"That would be great, thanks. I'm sorry I can't help. I can call some of my dance friends and see if I can find someone to help you," I offer.

"Thank you, I'd appreciate that. Unless..." Miss Lucia is silent for a moment. "It might take some time to find someone right away, so in the meantime, if I give you a student teacher to help, could you conduct the lesson and critique the class while the helper performs the steps?"

I bite the side of my cuticle. "I'm not sure."

"You can start off with the younger classes, so it won't be too technical."

Maybe it could work. Helping Miss Lucia sounds better than spending the next who knows how many weeks couped up in my apartment. "Okay, I'd love to do it."

"Excellent. Thank you so much."

"When would you like me to start?" I ask.

"Is tomorrow afternoon too soon? The first lesson starts at four PM. They're seven, eight, and nine year old girls and boys who have done a couple of years of classes, so they know what they're doing."

That sounds easy enough. "I'll see you then."

"It will be like the old days when you used to teach classes for me. You had such a skill for teaching. The kids will love you."

I hope so. It's been a while, and I remember young students were a handful. I taught classes after school for pocket money. It was the best job in the world.

"I'll see you tomorrow," Miss Lucia says.

"Can't wait!" I'm already looking forward to a new challenge. It will pass the time until my ankle is healed.

Once I'm fit, I'm going to hit the auditions hard. I will land a role on Broadway even if it kills me.

Chapter Six

HAYDEN

"Dad, these tights are going up my butt. They're too small and make me look stupid!" Lily, with a disgruntled expression, stomps into my bedroom.

Ever since I picked her up from school, she's complained about everything. From the car being too warm. The ride home too long. Not having her favorite cookies, and the list goes on. Is she eight or eighteen? If her moods are this bad now, what will they be like when she hits her teen years?

"Your tights are not too small, and they are not going up your butt. They're fine," I assure her.

Lily huffs, blowing her hair from her face. "Ruby's mom buys her better tights. I want those ones."

Where is this attitude coming from? "There's nothing wrong with your tights. Now, hurry and pack your bag for ballet or you'll be late."

"Only moms know the right ones to buy. Dads don't know this stuff."

An icy shiver stiffens my spine. This is the first time Lily has compared moms and dads. "I've bought the right ones. There's a uniform list on the studio's website. I checked."

"Well, they're too small. You don't know my size." With an eyeroll, she marches from the room.

What has put her in such a bad mood? And why is she talking about mothers? Hopefully her dance class will put her in a better mood. She loves ballet and always comes away with a smile on her face.

A few minutes later, Lily is back with her bag slung over her shoulder and an irritable expression. Even with a frown on her face, seeing her dressed like a little ballerina melts my heart.

"I'll do your hair, then we can go," I say, leading her into the bathroom.

As I glide the brush through her hair, she winces. "Ow, you're hurting me."

I take a deep breath and brush more gently then twist her hair up into a high bun. "How's that?"

"It's crooked." She crosses her arms over her chest. "Ruby's mom knows how to do hair better than you." The bun is sitting perfectly on her head.

She's eight, she doesn't know her words are slicing through my heart. I've done everything I could do to make her feel like she hasn't missed out on having a mother. Maybe it's not enough.

Looking at her in the mirror's reflection, I say, "Lily Pily, is something wrong?" This attitude has come from out of nowhere.

She frowns and shakes her head.

"You've been unhappy since I picked you up from school. Did something happen today?"

"Nothing happened. Can we go now?" Without waiting for an answer, she rushes from the bathroom.

During the car ride to the dance studio, Lily sits in silence. No matter how much I try talking to her, she stares out the window with barely a word to say. It's like talking to a brick wall. Eventually I give up. Something has happened. Whatever the problem, I wish she'd talk to me. How can I help her if I don't know what it is? I'll let it go for now and give her space. Hopefully, if it's something really bothering her, she'll come to me. Raising a baby on my own had been hard. I have a sinking feeling it won't get any easier.

We take the spiral stairs to the studio. Lily sits on a bench and digs out her ballet shoes from her bag. Normally, at this point, I'd leave her. Parents aren't encouraged to hang around. But I don't want to leave her in this mood. The kids in her class—some of them from her school—gather together talking excitedly as young children tend to do. Lily doesn't take part. This is her favorite place to be and seeing her not enjoying it breaks my heart. I want to fix whatever the fuck is going on.

A clap from inside the dance room catches the children's attention. Lily, with her ribbons tied, scurries away. Where is my wave goodbye? It's like she's upset with me. *What the hell have I done?*

Just as I'm about to leave, I hear Lily's teacher address the students. The voice stops me in my tracks. It's not Miss Naomi; she doesn't have the same sexy tone as the woman who's speaking—the woman who has been on my mind the last four days. Slowly, I turn to look through the window of the dance studio, and I see who that voice belongs to. My suspicions are confirmed. It's Alyssa.

"Hello class. My name is Miss Alyssa. With Miss Nikki's help, I'll be taking over from Miss Naomi while she takes time off to have her baby. I can't wait to watch you all dance." She looks over all the children. "We're going to have so much fun. Let's start with—" She stops mid-sentence as our gazes connect. A flicker of irritation creases her brow, her lips drawing into a thin line. What did I expect? A huge, cheerful smile?

"Excuse me for a moment. I'll be right back." She beams the class with a smile. As soon as she turns her back on them and heads my way, it drops into a frown.

She's dressed much like the girls in the class—a pink leotard with a sheer pink skirt over white tights. Under the fabric, her body is on full display. Slender, toned, and athletic. Gorgeous. My jeans tighten at the fly. Fuck. This is not good. I need to forget about her. How am I supposed to if she's Lily's teacher?

"I'm assuming you have a child in my class." Her tone is like a blasty chill.

I clear my throat. "Yes, my daughter Lily." I point to where she's standing away from the rest of the kids. My heart sinks.

Alyssa glances to where I'm pointing. "Parents aren't allowed to stay unless it's parent watch week. It distracts the children." She waves a hand in the direction of the stairs. "She'll see you in an hour."

Okay...I've pissed her off big time! I don't blame her. Guilt gnaws at me. What I did was inexcusable. I wish I'd acted differently. "Alyssa, about the other night—"

Her expression hardens. "I don't have time to chat. I have a class to teach."

Before she can walk away, I clasp onto her arm. She raises an eyebrow and glances at my hand. I drop my arm by my side. Okay, she doesn't want to talk about what happened, but I still need to tell her that Lily's not having a great afternoon.

"Lily is upset about something. I'd feel better if I can stay just in case she needs me."

She considers my request for a moment, then shakes her head. "I'm sorry, you can't stay. If I let one parent watch, others will want to."

"It's only for one lesson. Lily is upset."

"I'm sorry. No. If Lily has any problems during class, someone from the office will contact you."

Someone from the office. Is she so pissed at me she can't call me herself? From the icy expression on her face, I'd say yes. Gone is the fun, bubbly woman from the other night. I did that. I'm to blame for the change in her demeanor.

It's better this way. Better that she hates me. Because if she looks at me with a hint of desire, I may not pull away again. And I can't put myself in that position. There's a reason I don't have sex. Although, when I look at Alyssa, it's hard to remember what it is. She makes me want to finish what we started in her apartment and damn the consequences.

After all these years with no temptation, why now? Why with Alyssa? I hate how I weakened. Hate how she tempted me. I've spent the past eight years devoting myself to Lily and work, and one night I almost let my efforts crumble around me. Shame and irritation coil in my gut. I'm supposed to be stronger than that. "Speaking of the other parents, do they know what you do for a living?" I say. Alyssa's mouth gapes open. "Do you think they'd like their kids taught by someone who works in a strip club?"

"Excuse me?" Her lips thin. "Some of those parents have visited the club. Including you!" She jabs a finger into my chest. "If you have a problem with Lily taking my class, then you're free to take her home. Just remember, you'll be punishing her for your judgmental misconceptions." She crosses her arms over her heaving chest. "So, are you taking her out of class or not?"

Fuck! I'm so angry at myself for wanting her that I'm acting like an asshole. If that's what it takes for her to pull away from me, so be it.

"Hurry and decide. I have a class to teach."

Just because I need to stay away from Alyssa doesn't mean Lily should pay for it. I'll work out another way to keep my distance. "She can stay."

"Good." She spins away.

It's then I notice her limp. "Are you still having trouble with your ankle?"

"None of your business," she calls over her shoulder before disappearing into the studio.

Chapter Seven

—◦—

ALYSSA

My first day at the studio and I've already had a confrontation with a parent. Not just any parent, it had to be Hayden. Seeing him so unexpectantly had rattled me. Then he had the nerve to throw my job at The Temple in my face, like it was something I should be ashamed of. If I thought he was a jerk before, he's proven to be an even bigger one. Thank God I never slept with him. What a huge mistake that would have been.

I can't let my interaction with him distract me from the lesson. My attention is now only on my students. Hayden Alessi can take a hike from my brain.

I slide onto the wooden stool in front of the class to stay off my ankle and run through the warm-up routine I want Nikki to do with the class. As I watch the kids go through the drills, they're all smiling and having fun except for one girl. Lily is standing at the back of the room, her expression sad. It looks like she's about to burst into tears at any moment.

Maybe I should have let Hayden stay. I let my anger at him get in the way of what is happening with Lily. I keep a watchful eye over her. As the warm-up changes into steps down the room, once again, she's keeping away from the other kids, not mingling in with their playful chatter.

One by one, the students pirouette the length of the room. I smile, clap, and praise their wobbly attempts. They're so cute. I love their enthusiasm. Next is Lily's turn. Her arms are positioned perfectly, her spotting as she spins is lovely. She's a beautiful, little ballerina.

As she twirls down the room, I notice four girls whispering, giggling, and pointing at her. Lily must have noticed them too, because she stumbles and loses her posture. She hangs her head and walks the rest of the way and back into line.

"Girls! What is so funny?" I didn't want to use my stern teacher's voice on my first day, but these girls need to stop this behavior. It's clear it's upsetting Lily.

The girls' smiles drop, and they shake their heads. "Nothing, Miss Alyssa," they say in unison.

"Then please pay attention to the lesson."

For the rest of the class, there are no more incidents with Lily and the girls, yet she still looks miserable. No matter what I try, I can't pull a smile from her. When the class is over, I say goodbye to the students as their parents arrive. I'd forgotten how much I loved teaching. I only wish I could have danced along with them.

Among the parents gathered in the waiting room, Hayden is the first person I spot. It's easy when he's a head taller than any other person. To my annoyance, my heart races. As much as I want to avoid him, I need to speak to him about Lily. While she's busy taking off her ballet shoes, I nod for Hayden to follow me so we're out of earshot.

He's standing close to me, and my stomach muscles flutter and I take a step back. Will this reaction to him ever go away? An hour ago, he insulted me. I should not feel this way. I focus on what I need to say to him and will my body parts to calm the hell down. "I wanted to let you know Lily might have a problem with a few girls in class."

"Who are they? What did they do?" Hayden swings his head from side to side, looking ready to hunt the culprits down.

I put my palm on his chest to calm him—big mistake. The firm muscles remind me of what's underneath the shirt. I drop my hand. Lowering my voice so no one can overhear our conversation, I explain what had happened in class.

With a hardened expression, he scans the room. I'm not convinced he won't try to find the kids. It's a good thing I didn't give him names.

"I put a stop to it. I won't have that kind of behavior in my class. If it happens again, I'll be speaking to their parents." Hopefully that will help calm him down.

He scrubs his fingers through his hair. I can only imagine how hard it must be to hear that kids have upset your child. A small piece of my heart softens toward him. And when his gaze holds mine, it's hard to remember what a jerk he can be.

"Thank you for letting me know. I appreciate you watching out for Lily."

"I'd do anything for—" Shit! Was I about to say *I'd do anything for you*? What the hell! No. I wouldn't because that's ridiculous. "I'd do anything for Lily...she's sweet."

"Can we go now?" Lily sidles up to Hayden.

I'm so thankful for the interruption.

Hayden places a loving hand on his daughter's head. "Sure, Lily Pily."

"You did a fantastic job in class, Lily. You're a natural ballet dancer."

A ghost of a smile twitches at her lips. Hopefully I can pull more of them out of her at the next lesson.

"See you next week, Alyssa?" Hayden asks like he's questioning whether I'm going to keep teaching now that I know his daughter is in my class.

I pull my shoulders back. "I'll be here. Will you?"

He grins. "See you then, Twinkle Toes." He turns and leaves.

As much as I want to hate that nickname coming from him, it makes me smile. And damn it, now I'm looking forward to Lily's next lesson.

<hr>

Later that evening in my apartment, I order sesame chicken and steamed vegetable dumplings from a nearby Asian restaurant. After teaching three classes of young children, I'm too exhausted to cook, and I didn't even dance! Teaching is more draining than auditions, yet it gave me a buzz no audition ever has.

Seconds after placing the order, my phone rings. Looking at the screen, my shoulders sag on a heavy sigh. Whenever my mother calls, she always has a million questions about my auditions. Her favorite: *Why aren't you cast yet?* Or *What are you doing wrong?* I don't have the energy for her interrogation, so I let it go to voicemail. I'll message her later.

Placing my leg on the coffee table and trying to get as comfortable as I can, I don't have time to turn the TV on before my phone rings again. I better answer in case it's something important.

"Hey, Mom. Is everything okay?"

"No. Everything is not okay." Irritation laces her French-accented words.

I straighten. "What's happened?"

"Why did I have to hear from Davey about your accident? You had to cancel an audition because of it! It's not like they're falling at your feet."

I sag against the couch cushions. Nothing serious has happened except for her disappointment in me. What's new? She's more concerned about the missed audition than my injury. Typical.

"You've been talking to Davey about me?" I'll have to remind my agent to keep his big mouth shut. Just because he and my mother are friends, doesn't mean he can tell her my business.

She tsks like I've said something silly. "You make it sound like we're gossiping. I called to chat, and he told me you had to miss an audition."

I was born into a high-performing family. My parents are retired ballet dancers, and both performed in principal roles around the world on the most prestigious stages. They expect the same standards from me and my sister Christina.

Well, they have one daughter who's making them proud. Christina dances with the School of American Ballet, and they love to remind me I haven't made it yet. Although I know Broadway isn't their dream for me—nothing compares to ballet—they've sucked it up and find it somewhat acceptable. It's better than nothing, they often say.

"When did the physiotherapist say you can dance again?"

What about asking if I'm okay? Or what happened? I should be used to the lack of interest in my life and well-being. Performing is what's important. And if I'm not doing it, I should do everything I can to get there.

"I haven't seen a physiotherapist yet, so I'm not sure when I can dance."

"What!" she screeches through the phone, and I hold it away from my ear. "Why not? It's the first thing you should have done. The longer you leave it, the worse it will get."

"It's not so bad," I say to calm her down. "It's just a sprain."

"Oh...well..." I hear her sigh of relief. "If that's the case, strap it and take pain killers. Audition on one leg if you must. God knows how many times I've danced with broken toes, and I never let it stop me." It's not the first time I've heard that story.

I look at my swollen and bruised ankle propped on a pillow. "You're right. That's what I'll do," I lie. I'm not risking more damage.

"I'm assuming this means you're not working at the strip club?" I can picture her screwing her nose at the words 'strip club.' If my parents are embarrassed because I haven't made a big name for myself on stage, they're mortified that I'm dancing at The Temple. Even though I don't take my clothes off, they find it degrading.

"I asked for time off."

"Just time off? Maybe this is an excellent opportunity to quit. Then you can focus one-hundred percent on *real* dancing and get your career on track."

I pinch the bridge of my nose. *Breathe in, breathe out.* I know she thinks she's being encouraging, yet her words make me feel like crap. She'll never accept the way I make money.

"I have bills, Mom. Like rent and food. I need the job at The Temple."

I don't tell her about my temporary job with Miss Lucia, because she'll only tell me that's where I should stay. I do love it there, and Miss Lucia would give me a permanent job if I wanted one. In my mother's eyes, it's a more 'respectable' job than the club. And damn it, I don't want to give her the satisfaction.

"Oh, please. We have a perfectly good apartment in the Upper West Side where you can live. We'll provide it fully stocked with food and whatever else you need each week. You won't have to worry about anything except auditions."

I take a deep breath. "Mom, thank you, but I don't need the apartment. I can take care of myself." After all the dance, singing, and acting lessons they paid for when I was growing up, at twenty-four I want to support myself. I'm doing a damn good job too. The Temple is far from the classiest club, but the tips are great.

I can't keep having this conversation with my mother. It only reiterates what a failure I am. How my work is degrading and distasteful. If I'm to be accepted in the family, I have to aim higher in my career. Grace the stage with my name up in lights. To them, it shouldn't matter if I work in a strip club or Broadway. Why can't they love me and be proud of who I am? Not what I do.

Before she can lecture me more on my living conditions, I say, "Gotta go, Mom. Someone's at the door. Love you. Bye."

I hang up, toss the phone on the sofa next to me, and scrub my hands over my face. No one is at the door. I'm still waiting for my food to arrive. Although, I don't think I can eat anything. Nausea rolls in the pit of my stomach. It often happens when I talk to my parents.

If I don't make it on Broadway, I'll always be a disappointment to them. So I *must* make it. There's no other choice. As soon as my ankle is healed, I'm focusing all my attention on a Broadway career. I'm not letting any distractions get in my way. I want this. Been dreaming of performing since I watched my first show, *The Phantom of the Opera*, when I was five.

While picturing my life on stage, why does my chest feel heavy?

Chapter Eight

—◦—

HAYDEN

When we arrive home after ballet class, Lily dumps her dance bag by the front door and stomps up the stairs. The slamming of her bedroom door soon follows. What is wrong? I couldn't get a word out of her on the car ride home. If she doesn't talk to me, how can I help her?

Making my way to her room, I knock on the door, and I enter. Lily is lying on her back, staring at the ceiling. As soon as she sees me, she flips onto her side to face the wall.

"Hey, Lily Pily. Can we talk?" I take cautious steps toward her, like I'm approaching a wild animal. When she doesn't answer, I sit on the edge of the bed, facing her back, and rest a hand on her hip. "Have I done something to upset you?"

Is she at the age where all I need to do is breathe and I'll annoy her? No, there's more to it. Something must have happened at school, and for some reason, she's taking it out on me.

I hear her sniff, and she shakes her head.

"Are you having trouble with your friends from school or in ballet class?"

Another sniff. She doesn't deny it.

"Have you had a fight with your friends?"

She shakes her head. *Then what the fuck is going on?*

"Lily Pily, please turn around and talk to me. I want to help you."

She hesitates a second before she sits up. Her cheeks are flushed pink, and tears are filling her eyes. It breaks my heart to see her so sad. I gather her in my arms, resting her head on my chest. She's so small and fragile in my embrace, I want to protect her from all the bad things the world throws her way.

"Sweetie, what's wrong? Please tell me why you're crying."

Pulling away, she wipes her eyes with the sleeve of her t-shirt. "It's nothing."

"You're upset. If you tell me what the problem is, maybe I can help."

Dropping her head, she clutches onto her blue stuffed penguin. "We're having a mother and grandmother day to celebrate Mother's Day at school on Friday."

My heart sinks at my feet. I dread this time of year. I usually take her out of school and we do something fun together so she doesn't have to see all the mothers with their kids and feel like she's missing out. She's normally excited about skipping school and has never looked upset about the day approaching. What's changed?

"What do you want to do on Friday?" I say to deter the conversation away from Mother's Day. "We can even make a long weekend out of it. Spend a few days out of the city." I'd fly her to the damn moon if it made her happy.

Instead of getting excited about a day off school, she says, "Why don't I have a mother?"

Shit! This is what her bad mood after school was about and why she'd mentioned what mothers are better at when getting ready for ballet. I knew this day would come. Dreaded it. I'm surprised she hasn't asked about her sooner. I thought I was prepared. Even had a speech played out in my mind. Now, as Lily stares at me with a tearstained face, I freeze. My mouth grows dry. Words are a jumbled mess in my head.

"All my friends have a mom," she continues. "Freya, Serena, and Daphne teased me because I don't have one. They said there must be something wrong with me." Those girls are in Lily's ballet class, which would explain why she was upset during her lesson. "Is there something wrong with me? Is that why I don't have a mom?" Her bottom lip trembles.

God, kids can be fucking mean. I tilt her chin up to look at me. "No. You are perfect. They should never have said that. Making fun of someone is never okay. Don't let what they say get you down. You are perfect the way you are. You are smart, funny, kind, and beautiful. That's all that matters."

"But why don't I have a mom?" Her eyes search mine for the answer. It's like what I said doesn't matter. Of course it doesn't. Not when she wants answers. Answers I should have given her by now.

I'd love to tell her that Rachel, her mother, is dead. Abandoning her newborn daughter because of the inconvenience a child was to her life doesn't make her a mother. But what if one day the truth came out and Lily found out she's alive? Would she hate me for lying? Probably. It would fuck with her mind, that's for sure. That's why I can't do it. When Lily's older, she might want to look Rachel up and ask her why she left. I can't take that away from her.

I gather her hands in mine. There's no other way to say this. I just need to get it out. "You do have a mother."

Lily's eyes widen. "I do?"

I clear my throat. "Yes. When you were born, she couldn't take care of you—" More like she didn't want to, but I'll keep that part to myself. "—and she gave you to me."

Her brow creases. "Why?"

I take a deep breath to settle the anger clutching at my chest. "Sometimes mothers or fathers don't know how to look after children and need someone else to do it." Fuck! That excuse sounds so lame. I can't tell her that Rachel had another life. A husband. A baby didn't fit into her plans. "She gave you to me because I could give you the best life possible and take care of you by giving you everything you need."

Christ! Bullshit keeps pouring from my mouth. I didn't know the first thing about babies. Had to learn on the spot. At times, I still have no clue. I only hope I'm not fucking up her life. The reason I'm sugar-coating the truth is to protect Lily. I don't give a fuck about Rachel. If Lily knew the truth, it might break her heart. And I will do anything I can to stop that from happening.

"Can I get another mom one day?" She glances up at me with hope in her eyes.

"Umm...well—"

"Daniel in my class has two moms."

"That's because after his parents divorced, his dad remarried."

Lily nibbles her bottom lip. "If you get married, does that mean I'll have a mom?"

This is not how I expected this conversation to go. "Yes, if I got married, you'd have a mother. But I'm not getting married."

Lily's shoulders sag with disappointment. "Why?"

Why? Because what I went through with Lily's mother traumatized me enough to never want to go down that road. "Because I don't have a girlfriend," I say.

"If you had a girlfriend, would you marry her?"

"If the woman was someone special, then maybe I would." I'd never get close to anyone for it to get that far. A vision of Alyssa enters my mind. The only woman who I've let past my walls. I brush my hand over the top of Lily's head. "Are you feeling better?"

Lily smiles for the first time since coming home from school. "Yes."

"If you have any more problems at school, you tell me, okay? Because your friends shouldn't be teasing you."

She nods. "Okay."

I'm sure when she gets older, she'll have more questions. For now, this is all she needs to know. Hopefully by then, she'll be more mature and will be able to handle the truth. Although can anyone really handle the fact that their mother didn't want them?

I give her cheeks a playful squeeze, making her giggle. The sound swells my heart. "Wash up, and I'll see you in the kitchen for dinner."

"I hope you're not making lasagna again, because that didn't taste good." She screws up her nose in disgust.

I feign a shocked expression. I'd forgotten to boil the noodle sheets and the dish was crunchy. My culinary skills are lacking. "No, I'm making a big bowl of broccoli just for you!" I tickle her stomach, and she wiggles around, her laughter filling the room. God, I love this girl. Would die for her.

Rachel leaving her with me was hard, but damn if it wasn't the greatest gift. I couldn't imagine loving anyone as much as I love Lily. Again, Alyssa's face flashes in my mind. I must stop thinking about her. Nothing can come of it. It's a good thing she hates me now. After running out on her, and what I said about where she works, I doubt she'll ever want to talk to me again—except for when it's about Lily. I never meant to be such a prick. It's like I'm mad I'm attracted and I'm taking it out on her.

Attracted to her is an understatement. I'm drawn to her. The air sizzles whenever she's near. Just the thought of how I kissed her, touched her, causes my dick to twitch behind my jeans. Since the night in her apartment, it's not the first time I've needed a cold shower and a hard-working hand.

Chapter Nine

———◆O◆———

ALYSSA

Sitting in Harper's living room, I bury my nose in Avery's neck and breathe in her precious baby scent. "If we could bottle this smell, we'd make millions," I say taking a sniff.

"I know!" Harper smiles lovingly at her daughter. She's curled up on the couch. Dark shadows from lack of sleep are under her eyes. She's never looked happier. "I just want to eat her."

I giggle. "Can we do that?" I nibble on Avery's foot. "Can we eat you?" Avery makes gurgling sounds that make my heart swell.

If I weren't chasing the Broadway dream, would I want a family? I'm young and still have years ahead of me, but is this something I want? I've never given it a thought because I'm so focused on making it. I can't see myself living this kind of life. Not any time soon.

"A baby suits you," Harper says like she's reading my mind.

"I love being an aunt. That's all. I'm happy to give her back," I joke. I lift Avery into the bassinet.

"There are days I'd like to give her to someone." Harper chuckles around a yawn. "Then I look at her squishy face and I melt."

"Is Finn not stepping up?" I know she's joking about giving her baby away, but maybe he's not doing what's needed of him.

A smile lights up her face. "He's amazing. He fights me for more time with her."

"Where is Finn?" It's not like him to not be hovering over his daughter.

"He's with Hayden and Lily, picking out ballet stuff."

I raise an eyebrow. "Ballet stuff?"

"Mirrors and barres. Hayden is turning a guest bedroom in their house into a dance studio for Lily. Apparently, after you told her she has talent, she wants to practice all the time."

Well...It's no surprise Hayden would do that for his daughter, he has a sweet side. I witnessed it the night I'd fallen. I also know that underneath that sugary coating is a rotten core. One I won't take a bite from again.

Like we've conjured them up, their voices drift from the front of the house. They're home. Shit! I wasn't expecting to see Hayden here. Since Finn and Harper moved in together, I've never run into him. It's just my luck that the last person I want to see is about to stroll into the living room.

Damn my injured ankle. Sprinting for the back door to make a getaway is not an option. I'm lucky to hobble to the edge of the room. I will have to suck it up and try my hardest not to blast his ass. Better yet, I won't talk to him. Pretend he doesn't exist.

The trio walks into the room. My gaze zeroes in on Hayden. His eyes widen when he sees me. Obviously, he wasn't expecting to see me either. Dressed in faded jeans that wrap snuggly around him, and a navy t-shirt that molds his toned body, I'm finding it hard to pretend he doesn't exist. In fact, his presence fills the room and I want to drink him in. *Damn it! Stop it. You can do better. And you don't have time for men. Especially hot and cold ones.*

Finn beelines for Harper, giving her a gentle kiss on the lips. "How's my girl?"

"I'm great," she answers, looking at him with loved-up eyes.

"Is Avery behaving?" He looks in the bassinet, whisking a finger around his daughter's face. So much love is pouring from Finn and Harper it's palpable.

"Always," Harper answers.

Finn chuckles. "Hmm. I find that hard to believe."

"Can I hold her, Aunty Harper?" Lily asks.

"Sure you can. Sit next to Alyssa." Lily shuffles onto the couch, and Harper picks Avery up out of the bassinet and gently places her in Lily's arms. "Remember to support her neck."

"I wish Dad would get married, then I'd have a mom and a baby brother or sister."

Finn laughs, walks over to Hayden, who's still standing in the doorway, and nudges him in the ribs with his elbow. "Better get working on that."

I chance a look at Hayden, and he's scowling at his brother.

"Not happening." Hayden nudges him back.

"You said if you get a girlfriend you'll marry her." Lily looks at her dad like she's challenging him to deny it.

"I said *if* I found someone special enough." His gaze flicks to me, and for that brief, intense moment I feel like I could be that 'someone special.' "I haven't found her yet." Just as fast, the look is gone, replaced with a shuttered expression. Damn him and his mixed signals. Or damn me for seeing things that aren't there.

"Must be your charming personality keeping them away." I smile sweetly at him.

He leans a shoulder against the doorjamb. "Maybe I'm not interested in the company I've been keeping with lately."

A raging hot flush creeps over my skin. "Maybe you should stop lurking around strip club doorways!"

Lily looks up and asks, "What's a strip club?"

Hayden's cheeks turn red. "It's a bar for adults where they sell drinks," Hayden says through gritted teeth, his eyes throwing daggers my way.

I smirk.

Harper's gaze flicks from Hayden to me and back to Hayden. Concern is etched on her face, like she's worried a smackdown is going to start. "So, Hayden. Did you get everything you need for Lily's dance studio?" she asks, like she must defuse the situation before things get out of hand.

The question draws him into the room. He props a hip on the couch on the opposite side of where I'm sitting. Like he needs to keep his distance from me. *Yeah, buddy, I might bite.*

"I think so. I'll google the height for the barres and work out where everything needs to go, then I'll put it together."

Lily's head springs up. "Miss Alyssa can help you, Dad. She's a ballet teacher, so she'll know how to set it up."

"Oh...umm...I..." Lily has put me on the spot.

"Miss Alyssa can't help," Hayden cuts through my stuttering.

Lily's eyebrows crease. "Why?"

"She doesn't have time." He stares hard at me and crosses his arms over his chest, challenging me to object.

I narrow my eyes at him. For whatever reason he doesn't want me around, he doesn't have to be a rude prick about it. Although I'm thankful he was quick with an excuse. Because spending any more time around Hayden is not a good idea. We're likely to kill each other.

Lily looks at me with disappointment lining her little face. "Why don't you have time?"

Before I can answer, Hayden jumps in to say, "She has a job that keeps her very busy."

Hayden is quick with excuses, but the way he keeps answering for me is rubbing me the wrong way. "I don't work all day, every day."

Lily's face brightens. "So can you help my dad?"

I glance at Hayden, waiting for him to come up with another excuse. When he presses his lips together and stays silent, I rack my brains for something. If only I'd kept my mouth shut and agreed with Hayden, I wouldn't be in this position. I can't think of anything quick enough to get me out of it. And with Lily staring at me with hope on her sweet face, how can I say no?

"I can help if it's okay with your dad." Let Hayden be the one to say no and break his daughter's heart. My chest puffs out with pride at throwing it back at him.

"Can she, Dad? Pleassse!"

Hayden gives Lily a smile. Then he turns to me, and it tightens. "I'll be happy for the help."

"Yes!" Lily cheers, jostling Avery from sleep.

"Let's put Avery in her crib." Harper rises from the armchair and lifts the baby from Lily's arms. Lily shuffles off the couch to follow. "Finn, can you help us, please?"

Finn stares at Harper with confusion, like he's wondering why she needs help putting Avery to bed. When she gives him a not-so-subtle head nod toward the stairs and communicates with a wiggle of her eyes, he mutters, "Arrhh...yeah...sure." And he follows her from the room.

When the room is clear, Hayden says, "You could have said no."

"Unlike you, I don't enjoy disappointing people."

He cocks an eyebrow. "What's that supposed to mean?"

Is he clueless as to how he's treated me? He's the one who ran. Criticized my job. He's left me wondering what I've done wrong when in fact he's the one with the issue—I don't know what it is, but he's aiming his problem at me. I shake my head. "Nothing. If you don't want my help, I'll make up an excuse to tell Lily I can't do it anymore."

"She's looking forward to it. I don't want to upset her."

I can tell Hayden would do anything for his daughter—even put himself in an uncomfortable position. Again, there's that redeeming sweet side of him. It makes me want to like him and kick myself for the thought at the same time.

"Thank you." A smile cracks through his stone-like expression. A smile that stabs me in the chest. Oh boy, I'm in trouble if a smile can do funny things to me. *He's a jerk. He's a jerk. He's a jerk.* This is my new mantra. One that will hopefully make me keep my distance.

"When do you want me to look at the space?" I ask.

Lily skips into the room. "Can she come over this afternoon?"

"We need to give Alyssa more notice." Hayden brushes his hand down Lily's hair.

"No, that's fine. I'm free." Better to get this over with. It's not like I have a raging Saturday night planned.

"Okay, great. I'll send a car to pick you up," Hayden says.

"That's unnecessary. I can find my own way. Just give me your address."

"It won't do you any good traipsing around on your leg." He points to my strapped ankle.

He has a point. "Okay. Thank you."

"I'll have my driver pick you up at five PM if that suits you."

I nod. "Perfect." Butterflies flutter in my stomach. More time with Hayden is probably not a good idea. Thankfully, we have Lily as a buffer.

"I'll give the driver your address. I know where you live."

Chapter Ten

———◆◇◆———

HAYDEN

At five-thirty PM that afternoon I'm pacing the living room, waiting for Alyssa to arrive. I don't need her help. How hard is it to put up a few mirrors and barres? Many times this evening I wanted to call and cancel. I insisted Alyssa give me her number before she left Harper's house in case things changed. I would have canceled if Lily weren't so excited—she hadn't stopped yapping about it all afternoon.

Lily thunders down the stairs. She's dressed in a pink leotard, tights, and ballet shoes. She looks ready for a dance class. "Is she here yet?"

"Not yet. Why are you dressed like you're going to class?"

"Miss Alyssa is coming over. Maybe she can give me a lesson in my new room."

"Miss Alyssa is only having a look at the space and advising where things should go. I still need to put it all together. That's not happening tonight."

Lily's face drops with disappointment.

Outside, headlights shine through the living room window as a car travels up the long driveway, stopping at the front of the house. As Alyssa steps out of the car, she glances up at the house, looking unsure. Like she's trying to decide whether to come inside.

When the car drives away, she makes her way to the door. The bell chimes, and Lily bounces on her toes. "I'll get it!" She races to answer the door, and I follow close behind.

Lily swings the door open. Even though I saw Alyssa through the window, my breath catches in my throat. Dressed in black cargo pants, and a tight, black tank top, with her hair pulled back in a messy ponytail, she's gorgeous. Every time I see her, her beauty smacks me in the face.

When I don't say a word, she smiles with uncertainty. "Can I come in?"

Fuck! I'm staring at her with my tongue glued to the roof of my mouth. Thankfully, Lily pipes up and says, "You can't look at my room from outside, silly." Lily holds onto Alyssa's hand and pulls her inside.

Alyssa takes in Lily's costume. "You look ready to dance on stage. Are you on your way to a performance?"

Lily swings her hips from side to side. "No, but I want to show you something I've been practicing."

"I can't wait to see it. I'm sure it will be amazing." Alyssa smiles with genuine interest. If this is how she is in class, I can see why Lily is infatuated with her.

"Can I show you now?" Lily asks.

Alyssa glances at me, looking unsure of how to answer. "How about we show Miss Alyssa your room first."

"Okay." Lily bounces on her toes. "Follow me," she says as she races from the foyer and disappears upstairs.

Alyssa giggles, and the sound squeezes something in my chest. "She's a little excited."

"She hasn't stopped talking about you designing the room all afternoon."

"Designing is a bit of a stretch. It's easy putting a few mirrors and a barre against walls."

"Well, thank you. You've made her a happy girl."

"You're welcome."

We stare at each other as awkward moments of silence follow. I feel like I need to apologize for the shitty things I've said and done to her, yet isn't it better that she think I'm an asshole? If she hates the sight of me, can't stand to be around me, there'll be no chance of anything happening again. Then I can put her out of my mind, get on with my life, and forget I had a moment of weakness. As she looks at me with her big brown eyes, I have a feeling it may take a while.

"I'll take you to the guest room." As we make our way to the stairs, I notice Alyssa limping. "Your ankle still hurts? Do you need to sit down?"

"No, I'm okay. It's better than the night you..." She bites her bottom lip, stopping herself from finishing the sentence. "It's better."

Better than the night I'd taken her home, I'm sure she was going to say. The night I'd nearly fucked her. And I've been tearing myself in two over it. When I look at her, one half wants to kick myself for not staying and finishing what we started. The other half is relieved I didn't go through with it. Because I have a feeling that one night with Alyssa wouldn't be enough. And that's something I can't get involved in.

"Are you coming!" Lily yells from the top of the stairs.

I roll my eyes and Alyssa giggles. "On our way," I call back. "Will you be okay walking up the stairs?"

"Yes, thank you." If she had said no, it would have given me the chance to touch her again. Hold her. I mentally slap my forehead. I need these thoughts to stop. Having her so close is clouding my judgement. I have my life planned. There's no time for romance.

We make our way slowly up the stairs. Alyssa uses the handrail for assistance. I keep two steps back so I'm not too close, yet from this distance, I get a nice view of her pert ass. I pinch the bridge of my nose. How am I supposed to control where my thoughts drift off to if I can't control what my eyes focus on? The more I spend time with her, the more I feel like I'm losing the battle. After tonight, I'll only see her when I take Lily to dance class. Nothing can happen in a room full of students and their parents. Things will go back to normal.

Just before we reach the top, Alyssa trips on a step and stumbles. Rushing toward her, I wrap my arms around her waist, stopping her from falling. With my chest pressed against her back, I breathe in her floral scent. Heat explodes over my skin. Like the universe knew what I wanted, I got to touch her, hold her. She turns her head over her shoulder. Not ready to let her go, my gaze drops to her lips. Her mouth opens slightly. Wanting to taste her again is more important than breathing.

"What's taking so long?" Lily calls.

At the sound of her voice, I pull away. Clearing my throat, I say, "Miss Alyssa has a sore ankle, we need to take it slow." To Alyssa, I say, "Are you okay to continue?"

She doesn't turn around to look at me when she nods.

Thankfully, we make it to the guest room without another incident. Lily is waiting for us, excitement beaming over her face. "Is this room good for a dance studio?" she asks Alyssa. "Dad took the bed out before you got here."

With the guest room now a ballet studio, is it time for a bigger house? No. I have no plans on adding to the family, so we'll make this work.

Alyssa takes in her surroundings. "It's perfect. Plenty of room to move around. You're lucky your dad is doing this for you." She smiles at Lily.

"So, where do you think everything should go?" I ask.

Alyssa scans the room. "You should put mirrors along this wall. That way the afternoon sun won't reflect in them." She gives me the measurements for the barre height and the best way to secure it. "There's enough room to leave the closet in here for any costume changes you might have. It's not just about practicing. You can choreograph your own performances too."

"I love that idea!" Lily says. "Can I show you what I've been practicing now, Miss Alyssa?"

"Maybe another time, Lily Pily. Miss Alyssa can't stand on her ankle for long."

"I can sit on the floor. I'd love to see what you're working on."

"I can get you a chair."

Alyssa waves her hand. "Not necessary." She sits on the floor and crosses her legs pretzel style.

Propping my shoulder against the wall, I wait for Lily to begin. She takes a couple of deep breaths like she's nervous and begins to dance. Alyssa watches like she's being entertained by the American Ballet. Her face is alight with joy.

When Lily finishes, Alyssa claps her hands. "Well done. That was amazing. I can tell you've worked hard."

Lily's face splits into a smile. "I don't think I had my arms in the right position when I did my pirouette."

"It was close. Here, let me show you." Alyssa struggles to get up from the floor. I hold out my hand to help. She hesitates for a moment before taking it. I try to ignore the jolt of electricity that passes between us when our hands touch. As soon as she's on her feet, I let go and step away.

She places Lily's arms into position. "Hold them like this to start. As you're stepping into your spin, pretend that you're hugging a giant beach ball and hold them up just about here. Don't forget to drop your shoulders. Okay, give it a try."

Alyssa steps back so Lily can pirouette.

"Is that better?" Lily asks.

"Perfect. Now try it again."

Lily shuffles her feet and spins into an eloquent move.

"That's it. That looks so much better. Great job."

Lily stops and curtsies with a smile. "Thanks, Miss Alyssa."

"Any time." Alyssa curtsies back.

"Hey, Dad." Lily skips over to me. "When my room is done, can Miss Alyssa give me private lessons?"

"No." The word booms through the room louder than I'd meant. Lily and Alyssa's eyes widen at my harsh response. The last thing I want is for Alyssa to come to my house on a regular basis, tempting me. I soften my tone, "Miss Alyssa is busy with her job at the studio. Also, she has an injured ankle she needs to rest so it can heal."

Alyssa narrows her eyes at me before putting a smile on her face for Lily. "If you'd like, I can ask around the studio to see if another teacher is available."

Lily sighs heavily. "No. That's okay. I really wanted you."

"I'm sorry, sweetie. If things change, I'll let you know." She gives me another narrowed look over Lily's head. "Well, if you don't need me for anything else, I'll head home."

I can think of a dozen things I need her for, and they're all off limits. So I don't stop her as she walks to the door.

"Goodbye, Lily. I'll see you next week."

"I'll get a car for you," I say.

"Don't bother, I'll call an Uber." With her shoulders pulled back, she steps from the room.

Instead of letting her leave, I rush after her and catch up with her at the top of the staircase. Grasping her wrist, I stop her. She glances at her arm and back at me with a raised eyebrow. I let go. "I can have a car here in minutes, an Uber might take longer."

Alyssa's eyebrows slam together. "You're unbelievable. If you're in such a hurry to get rid of me, you should have said something." She pushes past me and takes the stairs.

Shit! She thinks I'm rushing her out of here. I reach out and stop her again. "No...I didn't mean—"

"Look, I don't know what I've done to annoy you. *You* were the one who approached *me*." She points a finger at her chest. "I was happy minding my own business until you came along."

"Happy dripping wet in a puddle of dirty water?"

She glares at me. "I was doing just fine."

"You couldn't walk," I remind her.

She tilts her chin. "I would have managed. Crawled home if I had to."

"I helped you."

She tosses her head back and scoffs. "So, are you pissed with me because I didn't say thank you? Although I'm quite sure I did. Don't forget I thanked you by letting you in my bedroom to..." She looks over my shoulder, probably watching out for Lily, who has thankfully stayed in the room. "...fuck me. Wasn't that thanks enough? Oh, but you must want a written thank-you note, because spreading my legs for you wasn't enough. I'll send something in the mail. From now on, you don't have to deal with me again. If it weren't for Lily, I wouldn't be here tonight. She's sweet. I guess she gets that from her mother."

My blood turns cold. I drop my hand from her arm and don't stop her when she rushes as best as she can down the stairs. The sound of the front door slamming behind her travels up the stairs.

She's sweet. I guess she gets that from her mother. Does Rachel have a decent bone in her body? Selfish, calculating, and heartless are her qualities. Sweet? I doubt it.

Lily walks out of the room and tugs at my hand. "Do you think Miss Alyssa will ever have the time to give me private lessons?"

"Maybe," I say to not squash her hope.

"She's a great teacher. I really want her," she says then goes back into the guest room.

I really want her too.

But we don't always get what we want.

Chapter Eleven

ALYSSA

I give a quick knock on Harper's front door and cautiously walk inside the house. Not because I'm worried Harper won't like me letting myself in—she's given me a key—but because I'm worried I'll bump into Hayden. It's the middle of the day, and he should be at work, but I don't want to risk seeing him.

So far, I've avoided any contact with him. When he drops off and picks Lily up from ballet class, I don't give him any of my attention. Lily seems to have resolved her problems with the kids in class and is happy, so there isn't anything I need to discuss with him.

"Harper," I call in a whisper as I search for her, ducking my head around walls before I enter a room.

"What are you doing?" a voice says from behind me.

I jump, put a hand over my racing heart, and turn around. Harper is staring at me with a confused look on her face.

"God, you gave me a heart attack."

"Why are you sneaking around the house?"

"I was looking for you."

She giggles. "You normally barge in demanding to see Avery."

We walk into the living room, and I plonk onto the couch. "Well, I'm trying to be more considerate. She's getting older, noise will disturb her."

Harper raises an eyebrow. "What's the real reason?"

She can always see through my bullshit. There's no point lying. "I don't want to see Hayden. I was making sure he wasn't here."

Flicking out her wrist, Harper checks the time on her watch. "Finn won't be home for another couple of hours. I'm not expecting Hayden to drop by, so you're safe."

"You saying 'I'm not expecting to see him,' doesn't reassure me that he won't drop by. Call Finn and make sure. Or I'm leaving."

"Why are you running away from Hayden? Weren't you there the other night helping with Lily's dance studio?"

"Yes, and then he kicked me out of the house."

"What!" Harper's eyes widen.

"I'm exaggerating, but that's how it felt. He couldn't get me out of the house quick enough."

Harper sits next to me. "You need to explain what happened."

I tell her about arriving in a car he sent for me. Giving my advice about the room, and how he wanted to send me home with his driver because it was quicker than an Uber.

Rubbing her fingers across her brow, Harper says, "You think he kicked you out because it was quicker to get you home with his driver and car?"

I nod. "He couldn't make it more obvious that he wanted to get rid of me."

"Maybe he offered you his car and driver because it was the safest option? Or more convenient for you?"

I take a moment to think. Shit. Could that have been the reason? "If that's the case, I feel like an idiot."

"Hayden isn't a bad guy. He's just been through a lot."

I'm curious as to what he's been through but don't ask.

The phone on the coffee table rings. Harper picks it up and says, "I don't have to call Finn—he's Facetiming me now." After swiping to answer, she beams with a smile as she looks at her phone. "You know, now that you're back at work full time, you don't have to FaceTime me every hour to see if I'm okay."

"I know I don't have to. I want to. Your face is better to look at than these two ugly mugs behind me."

Harper giggles. "Say hi to Hayden and Lucas for me."

"Are you and Avery okay? Do you need me to come home early?" Finn sounds like that's exactly what he wants to do. He's so in love with Harper and Avery it's beautiful to see this little family in their own bliss bubble.

"We're fine. Avery is in her room sleeping. Stop worrying about us. Besides, Alyssa is here. She's going to help me with the last-minute details for when the party planner arrives."

"Call me if you need anything. I'll come straight home."

"I will. Love you."

"Love you more."

"Come on, Finn, that mushy talk is making me sick," someone says in the background.

"Fuck off, Lucas. You'll get your turn one day," Finn grumbles.

"No fucking way."

Harper giggles. "I'll let you go so you can deal with Lucas."

They say their goodbyes and end the call. Harper tosses the phone on the coffee table, a smile still on her face. "Those boys are like big kids sometimes. But I wouldn't have it any other way." She slaps her hands on her thighs. "Now, I have things to show you before the party planner arrives."

"I wouldn't call Penelope Aldin a party planner." More like Martha Stewart on steroids. This woman is a global phenomenon. "How did you manage to snag her?" She's taken on the world with her cooking, decorating, crafts, and organization skills. There is nothing she can't do.

"She's a client of Finn's. She wears Alessi Fashion to all her major events. I still can't believe Finn asked her to help with such a small party. There's nothing newsworthy about Avery's name day. She'll get no publicity out of this."

"I'm sure Finn will make it up to her with a gorgeous gown. I can't wait to meet her. I've watched her Netflix series and want to redo my apartment, learn how to cook, and make Christmas decorations."

Harper laughs. "Good luck with that. I've seen you cook—you can burn water."

I feign an offended expression. "A girl can learn."

"Just practice a few hundred times before you ask me to sample anything," she teases.

"When I get good at cooking, you'll be begging me to cater your next event."

Harper laughs. "I'm sure I will."

While we wait for Penelope Aldin to arrive, Harper shows me the soft pink, pale gold, and white color scheme for the party. It's pretty and girly and perfect for the occasion. Why she needs my help I don't understand. There's nothing I can add that Penelope hasn't already thought of. Although, I love being included in Harper's family. She's more like a sister to me than my own. There's so much love and affection for one another. This is how a real family behaves.

Growing up with my parents and Christina felt more like a business. Perform well and there was praise. Underperform and you aren't worth associating with. Climbing the 'performing' ladder is the goal.

Reaching the top is where the 'love' is. Is it love though? It's all I've ever known. Until I see Harper and Finn together and witness how a family really loves. There's no way they'll make Avery into something she's not.

There's a knock at the door. "That will be Penelope," Harper says.

Harper leaves to let her in, and I'm surprised to find I'm nervous about meeting someone so famous. Finn and Hayden are famous in the fashion industry. My parents are famous in their performing world, but that doesn't compare to being a household name. I should have dressed up for the occasion. Worn my best black cargo pants. The ones I'm wearing are fraying at the seams. Oh well, there's nothing I can do about that now.

As they enter the living room, my breath catches. Penelope Aldin is gorgeous. It's true when they say people are better-looking in person than they are on TV. She's shorter than I thought and wearing a navy-blue skirt that flows to her knees with a pale denim shirt tied in a knot at her waist. Her long, auburn hair falls in soft waves down her back. Blue eyes shine from her alabaster, smooth face.

"Penelope I'd like you to meet my best friend, Alyssa Martinez. Alyssa, this is Penelope Aldin."

I jump to my feet, wipe my clammy palms down my pants, and hold out my hand. "I'm a huge fan. I can't wait for your next series to come out."

Shaking my hand, she smiles and it lights up her face like it's the first time she's heard the compliment. "Thank you. It's lovely to meet you. Harper tells me you're a dancer. How exciting. I wish I could dance. I have two left feet."

I blush and giggle. Am I fourteen meeting my rock star celebrity crush? *Get a grip, Alyssa.*

"Let's take a seat. Can I get you a drink, Penelope?" Harper asks.

"No thanks. I'm all good. And please, call me Penny. All my friends do."

We take our places, and I'm not too ashamed to say I beat Harper for the seat next to Penny—my new friend. Harper rolls her eyes with mirth and takes the armchair opposite us. I listen as they discuss the details of Avery's naming day, piping in when Harper wants my opinion on something. Really, what more can I add? The celebration is in two days, and everything looks perfect.

"I'm so happy with how it all looks," Harper says to Penny. "Thank you so much for taking the time to do this."

"It's my pleasure. It's been fun doing something like this. You're not demanding and wanting a million things done in the smallest amount of time. I've missed doing smaller events."

"Will you and your fiancé be joining us?" Harper asks.

Penny picks up a folder from the coffee table. "This is a family occasion. I'd hate to intrude."

"You've done so much for us, and we'd love to have you."

Before Penny can reply, the sound of the front door opening and closing echoes in the distance.

"Why is Finn home so early?" Harper frowns.

A moment later, Finn walks into the room, followed by Hayden and Lucas. Harper jumps to her feet. "Why are you all home? Is something wrong?"

At the sight of Hayden, my traitorous heart skips a beat. Dressed in a well-tailored charcoal suit and black shirt, he slides his hands into his pockets. The jacket fits snuggly across his broad shoulders. Two buttons of his shirt are undone, exposing his tan neck. I wonder if he wears a tie to work. If he does, would he take it off to tie my hands together above my head, shrug out of his jacket, and—

"Nothing's wrong, babe." Finn places a reassuring kiss on Harper's lips, breaking me out of my fantasy. God, is it getting hot in here? "Hayden insisted he needed to see Avery." Mirth shines from Finn's eyes.

Harper gives him a dubious expression.

Hayden adjusts the cuffs of his sleeves. "Lily is bugging me to bring her here for a visit."

Harper looks behind Hayden. "Where is she?"

He clears his throat. "At school. I'll pick her up when she's done."

Finn takes a seat and drops an ankle on top of his knee. "Hayden didn't want to wait at the office for school to finish."

Hayden throws Finn a dark, dirty look, like he wants him to keep his mouth shut. What is going on?

"Oh...well...You and Lily are welcome to come over whenever you like." Harper sounds just as confused as I am as to why the Alessi brothers are all in her living room in the middle of the day.

Hayden and Lucas are yet to make themselves comfortable, choosing to stand rigid by the doorway. Lucas is usually so laid-back and jovial, it's so strange to see him this way. Something weird is happening.

"Hayden and Lucas, you know Penny Aldin," Harper says. I glance at Penny; she's sitting on the edge of her seat like she wants to bolt for the door. Things are getting weirder and weirder.

"Nice to see you again," Hayden says with a smile.

"Hello, Penny," Lucas says stiffly.

"Hello, Hayden...Lucas." She returns her gaze to Harper and says, "We have everything ready and confirmed for the naming day. Call me if you have any questions or concerns." She rises, tucks the folder under her arm, and picks up her purse from the coffee table.

"Will we be seeing you on Sunday?" Harper asks.

"Don't you have fancier parties to attend to?" Lucas says with a sharp tone to his voice.

Everyone swings their heads toward him. What is the matter with him? I don't know him well, only met him a couple of times, yet I've never seen this side of him. Do all the Alessi brothers have a dark edge to them? Even Finn had some demons to clear out before he could commit himself fully to Harper.

Penny narrows her gaze at Lucas. "Beyonce's album release party isn't until next weekend, so I'm free." She turns to Harper. "I'd love to join you. See you Sunday. I'll see myself out. Goodbye, everyone." She struts from the room, not giving Lucas a glance as she brushes past him. His eyes, however, dropped to her swinging ass. What in the world is going on there?

"Are you ever going to tell us why you have a stick up your ass whenever you see Penny?" Finn asks.

"I don't have—"

"Don't deny it," Finn cuts in. "She's been a bug in your butt ever since high school."

Lucas strolls further into the room and drops into an armchair. "By the way you're gossiping, you sound like *you're* in high school."

Hayden stands by the doorway, not saying a word. When I look at him, he turns his head like he's engaged in Finn and Lucas' conversation.

I'm not going to let him ignore me. "Hayden, how's Lily? She seems happier in class, and it appears she's getting along with the kids. I hope whatever was bothering her has been resolved."

Barely giving me eye contact, he answers, "She's good, thanks."

"Is her studio at your house set up?"

He crosses his arms. "Finished it a couple of days ago."

"I bet she loves it."

"Yep."

Oh, he's freaking unbelievable. Why am I even bothering trying to have a conversation with him? That's it. I'm done playing nice. He can suck on a fat squirrel's nut for all I care.

"As enlightening as our little talk is, I need to go," I say. He has the good grace to look sheepish. *Yeah, you jerk. Hope you feel bad.* Looking over at Harper, I say, "I'll see you Sunday unless you need me for anything before then. If you do, it's better that you come to my apartment. Your house has an icy draft."

I get to my feet and stomp—as much as my ankle will let me—out of the room. Before I reach the door, a hand lands on my shoulder. I turn around to find Hayden. I raise an eyebrow.

"Alyssa, I didn't mean... I shouldn't..."

"Hayden, stop. I don't want to hear what you have to say, because every time you speak to me, you just piss me off. You act like I've done something wrong. I don't know what you're punishing me for, but whatever it is, it's on *you* not me. So sort yourself out or never speak to me again." I spin on my heels and rush from the house.

Chapter Twelve

⸻◦⸻

HAYDEN

On the day of Avery's naming ceremony, all of Finn and Harper's guests have gathered in their transformed backyard to celebrate the occasion. All this fuss over a baby that won't remember any of it. "I'll show her photos when she's older." Finn had said when I'd mentioned it. That little girl is going to get everything her heart desires. Isn't that what I'm doing with Lily? Daughters burrow into their father's hearts and we'd give them the moon if they asked.

Guests gather around Avery under shade sails surrounded by delicate flowers and lanterns, listening to the words from the celebrant. I should watch and listen too, but I can't keep my eyes off Alyssa. She was right when she said I'm punishing her and that I need to sort my shit out. I know I shouldn't take out my problems on her. Every time I do I feel like the biggest asshole and justify it by telling myself she's better off hating me.

Like she feels my eyes on her, she turns her head toward me. I give her a small smile, hoping she takes the gesture as an apology. Lines crease between her brows and she turns her head away. Not the reaction I wanted, but what did I expect?

When the ceremony ends, the guests mingle around the yard at tables while the catering staff hands out canapes and champagne.

"Can I get cotton candy please, Dad?" Lily tugs at my hand, pulling my attention away from Alyssa. A few kids are lining up, watching a woman at a machine twirl a big stick inside the spinning sugar.

"Sure, but don't eat too much or you'll feel sick," I warn.

"I won't." She skips to the line.

Lucas sidles up to me and points the glass of amber liquid he's holding toward Finn. "I never thought I'd see the day two females would have Finn wrapped around their fingers."

"He looks happy, that's for sure."

"You should get yourself some of that happy juice Finn is on."

I swivel my head toward Lucas. "I'm happy the way my life is. I don't need what he's having."

"Are you sure? Because from the second Alyssa walked into the party, your eyes have followed her around."

It's true. I haven't stopped staring at her. And right now, I'm not liking what I'm seeing. A man has walked up to her. She places her hand on his shoulder and gives him a kiss on the cheek. He leans close to her face; she tucks her hair behind her ear, and he whispers something that makes her toss her head back and laugh. My hands clench by my side, my chest heaves. That fucker needs to back the fuck up.

Lucas nudges my shoulder. "Yeah, you look so happy," he says sarcastically. "They do make a good-looking couple."

I turn my attention to Lucas and pin him with a shut-the-fuck-up warning glare. He just laughs, not intimidated one bit.

To steer the conversation in another direction and to stop myself from slamming the man talking to Alyssa to the ground, I say, "Speaking of good-looking couples, Penny and her fiancé Darren are picture-perfect. The successful businesswoman and the football jock. The media's golden couple. Wasn't she in your year in high school?"

"Yeah, she was." Lucas' jaw tightens.

Why does he look so tense at the mention of her name? "What's the story with her?"

"No story." Lucas' gaze trails to the couple as they mingle with the guests.

"That scowl on your face says something different."

He huffs and pulls his attention away from Penny. "We didn't get along. That's it."

I raise an eyebrow. It sounds like there's more to the story, but I let it slide. It's not the time or the place to bring up old wounds. I hate it when Lucas and Finn bug me for information, so I'll leave Lucas alone. He already looks pissed enough without me adding to it.

Plucking a glass from a passing waiter, my attention is again drawn to Alyssa. She's still talking to the guy who is too much in her personal space. He brushes his hand down her arm. *Who the fuck is he? And why the hell is he touching her?* Seeing red, I drink the champagne in one swallow and set the glass on the table.

"Where are you going?" Lucas calls after me when I leave him.

My jaw is clenched too tight to answer.

When I reach Alyssa, I stand between her and the guy she's talking to. Her smile drops and her eyes widen. "Hayden, can I help you with something?"

"Yeah, we need to talk."

"I'm speaking with Michael at the moment. Can it wait?"

"No. It's important." Getting her away from this asshole is urgent.

"Oh, okay. Excuse me for a moment, Michael. I'll be back in a minute."

Like fuck she will. I have no right to feel this possessive rage, yet it's blistering under my skin. I lead her to a quiet spot by the pool. The flickering candles floating in the water are competing with the afternoon sun.

"Hayden, what's wrong?"

"Who's Michael?" That's not what I meant to ask. When I stormed over to her, I didn't know what I was going to say, yet the words fly from my mouth.

Alyssa turns her head back to Michael. *Don't look at him. Look at me.*

With a frown on her face, she says, "Why do you want to know?"

"Who is he?" I demand.

She slams her hands on her hips. "Why do you want to know?"

I lean forward, our noses almost touching. "Are you going home with him?"

Sucking in a startled gasp, her eyes narrow, her face darkens. "What did you say?"

"Or are you throwing him in my face to make me jealous?" Because if so, it's fucking working.

Stepping closer, she digs her finger into my chest. "Who do you think you are? What business is it of yours who I'm talking to or who I'm taking home?"

Another hard jab to the chest. The force pushes me back a step.

"You don't want me. You've made that perfectly clear. So I can talk to and fuck whomever the hell I want. You have no right to pull me away like some jealous lover. I told you to sort your shit out or never talk to me again. Clearly you haven't, so leave me alone."

Her finger pokes harder. I take another step back and find air. I tilt backward, my arms flap like a bird, and a second later, I fall into the cold pool.

Splashing and sputtering to the surface, I shake the water from my hair and pull in deep breaths. The guests gather around the edge of the pool with shocked expressions. Alyssa folds her arms over her chest, a huge smile spreading across her face.

I rake my fingers through my hair and grin back. Nothing like cold water to smack some sense into you to cool off. Fuck, what was I thinking acting like what Alyssa had accused me of being—a jealous lover? This has never happened to me before. I don't know what the hell I'm doing. Everything I'm feeling is foreign. It's making me nuts and has me doing things I don't normally do.

"Have you cooled off?" Alyssa looks down at me and giggles.

"Yeah. I'm good," I reply, embarrassed that I've caused a scene at Avery's party.

Alyssa reaches out her arm. "Need help getting out?"

Not really, but I take her hand anyway. As she tries to pull me up, I grip on tighter and tug her toward me. She squeals before she hits the water. A second later, she pops her head out of the water, coughing and sputtering. The guests laugh at our watery display.

"What the hell was that for? I was trying to help you?" Her drenched hair is plastered to her face and mascara is running down her cheeks. She looks fucking adorable.

"You pushed me in," I accuse.

Her mouth falls open with exasperation. "I did not."

"You kept poking me in the chest. That made me fall in."

"It was an accident. You didn't have to pull me in with you." She splashes water in my face.

I splutter and wipe water from my eyes. "You did not just do that."

"Yep, I did." She pulls a smug expression before hitting me in the face with water again.

"Oh, you're going to get it now." I aim a missile of water at her. She squeals with laughter.

We keep splashing at each other until candles are flying around the pool.

"Hayden! Alyssa!" a stern voice snaps from the edge of the pool. I look up to see Harper glaring at us. Oh shit. For a moment, I'd forgotten where we were. "What are you doing?"

Alyssa swipes water from her face. "Hayden pulled me in," she explains sheepishly.

"That's because she pushed me in," I defend myself. We're sounding like two kids trying to get out of trouble.

I'm rewarded with another splash of water to the face.

Before I get my revenge, Harper holds her hand up like a stop sign. "Go dry off in the pool house. There are plenty of towels in the cupboard. I'll bring you some clothes to change into." Harper shakes her head at us before storming away.

Finn squats at the edge of the pool. "You're going to make it up to Harper big time."

First thing in the morning, I'll arrange flowers.

Lucas is standing behind Finn, grinning from ear to ear. "Best party ever."

***

In the pool house, we avoid eye contact and don't speak. We find the towels and go into separate rooms to dry off. When I head back into the main room, Alyssa is sitting on a chair, waiting for Harper to bring clothes. A white towel is wrapped securely around her body, exposing a lot of dark olive skin. My tongue practically rolls out of my mouth.

Her eyes trail over me too, like she's liking what she sees. Her gaze lands on the towel wrapped around my waist. If she keeps staring, it will only take a second for me to give her something to look at. I need to divert her attention.

"You have a little drool." With a grin, I tap my chin.

"What? Where?" She swipes the side of her mouth.

When I chuckle, she narrows her eyes at me. "Do you like what you see?" I ask. Because I fucking *love* what I'm seeing.

She shrugs her shoulder. "You look okay for an old man."

I choke on a laugh. "An old man? How old do you think I am?"

She taps a finger against her chin as she scrutinizes me. "Maybe around forty?" A twinkle of mirth shines in her eyes. I know she's playing.

I mimic her finger-tapping gesture. "Well, I'm not much older than you. You're around thirty-six, right?"

She gasps with a flash of irritation in her eyes. "I'm only twenty-four." Younger than I thought.

I squint my eyes like I'm trying to see it. "If you say so." I hide my grin. "I'm thirty-two. If you want to know."

"Hmm, interesting." She jokingly screws up her face like she doesn't believe me. Then with all seriousness, she says, "Are you going to tell me what happened out there?"

I lean my shoulder against the wall. "We fell into the pool." I know that's not what she's talking about. I don't know what to tell her. It's all such a mess in my mind.

"Not the pool. You tearing me away from Michael like I'm your possession."

That's exactly how it felt seeing her with another man. Like she's mine. That's crazy. I have no right to think of her like that.

"I should have come to you and apologized for acting like an ass lately, and I ended up behaving like a bigger one."

She stands and walks toward me, the towel just covering the curve of her butt. With a quick flick of my fingers, I can have the towel floating to the floor. I inwardly groan. *Keep it together.*

"Why do you act that way? Did I do something? Say something?" I hate the hurt shining from her eyes. The hurt I put there because I'm so screwed up.

I shake my head. "You did nothing wrong. It's me. There are things in my life that I'm sorting through. My focus is on Lily and work. I don't have time for anything else. I got distracted. And I hated myself for my weakness and took my frustrations out on you. I'm sorry."

A wet strand of hair is stuck to her cheek, and I brush it away and tuck it behind her ear. It's like I can't control myself when I'm around her. I need to touch her. My hand cups her cheek, her gaze drops to my lips, and I would give anything to forget about my life and take her into my arms and kiss her.

"Knock, knock," Harper sings out loudly from the door. "I've come bearing clothes. Lily is *also* with me." She calls out her warning like she has a feeling we're doing more than talking. If we'd been alone for a few seconds longer, maybe we would have been.

Alyssa walks back to the chair and sits. I glance down at my crotch to make sure I'm not going to poke anyone in the eye. When all is good, I call out, "Come in."

The door opens and Harper walks in holding a pile of clothes. Lily follows behind her with shoes. "Dad, you're so embarrassing." Lily giggles. "How did you fall in the pool?"

At eight years old, my daughter already thinks I'm an embarrassment. God help me when she's older.

I glance at Alyssa. We can have the same argument about who caused the commotion, instead I say, "I slipped and accidentally took Miss Alyssa down with me."

Harper places the clothes on a table. "These should fit. And please keep away from the pool." Thankfully she's smiling now. Although I'll still send her flowers. "I'll leave you to get changed."

Harper leaves and closes the door behind her. Lily takes a seat next to Alyssa. There's no chance anything can happen with my daughter in the room. She's the best cockblock I can ask for.

"Miss Alyssa," Lily says, looking up at her. "What are you doing after Avery's party?"

"Nothing. Why?"

"So you're not busy?"

"No, I'll probably watch TV. Why do you ask?"

I have a feeling I know where she is going with this. "Lily…" I say with a warning tone.

She doesn't hear it, or chooses to ignore it, because she says, "Then can you come to my house and give me a private lesson, please?"

"Oh…I…" Alyssa looks to me for help.

"Lily Pily. It's a lot to ask of Miss Alyssa."

"But Dad, the room is finished, and I really want Miss Alyssa to see it. She said she's only watching TV. I want to get better. Everyone in my class are better dancers than me." Her bottom lip drops in a sulk.

"That's not true. You're a beautiful dancer," Alyssa comforts.

"I still have trouble with some steps."

"If you want more practice, there's another class during the week you can join," she suggests. Is she suggesting that because she thinks I don't want her at the house? I haven't given her the impression I want her around.

"The class is for babies," Lily complains.

"They're not babies. They're about two years younger than you," Alyssa explains.

This is where I should jump in with a thousand excuses why giving her a private lesson is a bad idea. Instead, I say, "If it's not too much trouble and you don't have plans, it would make Lily happy." *And I get to see you again.* Fuck! Why am I doing this? Why am I putting temptation in front of me?

"You're okay with it?" Alyssa asks with a dubious expression.

How can I not be? Lily is trying so hard to become the best dancer she can be. She's already spending every spare moment in her studio practicing. How can I deny her? I can't. I'll just keep my distance from Alyssa. With Lily in the house nothing will happen.

"Sure, it's no problem," I reply.

"Yes!" Lily jumps from the seat with a broad smile.

"Do you want to go straight from the party?" God, I hope I don't regret this.

Alyssa shakes her head. "I'll go home and change and meet you there."

"Is six okay with you?" I ask.

"Perfect."

"Great," I say.

"Great," she repeats.

We're still wrapped in our towels, awkward as fuck. "Can I send the car to pick you up?"

She tightens the knot in her towel. "Yes, thank you."

"Right...well... We should change and go back to the party," I suggest.

Alyssa stands and heads to the bathroom. "I'll see you back out there."

When she disappears into the room, I sink onto the nearest chair. Dropping my head in my hands, I drag in a deep breath and remind myself why I've chosen the life I'm living. I'm not looking for anything else. I have all I need. Alyssa is only coming over to teach Lily. So why does my heartbeat gallop with anticipation?

Chapter Thirteen

HAYDEN

Like the last time Alyssa was due to arrive at the house, I watch for the car at the front window. The lights of the car wind up the driveway, stopping at the front of the house. Alyssa steps out of the vehicle and walks to the door. Lily, dressed in a pink leotard, rushes to open it before Alyssa can knock.

Alyssa steps into the foyer and my eyes drink her in. Dressed in her signature black cargo pants, black studded leather jacket, and chunky boots, she looks like a biker chick. A pink leotard peeks from beneath the jacket. With her hair twisted in a high bun, she carries herself with grace. Her long neck, perfect posture—she glides into the room like she's floating on air. Even with a slight limp, she's perfect.

My mouth is suddenly dry, and I swallow hard. "Thanks for coming. Lily has been bouncing off the walls with excitement."

"I'm excited to get started too." Alyssa flicks her gaze from Lily and lingers a little longer on me, her eyes holding me captive.

God, if she keeps looking at me like that, I'm screwed. "Well, I'll leave you two to it. Lily, can you remind Miss Alyssa where the room is please?" *Remember to keep your distance*, I remind myself.

"Sure." Lily holds onto Alyssa's hand, and they disappear up the stairs.

As I settle myself in my office to do some work, music floats into the room. It's not the usual classical music you associate with ballet but some up-tempo Michael Jackson song. Lily is going to love this lesson, I'm sure.

After about half an hour of trying to focus on the spreadsheet on the laptop, I give up and shut it down. I'm too distracted by the noise coming from the studio. I'm curious as to how it's going.

Making my way up the stairs to the room, I poke my head inside. A gasp catches in my lungs. Alyssa is stripped down to her leotard and tights and is demonstrating a move. With one arm above her head, another out to the side, the lines in her body are breathtaking. I prop a shoulder against the doorframe and admire the view.

"See how my heel lifts off the floor?" she says to Lily, not yet seeing me watching them. Lily nods as she looks intently at Alyssa's feet. "This allows for all my weight to be put on the ball of my foot. That way, when I spin, I'm not leaning back and tipping out of it. Let me show you."

Alyssa does a graceful twirl. Her body is athletic, yet soft in all the right places, the spin showing off her working muscles. I never thought ballet could ever look so fucking sexy. I groan out loud. When I realize what I've done, I cover it up with a cough. Alyssa and Lily turn to me, both wearing a querying expression.

I push away from the doorframe. "Should you be doing that on your injured ankle?"

"I'm putting weight on my good leg." She smiles. "Did you need Lily for something?"

"No, I'm just checking to see how's she's doing." *Liar! More like checking you out.*

"She's doing great." Alyssa smiles down at Lily. "Do you want to show your dad your pirouette?"

Lily nods, stands in front of the mirror, and positions her body before she spins.

"That's fantastic. You nailed it." Alyssa holds her hand up to give Lily a high-five. To me, she says, "She was struggling with it in class. Now she can do it with ease."

"You're a great teacher," I say.

Alyssa's head dips like the compliment embarrasses her. "Thank you. Although Lily's easy to teach."

"Have you got much longer to go with the lesson?" I ask.

"I can finish up now if you want me to." Alyssa picks her phone up off the floor, swipes the screen, and the music stops. Does she think I'm kicking her out again?

"There's no rush. Are you hungry? I'm putting some steaks on the grill. Nothing fancy, but you're welcome to join us for dinner." Where the hell did that come from? This is supposed to be about dancing lessons for Lily. But now that the offer is out, I can't take it back. Not that I want to.

"Oh...arrhh..." Alyssa looks like she's unsure how to answer. Things have been tense between us, so I can understand why she's confused by my invitation to dinner. I'm hoping this can be an olive branch for being such an asshole.

"Please stay." Lily tugs on Alyssa's hand.

Alyssa's gaze meets mine. "Only if you're sure it's no bother."

What's bothering me is not being able to touch her. "Lily would love for you to join us." *Yes, make this about my daughter.*

Lily nods vigorously.

Alyssa nibbles her bottom lip. "Okay, thank you."

"I'll see you in the kitchen when you're done." With that, I leave the room and head downstairs.

In the kitchen, I plant my hands on the cool stone countertop and drop my head between my shoulders. The more I try to keep away from her, the more I'm pulling her in. What the fuck is wrong with me?

⚊⚊◄O►⚊⚊

As I'm preparing the salad for dinner, I hear the patter of Lily's feet on the timber floorboards seconds before she barrels into the kitchen. Crashing into me, she throws her arms around my waist. "Thank you, thank you, thank you for letting me have a lesson, Dad." Seeing the smile on my little girl's face is worth all the agony I've put myself through.

Alyssa, walking at a slower pace than Lily, enters the room. Her leotard is covered up by her clothes. "She did well. A few more lessons and she'll have caught up with the more advanced kids in the class."

Lily tilts her face up at me with pleading eyes. "Can Miss Alyssa give me more lessons please?"

"Oh, I didn't mean to sound like I'm pushing for more."

"If you're available, it would make Lily happy. I'll pay you of course."

Am I testing my weakness? Having her here to see if I can control myself? For fuck's sake, I'm not a monk—although my brothers believe I'm living like one. My reason is solid. My celibacy has never been a burden until I laid eyes on Alyssa. Now, everything I've promised myself is slipping through my fingers.

"Can you come back tomorrow?" Lily asks as she slides onto a stool at the kitchen counter. Picking up an olive from the salad, she pops it into her mouth.

Alyssa giggles. "I think we should wait a few more days. I'll talk to your dad about when it's good for both of us."

"Okay." Lily reaches for another olive, and I playfully swat her hand away.

"I've set up the outdoor table for dinner. It's a warm night, and I thought it would be nice to eat outside."

"Sounds good. Can I help with anything?" Alyssa offers.

"You can carry the salad out, and I'll grab a couple of beers from the fridge. Oh, unless that's something you can't have. I read somewhere that ballerinas have strict diets."

She picks up the bowl off the counter. "I'd love a beer, thanks. And I'm not a ballerina. Just an all-around dancer." She chuckles.

I take two beers from the fridge, and we walk to the back patio. Lily follows close behind. I twist the lids off the bottles, and after Alyssa puts the salad on the table, I hand her one. Even pulling back on a beer, dressed like a biker chick, she looks graceful as fuck. My dick twitches behind my jeans. To drag my attention away from how Alyssa makes my body react, I prop my beer on the side of the barbeque and pick up the plate of steaks I brought out earlier. They sizzle as they hit the heat.

When the food is cooked, I dish the steaks onto the plates, and we begin to eat. When I'm done, I push my plate aside, then sit back to watch and listen to Alyssa and Lily interact. Lily is talking about dancing with so much animation. I never realized just how passionate she is about it. She asks Alyssa a million questions about performing on stage, auditions, classes, and if she gets scared dancing in front of hundreds of people.

"You're such a good dancer," Lily gushes. "I want to dance where you do."

Alyssa flashes me a smile, amusement spilling from her eyes. Like she knows that dancing at a strip club is not where I want my daughter to perform. Thankfully she doesn't mention her job. I'm not sure I'd know how to explain that to an eight-year-old.

"I'm not as good a dancer as my mother," Alyssa says as she pulls out a phone from her pocket. She swipes the screen a couple of times to pull up a video and holds it out for Lily to see. "This is my mother performing *The Nutcracker* in London."

Lily slides off her chair and lifts herself onto Alyssa's lap to get a better look. Oh fuck. Seeing Alyssa with my kid is making my heart beat out of my chest. She looks so good with her, like she could easily fit into Lily's life—my life.

"Wow." Lily's eyes widen with awe. "She's amazing. Do you think I can dance like her one day?"

Alyssa playfully taps the end of Lily's nose. "If you practice and work hard, it's possible."

"Dad, I'm really going to need more private lessons." She looks at Alyssa and asks, "Can we go back upstairs and dance again?"

Alyssa chuckles. "I love your enthusiasm, but save your energy for another day. Sometimes you can overdo it with too much training and injure yourself."

"Is that how you hurt your ankle?" Lily asks.

Alyssa's gaze flicks to mine, a spark of mirth glittering in her eyes. "No, I fell when I tripped during a storm."

Lily's eyes widen. "Oh no!"

"Luckily a nice man stopped and helped me." Her lips twitch.

"How?"

"Okay, Lily." I clap my hands. "Enough chatter. It's time for bed." And time to end this conversation.

"Can I stay up a little longer? I'm not tired," she says around a yawn.

"It's getting late. I'm going to need a marching band to wake you up for school."

Lily giggles, slides off Alyssa's lap, and kisses my cheek. "Goodnight, Dad." Throwing her arms around Alyssa, she says, "Thanks for the lesson."

Alyssa brushes her hand down Lily's head. "You're welcome. I had fun."

We watch Lily bound away. "That kid of mine has way too much energy."

"If I could siphon just one percent of a child's energy, I'd be supercharged for a week." Alyssa giggles. "She's lovely. You must be so proud."

My heart swells with love for my little girl. "Some days she can be a little devil. I'm dreading the teenage years."

"Her mother—"

"Is out of the picture," I cut her off.

Her eyes widen at my tone. I hadn't meant to sound so harsh. Thinking of Rachel brings it out of me.

Softening my voice, I say, "She left when Lily was born." Before Alyssa can ask any questions, I ask, "Would you like another beer?"

She shakes her head. "No thank you." Thankfully she doesn't ask anything more about Lily's mother.

We sit in silence as the night air cools, the sounds of crickets surrounding us. It should feel awkward and uncomfortable, yet there's nowhere else I want to be right now.

After a few minutes, Alyssa says, "How are things between you and your father? Harper tells me Finn still refuses to take his calls." Alyssa would know the story about my father because it involved Harper and she had needed Alyssa to lean on through the difficult time.

"He's still in France. He keeps reaching out, but I'm not ready for him to be in my life."

"Do you think you'll ever forgive him?" she asks.

"He cheated on my mother for years. Left her to die while he was screwing his mistress. How do I forgive that? Then to top it off, he almost ruined Finn and Harper's relationship with the lies he told. Telling Finn that Harper was trying to seduce him was fucked up. Thank God they pulled through it."

"I'm so glad it all worked out. Harper is happier than I've ever seen her."

"Yeah, Finn has heart-shaped eyes over her too." I chuckle. "I'm happy for them. Quite the party they threw for Avery."

"Can you believe they had Penelope Aldin as their party planner?" Alyssa says with awe.

"A little over-the-top for a baby," we say at the same time. Our eyes connect as we chuckle. I can't pull away. Thankfully, she can.

"I better get going. I'll help you clean up before I leave."

I don't need help, yet I let her collect the plates while I gather the remaining dishes and bring them into the kitchen. I want a few more minutes with her. Rinsing the dishes, I stack them in the dishwasher. All too soon, the job is done and there's no reason for Alyssa to stay any longer.

Like she knows her time is up, she says, "Well...I should go." She shuffles toward the door, looking reluctant to leave. "Thanks for dinner."

"Would you like a coffee?" Why can't I let her go?

"Sure, I'd love a cup." Is she holding onto as many minutes as she can too? Why would she? The way I've treated her, she shouldn't give me the time of day.

I put the pot on to brew and pull two cups from the cabinet. Turning my back toward her, I busy myself with the task. The more I look at her, smell her sweet perfume, hear her laughter, the more I want her.

When the coffee is ready, I pour it into the cups and hand one to Alyssa. "Would you like cream or sugar?" I ask.

"No, thanks. The hotter the better."

"The way I like mine too. Let's sit in the living room. It's more comfortable." We walk into the room and take our seats. Alyssa's elbow accidentally knocks my arm and hot coffee splashes over my chest. "Shit!" I hiss.

"Oh God! I'm sorry." She jumps from the couch, grabs my cup from my hand, and puts both cups on the coffee table. "Did it burn you? Of course it burned you. Let me see. Take off your shirt." Not waiting for a response, she tugs my t-shirt over my head. Looking at my chest, she covers her mouth with her hand and gasps, "I'm so, so sorry. Your skin is red. Where's your bathroom? We need to run cold water on it now!" Grabbing my hand, she tugs me to my feet. "Quickly, before it gets worse."

I lead her to the bathroom, not letting go of her hand. It feels small and fragile, and I like how it fits in mine, almost making me forget the burning sensation across my chest.

She turns the cold water on in the shower. "Get in," she demands.

When I step inside, she stops me with a hand on my shoulder. Her gaze trails over me. "Do you want to...arhh...take your jeans and shoes off first?"

I kick off my shoes but leave on the jeans. I can't promise, even with the pain, I can control my cock with her standing so close. Stepping into the shower, I give a sharp hiss as the cold water touches my skin.

"Oh God." She covers her face with her hands, peeking through separated fingers. "Are you in a lot of pain?"

Fucking hurts like a bitch. "I can hardly feel it."

She drops her arms by her sides and gives me a dubious look. "I doubt that."

"Okay, it stings a little."

She raises an eyebrow like she still doesn't believe me.

"How long do I have to stand here?" The water is cold, and I'm shivering.

"I think twenty minutes."

"Then what?"

She shrugs. "My knowledge doesn't go past running cold water over a burn. Maybe see a doctor?"

"It's not that bad. My shirt took the brunt of it." I turn my body slightly and wince as the spray hits me directly on the burn.

Noticing my discomfort, she says, "The pressure is too strong."

The shower is big enough for her to reach inside while avoiding the water spray, and she twists the faucet, but instead of softening the pressure, it hits me in the chest at full force.

"Oh crap." Alyssa steps further into the shower, either not caring or not thinking she'd get drenched.

In her panic to fix the water pressure, she fumbles with the faucets. The water turns off then on. Cold then hot. With her back toward me, I reach over her shoulder and lay my hand on top of hers, stopping her from boiling us alive. I turn the hot water off and put the cold back on. Alyssa is standing so close to me, her back pressed against my chest. I no longer feel the sting of the burn. Now I'm burning up in a different way.

Instead of pulling away, I stand statue-still, waiting for Alyssa to move. When she doesn't and remains just as still, I place my hand on her stomach, bringing her closer. She doesn't object, so I place my other hand on the curve of her hip. Our heavy breathing is competing with the sound of the shower.

The water is bouncing off Alyssa's jacket, and I take my hands off her long enough to slide it down her arms. It lands with a heavy thud at our feet.

Does she want me to touch her again? She hasn't run from the room. Or demanded to know what the hell I'm doing. That must be a good sign, right?

As I'm mentally debating what to do, Alyssa drops her head back onto my chest. I'll take that as a sign that we're on the same page. I splay my hands on her stomach and once again pull her closer to me. Our bodies are pressed together so tightly there is no hiding how much I want her. Even through my jeans, my cock is branding her lower back.

Glancing down the front of her, I see that the water has soaked through her leotard, almost making it transparent. Her nipples are spearing through the thin fabric, and I can make out the dark areolas. I groan with the desperate need to suck them into my mouth.

"Do you know how much I want to fuck you right now?" My hands skim up her torso, and I cup her breasts. They're not large but they fit perfectly into my hands.

"Tell me how much," she says on a husky whisper.

"More than I need to breathe." I pluck and twirl her nipples between my fingers, making her moan. My cock twitches at the sound, ready to plow into her.

Her butt squirms up against me like she needs more connection. "I wouldn't want you passing out from lack of oxygen." She reaches her hands behind her and links her fingers at the back of my neck, arching her back and pushing her breasts harder into my palms.

"Do you want me to fuck you, Twinkle Toes?" I suck water from her neck and lick my tongue over her racing pulse.

"Yes," she moans.

One hand massages her tits while the other travels south. I slide my fingers behind the waistband of her pants and under her tights. I ghost a finger over her panty-covered pussy.

"Yes, what?" I want to hear her say it.

"I want you to fuck me, Hayden."

Hearing the words and my name from her lips shoots pure desire to my cock, making me harder than I thought possible. But a thought niggles at the back of my mind. There's a reason I shouldn't be doing this. I've spent eight years keeping away from temptation. Alyssa is the biggest temptation of them all. One I can't deny. I've tried. It doesn't work.

Why should I? We both want this. I shouldn't be so terrified to take the next step. Nothing will happen except a mind-blowing orgasm. It will be good to feel one again that doesn't come from my hand.

With her back still toward me, I unlink her fingers from my neck and lower her arms by her sides, pushing the straps of her leotard down along the way, exposing her breasts. I cup them in my hands again, and like she's lost the energy to stand on her feet, she slaps her palms on the tile wall, causing her to bend slightly at the waist.

"Christ." I grit my teeth as she pushes her butt against my cock.

She wiggles her hips, silently telling me what she needs. And I want to give it to her. What is it about Alyssa that makes me throw all caution out the damn window? Making me forget why this is a bad idea. Maybe I'll regret this later, want to kick myself for being so reckless, but fuck it. This is what I want, and I'm taking it. I palm her ass and grind my cock into her. Her head drops forward on a long groan. Our clothes are too restrictive and getting in the way of her sweet spot.

Pulling her up straight, I spin her around. She slips on the wet floor, and I hook my arm around her waist to steady her. Water is pouring over our heads. Our chests are heaving like we've run a marathon.

When her gaze drops to my lips, all I want to do is taste hers. I have no idea who moved first when our mouths frantically collide. There's no finesse in the kiss. Lips, tongue, and teeth. Her hands run up and down my back. Mine are memorizing every part of her. Like they know this moment might never happen again.

She unzips my fly and reaches into my underwear. When she grabs a firm hold of my cock, my knees buckle. "Oh fuck." I drop my forehead onto hers and squeeze my eyes shut as she slowly strokes me. It feels so fucking good. *She* feels so fucking good.

Backing her against the tile wall, my lips travel across her jaw, down the elegant slope of her neck, across her collarbone, and to her pert tits. Her rosy, pink nipples pebble, waiting for me to suck them. As I flick one with my tongue, she releases my cock to tunnel her fingers in my hair, clasping me to her chest.

"Oh yes. That feels amazing." Alyssa sighs.

I should probably take her into my bedroom where it's more comfortable, but I don't want to break this moment. If we leave the confinement of the shower and step out of the room, it may shatter what we're doing. Taking a step back, I kneel in front of her.

"I like where this is heading," she says, her voice husky with need. She doesn't have to touch me; her voice alone can make my cock as hard as stone.

I unbuckle her boots and throw them into a corner of the shower. Next, I unzip her pants and tug them, along with the tights, down her legs, the wet fabric making it difficult to peel from her body. They too land with a splat next to the boots. All that's left is the pink leotard around her waist. It doesn't take long for it to be added to the pile of clothes.

Leaning back on my heels, I take in her nakedness. "You're gorgeous." The most beautiful woman I've ever seen.

"I don't exactly have all the curves in the right places. Actually, I lack any curves." She giggles.

No, she may not have voluptuous curves, but her dancer's body is strong and powerful. Her body can do amazing things. "You're pure perfection."

"That's sweet, but are you going to stare at me or are you going to put your mouth on me?" She sighs with frustration.

I chuckle. "Impatient are we, Twinkle Toes?"

"Yes, I am." With a sexy grin, she points to her pussy. "Get to work."

I choke out a laugh. "Yes, ma'am."

My mouth lands above her pubic bone, and I kiss the water from her skin. Her head falls back against the wall. Clutching her hips in my hands, I take small bites from her hipbones. I tilt my head up, because I want to watch her face the second I kiss her where she desperately wants me to. With open-mouth kisses, I head lower and cover her pussy.

Her eyes roll back in her head right before she squeezes them shut. Biting her bottom lip, she moans, "Yes, right there, Hayden. I need more."

The sound of my name spurs me on. I lick into her slit, twirling her clit and sucking it into my mouth. Trailing my hand along her inner thigh, I enter two fingers inside her.

Her hips arch from the wall and press against my hand. "I like the way you work."

I pull my mouth away long enough to say, "I do my best." Then I get back to laving her up.

"I'll make sure you're rewarded for a job well done," she says as her fingers tunnel through my hair.

Joking around during sex is something new to me. I'd had no connection with the women I'd hooked up with in the past. I would pick up someone in a club and we'd go somewhere to fuck. We barely made any small talk. Fucking women came to a screeching halt after meeting Rachel. No, I don't want to think about her now. Not when I have Alyssa in front of me. A woman, for the first time in years, I'm desperate to bury myself inside of.

"I'm not sure how much more I can take. Hayden, I'm about to come!"

Exactly what I want her to do, except I want to feel her orgasm clutching my cock. Rising to my feet, I push my jeans down my legs and kick them off. With her scent on my tongue, I kiss her so she knows how good she tastes. Fusing our mouths together, I place my hands under her ass and lift her.

Her legs wrap around my waist, and I press her against the wall. Cold water is running down our faces and bodies, yet I'm burning up like I'm in a fucking sauna. I grab my cock and position myself to enter her. Before I take the plunge, a thought smacks me hard in the head. *What about protection?* Fuck! How could I forget? I'm so enthralled with Alyssa, I almost forgot the most important thing.

I break the kiss. "I don't have a condom." I haven't needed one in years and don't keep any in the house.

"I'm on the pill."

My brain goes into overdrive. No contraception is one-hundred percent effective. I should know—I used a condom with Rachel, and she still got pregnant. Ice trickles down my spine. *I can't do this!* My hard-on deflates like a balloon.

Dropping Alyssa's legs to the floor, I step away, swiping water from my face.

"Hayden, what's wrong?" Her expression has gone from desire to concern. The fear I'm feeling must be clear on my face.

Reaching around her, careful not to touch her, I turn the water off. "I don't want to do this."

As I step from the shower, she follows, and I pass her a towel. She wraps it around her body. I grab another one and wrap it around my waist. Placing my palms on the vanity counter, I take a deep breath to collect myself. I thought I wanted to do this—I *did* want to do this, more than I've wanted anything. When it came down to it, the experience with Rachel still literally scares the fuck out of me. I'm pissed at myself for letting this affect me the way it does.

"Hayden, what's going on?"

I hate that I've done this to her again. Leading her on only to pull away. She deserves better. "You should go."

"What?" I hear the incredulous tone in her voice. "You want me to leave?"

Turning toward her, the hurt expression on her face stabs me in the chest. "I'm sorry. This isn't what I want."

She frowns. "You acted like it was exactly what you wanted."

I drop my head with shame. "I was wrong."

Pointing a finger toward the shower, she says, "*You* were the one who started this. *You* were the one who told me you wanted to fuck me."

I push my hair from my face. "I know. I'm sorry."

"Why do you keep running hot and cold with me? Tell me what's wrong."

The hurt is back in her face, and it kills me that I'm doing this to her. I can't talk about Rachel. If I had my way, I'd never speak about her again. All I want to do is pull Alyssa into my arms, but I can't do that either.

I stiffen my spine and do what I must do—distance myself from Alyssa. "There's nothing wrong. I changed my mind."

"You changed your mind? I'm not buying it. There's something more you're not telling me. I never asked for this. You keep coming on to me with the looks, touches, and kisses. You wanted to fuck me. Something happened. What is it?"

"Nothing happened. I made a mistake."

Her eyes narrow at the words. "So, you don't want to fuck me?"

"No." *Liar!*

"You don't want me?"

"No." Fuck. I should never have taken things so far.

She nods. "Okay. Fine. You like playing games. Got it."

She yanks a robe hanging from a hook on the wall and shoves her arms into the long sleeves. Unwrapping the towel from around her body, she tosses it onto the counter, then ties the belt around her waist.

"Next time you want to tell me you want to fuck me...don't. Play your games with someone else." She spins on her heels and storms from the bathroom.

"Where are you going?" I call as I follow her.

"Home," she throws over her shoulder as she jogs down the stairs.

"What about your clothes?"

She ignores the question and heads straight to the front door. I rush toward her, stopping her from opening it. "You can't leave dressed in a robe."

"Yes, I can." She tilts her chin up with defiance.

"You're naked under that thing. You're not leaving until you get dressed."

"Watch me." She pulls at the doorknob. I slap the door closed.

"Let me put your clothes in the dryer first."

"I'm not sticking around to wait for them to dry." Again, she pulls at the doorknob, and I again slap it shut.

"Then let me get you something to wear. Wait here, I have sweats and sneakers you can put on. They'll be too big, but it's better than a robe and bare feet."

She sighs heavily. "Sure. Thanks."

"I'll be right back." As soon as I reach the top of the stairs, I hear the door slam. I turn around.

She's gone.

Chapter Fourteen

———◆———

ALYSSA

"Tell me you're joking." Although Harper covers her mouth with shock, there's a sparkle of mirth in her eyes. I guess running out of a guy's house wearing nothing but a robe and no shoes does sound amusing.

I sink back into the couch and hug a pillow to my chest. "Does it look like I'm joking?" God, I've never been so humiliated in my life.

"You ran out of Hayden's house wearing a robe and got into an Uber," she says like she needs to set the scene.

"Don't forget no shoes. I damn near cut my feet on gravel on the sidewalk."

"Oh, Alyssa, how did you get yourself into this mess?"

I lean my elbows on my knees and scratch my scalp with my fingernails. "It's Hayden's fault. If he didn't get all 'I want to fuck you,' it never would have happened."

Harper's smile drops. All mirth is gone. "I can't believe he did that to you. That's not okay."

Tossing the cushion aside, I sigh. "Everyone has the right to change their mind. That's not what's annoying me so much. It's the way he's led me on only to tell me to leave. Like what happened is somehow my fault. He turned me on with his big hands and big…shower."

Harper grins, knowing what I really wanted to say.

"Then he has the nerve to tell me he doesn't want me." Am I not good enough? Why am I not what anyone wants? My parents. Broadway. Now Hayden.

Avery stirs in the bassinet sitting beside Harper, she picks her up and cradles her daughter in her arms. "Hayden has his reasons."

Wait, is Harper defending him? I sit straight in my seat. "What reasons?"

"It's not my place to say. If he's getting this close to you, maybe he'll eventually open up."

In the pool house he'd mentioned something about sorting through some things. "Whatever it is, he's still treating me like crap."

Harper sighs. "I know. I can talk to him for you if you'd like."

"God no. I don't want him thinking that this has bothered me."

Harper pats Avery's diaper-covered bottom. "It is bothering you."

I wish it didn't. A guy has never made me feel so rejected. My parents? Yes. A guy? No. "It stings a little. I'll get over it."

Harper gives me a dubious look but doesn't say anything more about it. "Since you're here, I'd love your help with something."

"Anything. What is it?"

"I need to head over to Alessi's and take a look at a fabric sample I'm interested in working with."

"You're working with Alessi Fashion now?" I ask.

Harper had tried working at the fashion house in the past. Being involved with Finn caused too much office gossip, and she decided to venture out on her own, hoping to stop anyone from accusing her of making it in the fashion world because of her husband's influence.

She'd put herself through school, had a baby, and got a job at a leading fashion house in New York City. I'm so proud of her.

"No, I'm still at Sempre. I've shown a design to Juliette Monet at Alessi's, and she says she has the perfect fabric for the gown. I'm desperate to see it."

"Do you need me to babysit Avery while you go?"

"I promised Juliette I'd take Avery into the office for a visit. Would you mind coming with me? This might sound silly, but now that Finn has gone back to work this is the first time I'm leaving the house with Avery on my own. I'm a bit nervous."

"It's not silly at all. Can't Finn bring the sample home for you?"

Harper gives a heavy sigh. "I've been stuck at home for days. Going to the office sounds like a trip to Disney World."

If I go to Alessi's, I might run into Hayden. That's the last place I want to go.

The expression on my face must tell Harper exactly how I feel about the request because she says, "I'm sorry. You don't want to see Hayden. I should never have asked. I'll manage. Moms do this every day. I need to start sometime."

"No, it's okay. I'll help you. I'll see him at Lily's dance class anyway. It's probably better to have our first encounter away from small children." I laugh, but deep down my stomach twists into knots at the thought of possibly seeing him today.

"Hopefully, he's stuck in meetings and you won't bump into him," Harper says.

I can only hope. "Fingers crossed."

The second we step out of the elevator into the reception of Alessi Fashion, of course Hayden is the first person I see. He's walking toward us with an older man. When he spots us, he does a double-take. *Bet you never expected to see me here, buddy.*

He shakes the man's hand, and the man enters the elevator we vacated. "Harper. Alyssa. What are you doing here?"

"Nice to see you too, Hayden," Harper says teasingly.

"I mean—"

"What you're really trying to say is 'What is Alyssa doing here?'" I cross my arms over my chest. "Don't worry. I'm not here to see you. I came to help Harper with Avery." To Harper, I say, "I'll wait for you here." Taking a seat in the waiting area, I pick up a magazine on the side table next to my chair and flick through the pages. Trying to ignore how good Hayden looks in a damn suit.

"You can come with me if you'd like," Harper says as her gaze flicks between Hayden and me with concern creasing her brows. Does she think I'm going to blast him in Alessi's reception?

"I'm fine here. I can take care of Avery while you look at the sample," I offer.

"That's okay, thanks." She brushes the top of Avery's head with her hand. The baby is strapped to Harper's chest with some kind of wrap.

"Take your time."

When Harper leaves, I'm hoping Hayden will follow. Instead, he stands next to my chair. I don't have to glance up to know he's staring at me. I can feel warm tingles along my skin. After a moment of silence, I look up at him. His dark hair is falling over his forehead, his face hard and expressionless. God, he's beautiful. Too bad he has a stone-cold heart.

"Can I help you?" I ask.

"You didn't answer my call last night."

"You called?" I play dumb.

"Yes, you know I did."

"I'm sorry, there was a call from an unidentifiable number, was that you?" I widen my eyes with mock surprise.

He frowns. "I texted you too."

"Yeah, that I chose to ignore." I glance back at the magazine and flip the page so hard I'm shocked it didn't rip.

He slides his hands into his pants pockets. "Can you come into my office so we can talk?"

"There's nothing to talk about. You said everything you needed to last night. If you need to add anything, you can tell me here."

He blows out a frustrated breath. Lowering his voice, he says, "Do you want me to discuss what went on between us with an office full of staff overhearing?"

Glancing up at him, I shrug my shoulders. "Sure, let's fill them in." God, I'm being such a bitch. The situation stings more than I'd like.

"Please." The word and the pleading way he says it, slices through me.

Closing the magazine, I slap it on the table next to me and rise. "Fine. Let's get this over with." The thought of rehashing last night's humiliating events makes my stomach churn.

He leads me to his office. The walls in the hallways are covered in glossy pictures of celebrities and royalty wearing gorgeous Alessi Fashion gowns. I can only dream of owning one of their designs. Thanks to my best friend, I can always borrow something from her closet.

Hayden's office is modern and sleek, overlooking central park. A photo of Lily on his desk is the only personal touch in the sterile-looking room. *Matches his personality.*

"Would you like to take a seat?" He points to a black leather sofa near the window.

"I'll stand." Suddenly I'm feeling nervous. Every time we've been alone in a room together, something sparks between us, and we do something that he obviously regrets.

Like he is thinking the same thing, he slides his hands in his pockets and keeps his distance. "You went home in nothing but a robe."

"Yes, so?"

"In. A. Bathrobe." He spits each word out like he's pissed.

I cock an eyebrow. "What's your point?"

Taking his hands out of his pockets, he tosses them in the air. "You were naked!"

"No, I wasn't. I was wearing a robe."

He rakes his hands through his hair. "You were *naked* under the robe. How the hell did you get home?"

"I called an Uber."

Pinching the bridge of his nose, he shakes his head. "You were naked in a stranger's car?"

"I wasn't naked, I was wear—"

"Don't you fucking say robe," he growls.

I roll my eyes. "It was no big deal. I'm sure my Uber driver has seen stranger things."

Hayden paces in front of the window. "I called you to make sure you got home safely. The least you could have done was answer your phone or reply to a fucking message."

How dare he be mad at me? "I didn't think you'd care how I got home since you were the one who kicked me out of your house."

He slams a hand on his hip. "I didn't kick you out."

I'm not sure how it happened, but Hayden is standing toe to toe in front of me, our noses almost touching. I need to strain my neck back to look at him. "You did! So you shouldn't care how I got home," I say, my voice rising to match his.

"Shouldn't care? I wouldn't let my worst enemy leave my house naked."

My hands dig into my hips. I yell into his face, "I was wearing a—"

"I fucking said, don't say robe!"

"Hey, what the hell is going on in here?" We both turn to find Lucas strolling into the office, closing the door behind him.

"Nothing," we both snap.

Lucas holds up both hands like he's been caught in a robbery. "Doesn't sound like nothing. I could hear you screaming at each other from my office. Something about someone being naked?" He grins. "Sounds like my kind of conversation."

I cover my face and groan into my hands. I didn't mean it when I told Hayden I didn't care if the office staff overhears our conversation.

Hayden narrows his eyes at Lucas. "Mind your own fucking business."

Lucas laughs, taking no offense at Hayden's harsh tone. "Hey, Alyssa. Good to see you." He smiles and saunters next to me. "I didn't get a chance to speak to you at Avery's party. Nice dive into the pool by the way." Oh God, lately my life has been one humiliating moment after another. "Are you still dancing at The Temple?"

"Not at the moment. I've injured my ankle and need time off." After two weeks and exercises from my physiotherapist, my ankle is feeling better. It won't be long until I've fully recovered. Hopefully I'll be back soon. I need the money.

"Hope it's not too serious. Let me know when you're back at work. I haven't visited The Temple in months. I'd like to say hi to a couple of the ladies." He grins.

"What do you want, Lucas?" Hayden interrupts our conversation.

"I wanted to let you know I finished looking through the proofs from the photoshoot. If you and Finn want to take a look, I've picked out the ones that will work the best for the campaign."

"I'll be in your office in a minute."

"Okay then." Lucas slaps the tops of his thighs. "I'll leave you two to discuss whatever it was you were discussing. Although, you might want to keep it down."

We wait for the door to close behind Lucas. My anger has subsided. "I'm sorry I worried you last night. It probably wasn't the best idea to catch an Uber in a bathrobe."

Hayden cocks an eyebrow. "You think?"

I narrow my eyes. "I'm trying to be the bigger person here and admit to my mistakes. You should try it sometime." The anger is boiling up again.

With a heavy sigh, his shoulders roll forward. "I shouldn't have—"

"Kicked me out?" Maybe I'm being dramatic. Harper did say he has his reasons.

He frowns. "Asked you to leave. After we...after what... Well, it was wrong. I'm sorry."

"Do you want to tell me what has you twisted in knots?" Will he open up to me like Harper said he might?

He drops his head to look at the floor. For a moment, I'm hopeful he'll tell me. When he lifts his head, his expression is closed. "Like I've said before, I have shit to sort through."

My heart sinks. We're not close enough for him to share his feelings. Just close enough to nearly fuck.

"So, I'll go find Harper." I hook my thumb over my shoulder toward the door.

He nods. "See you soon."

"Soon?"

"At Lily's dance class."

Of course. I fiddle with the button on my jacket. "Right, yes. See you then. Does Lily still want private lessons?" With what has happened between Hayden and me, I'm sure he'll cancel them.

"Yes, she does. If you're still available."

If I keep away from coffee and showers, I should be safe. "I'm still available."

"Great," he says.

"Great," I repeat. God, we're talking like strangers, not like two people who had their hands and mouths all over each other's bodies the night before. "Goodbye, Hayden."

"Goodbye, Alyssa."

I turn and head toward the door.

"Alyssa!" Hayden calls behind me. I slowly turn around. He walks over to a chair in the corner of the room and picks up a plastic clothing bag. "I had your clothes dry-cleaned. I was going to give them to Harper, but since you're here..."

My stomach drops to my knees. Was I hoping he stopped me to tell me to forget everything he said? That it was a big mistake letting me go? "Thank you. You didn't have to do that." I take them off his hands.

He picks up a canvas bag from the floor. "Your boots are still damp. I didn't know what to do with them, so I aired them out."

Plastering a fake smile on my face, I take the bag from him and thank him again.

As I get to the door, Hayden calls my name again. When I face him, he says, "I am sorry about last night. About all the times I've acted like a jerk." The sincere expression on his face tells me he's telling the truth. He's not some guy who likes to lead women on. Something is troubling him and holding him back.

"We'll pretend it never happened."

He nods, relief flooding his face.

When I leave the room, I lean on the closed door and drop my head back. We may pretend it never happened, yet I have a feeling I'll be reliving those moments over and over in my mind for years.

Chapter Fifteen

HAYDEN

The moment I sit down in the booth at the bar where Finn and Lucas are waiting for me, I know that this is going to be more than after-work drinks. The smiling assassins are eager to kill me with their questions. Lily is playing at a friend's house; I should tell them I don't have time for a drink because I have to pick her up so I can avoid what I know is coming. But they'll only keep badgering me about it, so it's best to get it over with.

Before they can fire their questions, the waiter comes to our table and I order a scotch. Something strong to get me through this conversation. When he leaves, I face my brothers. "Get it over with."

"Get what over with?" Lucas smirks.

"The twenty questions I know you're dying to ask."

Finn leans his elbows on the table. "I'm thinking more like fifty."

I roll my eyes.

"So, Alyssa..." Lucas says.

"What about Alyssa?" Just because they want information doesn't mean I have to make it easy for them.

"Something has happened between the two of you," Lucas states. I drum my fingers on the table. They both look at me expectantly. "Tell us."

"There's not much to tell." I sit back in my seat, enjoying their irritated expressions.

"Bullshit." Finn points a finger at me. "Harper knows something and is keeping her mouth closed. Lucas overheard an interesting conversation about Alyssa being naked. So, what's going on?"

"You know I don't have to tell you anything, right? What happens in my private life is none of your business."

They both pull a face like I'm talking shit. My brothers are my best friends. When something is happening in each other's lives, we know about it whether we're happy to share the information or not. We've always been close, but after learning about our father's lies and what he pulled between Finn and Harper, we've become even closer. There's nothing we wouldn't do for each other.

"Your business *is* our business," Lucas says.

We pause the conversation when the waiter arrives with our drinks. After he leaves, their attention is focused on me again. I take my time sipping the scotch.

"Okay, quit stalling and tell us what the fuck is happening with Alyssa," Lucas demands.

Taking another sip, I put my glass on the table and pull in a deep breath. I tell them about the night I helped Alyssa home after her fall. How things went too far in her apartment and I left without saying a word. I go on to tell them about Lily's private lesson, the coffee spill, and without too many details, what went on in the shower. Shame heats my face when I explain what happened next.

"You kicked her out of your house after you nearly fucked her?" Lucas says incredulously.

I blow out a frustrated breath. "I didn't kick her out! I asked her to leave." God, Alyssa and now my brothers believe I kicked her out. I guess no matter how I try to spin it, it doesn't look good.

Finn holds his hand up in a calm-down gesture. "Okay, okay. You asked her to leave. She got upset. You did lead her on. Not just once but twice."

I twirl the glass in my hand on the table. Christ, I am an asshole. Who does that to someone? Me, obviously. Because I'm fucked up. "One minute I'm remembering all the reasons why I don't sleep around, and the next, I'm almost fucking her. What's wrong with me?"

"You're a man who hasn't had sex in eight years," Finn says like the answer is obvious.

"It's never been a problem before. Why now? Why with Alyssa?"

Finn and Lucas stare at me like I've lost my marbles. Finn says, "Because you're obviously attracted to her. Maybe there's something more you're feeling."

I shake my head. "No, there can't be more. I don't have time. I have Lily and work and...and..." *Fear.* Fear that I'll be left with a newborn at my doorstep. I know I'm being irrational; what are the chances of it happening again? Yet the thought turns my blood to ice.

"You can have those things. It wouldn't hurt to let yourself go occasionally. Have some fun. Life isn't only about work and Lily," Finn says before taking a sip of his drink.

"A good fuck—hell, any fuck—would do wonders for you. I swear if you leave it any longer, you'll be a virgin again," Lucas jokes.

"Doesn't work like that."

"Might."

I roll my eyes.

"The last time I let myself have a good fuck, nine months later Rachel dumped Lily at my feet." My gut burns, not because of the alcohol but the feeling the memory evokes.

"Lily is great. Rachel did you a favor. The chances of that ever happening again are slim to none," Finn says. Exactly what I've been thinking. Yet fear takes over. Enough to not take the risk again. "Are you going to stay celibate for the rest of your life?"

After getting the biggest hard-on in my life with Alyssa, my desire is roused. Blazing like a bushfire out of control. Needing some relief. Something I can't provide for myself anymore. I don't burn for any woman. It's Alyssa.

"If you don't want a fling, what about a relationship?" Lucas asks. "Surely, you can't be against that too."

I scratch the side of my neck. Knocking back my drink, I signal to the waiter for another one. "I'm not against a relationship. It's just not the right time."

"I don't think the time is ever right. When it happens, it happens. There's nothing you can do about it," Finn says.

"It's not what I want right now. I have Lily to raise. I'm happy with how my life is." Am I? There was never a time I thought I needed anyone. Until Alyssa burst into my life with her black clothes and feisty attitude, turning everything I believe in upside down.

Lucas shrugs. "So, you're not ready for a relationship, but you'd fuck her if you weren't so terrified of getting her pregnant."

The waiter arrives, putting a glass of scotch in front of me on the table. I pick it up and take a long sip. "I think we're done with this conversation."

Finn gives me a scrutinizing stare. "I think you want a relationship. You're too set in your ways or too scared to admit it."

Rubbing my fingers over my forehead, I sigh. "No, I don't."

"I think you do," Finn says.

Gritting my teeth, I repeat, "No, I don't."

"Well, if you're not interested, maybe I'll ask her out. Maybe I'm ready for a relationship." Lucas grins.

I want to slap that smile off his face. "The fuck you will."

Lucas' grin grows wide. "I'm messing with you. Now I know there's something more than you just wanting to take her to bed. You have feelings for her, don't you?"

That was a shit move to make. I clamp my mouth shut. I can't answer that because I don't know what I'm feeling. All I know is it's more than wanting to sleep with her. The attraction is powerful. She's always on my mind.

Lucas slaps his hand on the table and chuckles. "Finally! There's life inside you. I was wondering if you'd turned into stone. You like her, and by the look on your face, I'd say a lot. You need to do something about it."

Sometimes I think my brothers know me better than I do. "I don't need to do anything about it because—"

"You have work and Lily to concentrate on. Yeah, yeah. We've heard it all before." Lucas rolls his eyes. "How about thinking about *you* for a change?"

"I don't need to complicate my life with a relationship."

"You might like it if you tried," Finn adds.

I shake my head. "Is this some kind of intervention? If I wanted to be in a relationship, I'd be in one. I don't need you two talking to me like I'm a freak because I haven't had a girlfriend in years."

"Or a fuck," Lucas mumbles under his breath.

Ignoring him, I continue, "This is my life. I'm happy. Move on."

"Geez, so much pent-up tension." Lucas smirks into his glass.

"One last thing and I'll drop the subject," Finn says with caution, like he thinks I'm going to bite his head off.

I sigh. "What is it?"

Finn twirls the ice in his glass. "If you're considering anything with Alyssa, she's a great girl. You'd be lucky to have her. Even though you're a grumpy asshole, I reckon she'd be lucky to have you too." Finn holds up his hands. "That's it. I have nothing more to add. I need to get home to Harper and Avery. Being away from them too long is hell."

We say our goodbyes and leave the bar. On the drive home, Finn's comment plays in my mind. *If you're considering anything with Alyssa, she's a great girl. You'd be lucky to have her.*

My life has revolved around Lily for so long, I'm not sure if I know how to fit in a relationship. Have I hidden behind the excuse of work and family long enough? Gotten too comfortable with my life? If I take that step, it's Alyssa I see in my future. She's the only woman who makes me feel this way. She makes me consider something more.

Chapter Sixteen

ALYSSA

Excitement is buzzing at the dance studio today. We're taking thirty of our students on a two-hour bus trip to attend a weekend workshop with Kai Hart. He's a fabulous dancer who has performed for multiple famous artists around the world. It's a trip of a lifetime for these kids. I must admit, I'm excited too. I might even fangirl over him. Too bad my ankle still isn't healed, or I'd take the classes alongside the students.

Parent helpers arrive at the studio, and my stomach twists in a knot. Two days ago, when Miss Lucia gave me the list of parents coming to help with supervision, one name stood out among them—Hayden Alessi.

He never mentioned coming on the trip. Probably because, since our talk in his office, when he drops Lily off at the studio, he greets me with a curt nod before leaving. When I arrive at his house for her private lessons, I get the same greeting. He doesn't come to watch, there's no offer of dinner afterward, and definitely no invitation for coffee. There's no conversation.

It's probably best this way. There are only so many times a woman can strip naked with the promise of sex only to have the man run screaming from the room. It hurts one's pride. I won't fall for his lusty eyes and roaming hands again.

Like always, when Hayden enters the room the air crackles with electricity. My body is hyperaware of him. I'm annoyed he has that effect on me. It doesn't help that he fills out a gray t-shirt and faded denim jeans like a GQ magazine cover model. Dragging my attention away from him, I make my way around the room to greet the parents, leaving Hayden for last.

"Good morning, Hayden. It's nice of you to join us this weekend."

His hair is damp and brushed back from his face like he's just had a shower. It has me thinking of our time in the shower, and my heart does a traitorous gallop in my chest.

"It's Lily's first dance trip. I wasn't comfortable letting her go by herself."

This is the most Hayden has spoken to me in two weeks.

Lily skips over to us. "Hi, Miss Alyssa."

"Hi, Lily. Are you excited about the workshop?"

Her grin spreads from ear to ear. "I can't wait. I packed a Kai Hart t-shirt. Do you think he'll sign it for me?"

"I'm sure he will."

Miss Lucia claps her hands to grab everyone's attention. "Our transport has arrived. Students, please follow your teachers outside and take your seats on the bus. Leave enough room for the parents to sit at the front."

"Let's go, Lily." To Hayden, I say, "See you later." Or not. If I can avoid him, I will. Hopefully, I'll be so busy with the kids and the workshops I won't give him a second thought.

As we get on the bus, Pippa Davidson, Kyle's mother, not so subtly elbows her way onto the bus to grab the seat next to Hayden. It's not like I wanted to sit next to him. He's all hers. I listen to Miss Lucia read out the roll to make sure everyone is on the bus. When everyone is accounted for, she puts the clipboard in her bag and sits next to me.

During the trip, my gaze involuntarily flicks over to Hayden and Pippa. She hasn't stopped talking the entire time. Hayden is nodding and smiling like she's telling him the most interesting story he has ever heard. At times, she places her hand on his thigh like she needs to touch him to emphasize what she is saying...*or* she just wants to touch him.

Doesn't she have a husband? I mentally shake my head. None of my business. Good luck to her. If she's trying to lure him into her bed, I hope she has better luck than I did. At the thought of them together, burning jealousy heats in my gut. I turn away to stare out the window.

"I'm so happy you're at the studio with us, *bella*," Miss Lucia says. I'd been so distracted by Hayden and I-want-to-jump-your-bones Pippa, I'd forgotten she was sitting next to me.

I turn to her and smile. "Me too. I'm having so much fun."

"I've been getting wonderful feedback from parents about you. The kids love having you as their teacher."

That warms my heart to hear. "I love teaching them too. I only wish I could dance with them instead of instructing Nikki to demonstrate." I haven't danced in three weeks. I miss getting lost in the music and movement.

"Hopefully it won't be too much longer. How is the ankle coming along?"

"It's a lot better. The swelling and bruising are gone, and I can walk on it without a limp. It causes me some pain when I try to dance and put pressure on it."

"Healing takes time. Have you any auditions lined up?" she asks.

"Yes, my agent has something set up for me." Normally, I'd be buzzing with excitement, nerves, or anticipation. This time, I feel nothing.

"I'd say that's exciting, but from the look on your face, it doesn't appear so. What's the matter, *bella*?" She looks at me with concern.

I give a tight smile and shrug my shoulders. "I'm just worried I won't be ready." That's not exactly true. I'll take pain killers and strap my ankle to get through the audition. Because I *will* be ready.

"It's normal to feel worried after an injury. You've got this," she says with confident encouragement.

I smile. "Thank you. Have you decided what you want to do with the studio? Are you still thinking about selling it?"

"I love that place so much. I've had so many wonderful memories there. It's my life. But I know I can't go on much longer. These old bones are getting tired."

I nudge her shoulder. "You're not old. But if you need to stop dancing, can't you hire more teachers to take the classes? Then you can just run the place."

"That won't work. If I'm there watching, I'll want to be in class." That's true. I've never seen a dance teacher so dedicated to her students like Miss Lucia. "Selling is the only option."

As much as I'd hate to see the studio run by a stranger, Miss Lucia deserves the time to rest.

After a few minutes, the bouncing of the bus is making me drowsy, so I lean my head against the window and close my eyes. What feels like five minutes later, Miss Lucia is shaking my shoulder. "*Bella*, we have arrived."

Cracking my eyes open, my gaze groggily sweeps the bus and connects with Hayden. A small grin tugs at the corners of his mouth. I turn away and stretch out my sore muscles from being cramped in a bus for two hours.

We usher the kids off the bus and meet the coordinator of the workshop. Once everyone is checked in, and bags are in the rooms, we make our way to the hall where the dance classes are taking place.

The kids cheer and clap when Kai Hart enters the room. Brown skin, bleached blonde hair, with baggy white pants, and a white and yellow tank, Kai Hart is one cool-looking dancer. I'm keeping my inner fangirl under control.

Looking around the room at the parents, the smiles on their faces tell me they're enjoying him too. Except for one person. Hayden. He is expressionless. I don't know what he thinks about the workshop.

Kai takes the students through a hip-hop routine, breaking it down so everyone, even the non hip-hoppers, can follow along. The weekend will be filled with different styles of dance. That's how good he is.

After they've performed the dance a few times, Kai claps his hands to grab their attention. "Who's ready to try something completely different?"

The kids' hands shoot into the air.

Kai glances around the room and smiles at me. "Miss Alyssa, can you help demonstrate with me, please?"

"Sure." I jump at the chance. Dancing with such a renown superstar is a dream come true. I make my way to the front of the room and stand next to him. "What are we doing?"

"The rumba. Now, I'll demonstrate the dance with a partner so you can see what it looks like," he says to the kids. "Then I'll break it down."

One boy groans. "Do we have to dance with the girls?"

Kai laughs. "No, you can do the steps by yourselves."

The boy sags with relief. Give him a couple more years and he might change his mind.

Kai holds my hand and puts his other hand on my shoulder blade.

"She can't dance with you." Hayden's voice shoots across the room. All heads swing toward him. He clears his throat. "She's hurt her ankle," he explains.

Kai looks at me then glances at my feet. "You're injured?"

"I was...am. It's a lot better. I can still dance." I'm not passing up this opportunity. I'll dance through the discomfort even if it kills me. Through the reflection of the mirror, I throw Hayden an annoyed look. Why did he have to speak up?

Kai gives me a dubious expression. "If it's not healed, you should keep off it. I'd hate to cause more damage."

"I'm fine." I bounce on my toes to convince him. A dull ache squeezes at my ankle. I smile to hide the pain.

"Are you sure?" Kai asks.

"She's in pain. I can see it all over her face." Again, all heads swing toward Hayden.

The parents and teachers all smile in a way that indicates they know something is going on between us but they're not sure what.

"Hayden, I'm fine," I say through gritted teeth.

"You're not." His jaw clenches.

Putting on a fake smile so I don't cause a scene in front of the children and parents, I say, "Thanks for your concern." I add extra sweetness to my tone. "It's lovely that you care so much about my well-being, but I know my body better than you do."

Hayden pushes off the wall he's leaning on and folds his arms over his chest. "I don't want to pick you up off the floor again when your ankle gives out."

My body tenses as I step out of Kai's arms. "I would have been fine without you." I'm using every muscle in my face to stop my smile from slipping.

"Really? I found you with your dress thrown over your a—" I know he stopped himself from saying ass. "—knees. In a puddle of water, barely able to walk."

"Will you ever let me forget that night?" It's not just the fall on the street I don't want to keep reliving, it's what happened in my apartment afterward too.

"Not when you keep doing stupid things."

The children are oblivious to our conversation as they chat and giggle among themselves. The parents, however, are swinging their heads between us like they're watching a tennis match, trying to hide their smiles behind their hands, entertained by our verbal sparring.

"Hayden, can you please follow me outside?" I don't wait for an answer, and as I walk out of the room, I'm aware that every adult's eyes are on us. In the lobby, I spin on my heels. The sudden movement shoots pain through my ankle, and I stumble. Hayden catches me around the waist, stopping me from falling.

With his arms still around me, he says, "And you thought you could do the *rumba*. You're not steady on your feet."

I point a finger at his chest. "What is your problem?"

"I don't have a problem. You do. Why would you dance on an injured ankle?"

"Oh, so you're only worried about my ankle?" I say with disbelief.

He cocks an eyebrow. "What other reason is there?"

I tilt my chin to the side like I'm thinking. "Oh, I don't know...maybe you don't want me dancing with Kai Hart?" I'm aware that I'm still wrapped in his arms. I'll step away any moment.

Averting his eyes for a beat, he looks back at me and frowns. "I don't care if you dance with him." Music drifts from the room, people are walking past us, yet we don't part. Hayden's hands are branding hot on my waist.

"I don't believe you. Try again."

He shrugs with a nonchalant expression. "The rumba isn't exactly appropriate in front of children."

I roll my eyes. "It's not dirty dancing. Well, it can be when it's done privately. I wonder if Kai gives private lessons," I tease to see if I can get a rise from him.

Hayden's hands tighten around my waist, and he pulls me forward so our chests touch. "You have children to supervise." His eyes darken. "There's no time for private lessons."

The way Hayden is staring at me causes the air to expel from my lungs. "Are you jealous, Hayden Alessi?" Why else would he act this way? My heart stops beating as I wait for the answer.

Dropping his hands, he steps away, scrubbing his fingers through his hair. "I'm...it's...whenever we're—"

The doors to the workshop swing open. Miss Lucia pokes her head out. Glancing at us both, she gives an apologetic smile. "I'm sorry to disturb you, but the children are having a break. We need help getting them to lunch."

I want to groan with frustration at her interruption. What was Hayden going to say?

"We'll be right there." When she ducks back into the room, I say to Hayden, "This conversation isn't over."

Chapter Seventeen

HAYDEN

The rest of the day is filled with more workshops. When Kai needs to demonstrate a dance with a partner, he calls on Miss Lucia or Miss Nikki for help. I'm not sure if he's not asking Alyssa again because of her ankle or because of the scene I caused. When I'd seen his hands on Alyssa's body, a surge of jealousy tore through me. I wanted to rip his arms off. I had the same reaction at Avery's party. Alyssa was right, I am jealous.

At the end of the day, we all gather at the hotel restaurant for dinner. Two tables are set for the children and another for the parents and teachers. Once again, Pippa Davidson from the bus sits next to me. If she slides her chair any closer, she'll be sitting on my lap. Alyssa takes a seat opposite us. Her eyes narrow in on Pippa. I'm not the only one with a case of the green-eyed monster. When our meals arrive, we start to eat.

"So," Pippa says, leaning toward me. Her warm breath fans over my neck. "Is there something going on with you and Alyssa?"

I glance over at Alyssa. Her head turns away like she doesn't want to get caught watching me. "Like what?" Our little scene has probably caused a lot of gossip.

"Are you two in a relationship?" she asks.

I fold my napkin and place it on the table next to the plate. "No."

Pippa slides her chair closer. "It looked like there's a lot of sexual tension between you two."

Picking up my glass, I take my time drinking the water. I put it back on the table. "We're just friends." Nothing I want to talk to Pippa about.

She puts her lips to my ear. "Friends who fuck?"

What the hell? I scan my gaze around the table to see if anyone heard her question. Thankfully, no one is paying us any attention. Not even Alyssa. She's fanning her face with a napkin like she's hot. Her skin is pale. Is something wrong?

"I don't care if you are. I can share." Under the table, Pippa trails her fingers up my thigh, brushing over my dick. Jerking, I scrape my chair back and abruptly stand. There's only one woman I want touching me, and she's sitting across from me, not looking the best.

"Alyssa, are you okay?" I ask.

Covering her mouth with her hand, she shakes her head. Then she jumps from the chair and dashes out of the room.

"I'll go check on her," I say to no one in particular. To Miss Lucia, I say, "Can you watch Lily please?"

"Of course. Let me know if you need any help," she calls after me as I rush out of the restaurant.

Scanning the lobby, I spot the restrooms and head toward them. If she were about to throw up, like it looked like she was going to do, that's where she'll be. Not caring that it's a female bathroom, I make my way inside. Thankfully it's empty. Only one cubicle door is closed. I knock on it. "Alyssa, are you in there?" The answering retching sound tells me she's inside. "Open up so I can help you."

"Go away," she croaks.

"Open up," I say again.

More retching, then a weak, "No."

"Let me in." I rap my knuckles on the door.

"I said go away."

I hear a slight thud. Shit! Has she passed out? Knocked her head? "If you don't open the door, I'll break it."

"I'm hideous. You don't want to see me this way."

I breathe a sigh of relief. She hasn't passed out.

It's driving me nuts that she won't let me in. "I'm warning you, if you don't open this door, I *will* break it down. That will really give the parents something to talk about."

I hear a heavy sigh. "Fine."

A few seconds later, the lock unlatches and the door swings open. Alyssa looks anything but hideous. She couldn't if she tried. Even after spewing her guts out. What she looks is tired...vulnerable. Like she needs someone to take care of her.

She squats next to the toilet. "How can you help me?"

"I can hold your hair back. Isn't that what your girlfriends do in public toilets?"

She gives a half-hearted chuckle before leaning over the bowl and heaving into it. Her hair is in a bun, so I squat next to her and rub her back.

When she's done, she rips off toilet paper from the dispenser and wipes her mouth. "Please go away and let me die in peace."

"I'm not going anywhere. Not until I know you're okay. What's brought this on? Was it the food?" Everyone else seemed fine.

Shuffling to get up, I help her to her feet.

"Not the food. I started feeling funny after the last class. I put it down to a busy, full day." She flushes the toilet. "I think I'm done."

Walking to the vanity, she splashes water over her face and rinses her mouth. "Thanks for checking on me."

Her face is pale with bright red patches on her cheeks. I place a hand on her forehead. "You're burning up."

Like she's run out of energy, she slides to the floor, resting her back on the tile wall. "Can I stay here and go to sleep?"

This is not good. She needs to see a doctor. "Let me get Miss Lucia to watch you while I call for a doctor."

Closing her eyes, she shakes her head. "I don't need one."

"You have a fever."

"I'll take Tylenol and sleep it off in my room. I bet it's just some twenty-four-hour bug."

"You're bunking with four kids and another parent. You might be contagious."

"I'll book another room," she says, closing her eyes and leaning her head on the wall.

"You can stay with me." There is no way she can stay in a room on her own. I could ask one of the teachers or parents to stay with her, but that would take them away from supervising the children. I'd booked a separate room for me and Lily—there was no way I was sharing one with a bunch of kids and another parent.

A ghost of a smile tugs her lips. "Are you trying to have your way with me again?" Then she frowns. "No, you don't want me. I'll be okay on my own."

Don't want her! Each morning I wake up with the biggest hard-on after having erotic dreams about her. If I weren't so fucked up, I'd have her in fifty different positions by now.

"You can't stay on your own," I say. "You're sleeping with me—I mean..." I pinch the bridge of my nose. "You're sleeping in my room."

"You said I might be contagious. I don't want to pass it onto you or Lily." She folds her legs to her chest and rests her head on her knees. I can't let her stay on the bathroom floor much longer. She needs a bed.

"Lily can bunk in with one of her friends. Don't worry about me."

"Are you sure?" She rolls her head to the side to look at me. My heart squeezes in my chest seeing her so sick.

"I'm sure. Wait here for a few minutes. I'll let Miss Lucia know what's happening. Will you be okay?" I don't like leaving her, but I can't take her with me.

She gives me a thumbs-up, like she's too tired to speak.

"I'll be back as soon as I can."

Rushing from the bathroom, I stop at the hotel's reception and ask them to deliver some Tylenol to my room. Then I race into the restaurant. Kneeling next to Miss Lucia, I fill her in on Alyssa's condition and what I have planned for her.

"Is there room in one of the other rooms for Lily to stay in? If Alyssa's contagious, I don't want her catching anything."

"I'd be happy to take Lily with me," Margo, a parent sitting on the other side of Miss Lucia, offers. "Unless Lily wants something specific from her bag, I'm sure I can find something for her to sleep in."

"Thank you, I appreciate it."

I'm anxious to get back to Alyssa. I hate I left her alone on the bathroom floor, but I need to speak with Lily. "Lily Pily, Miss Alyssa is sick. I need to take care of her. Margo said you can sleep with the girls in her room tonight if that's okay with you."

"Yes, that's okay."

I rub a hand down her hair. "Margo has something for you to sleep in. Do you have anything in the room you want to take with you?"

She shakes her head.

I give her a hug. "Call me any time of the night if you need me."

She smiles. "I will."

Kissing her cheek goodbye, I hurry back to the bathroom. Alyssa is where I left her. Still looking like death.

I squat next to her and tap her shoulder. "Hey, how are you feeling?"

She cracks her eyes open. "Sleepy," she mumbles.

"Are you sure you don't want me to call a doctor?"

"I'll be fine." She puts her hands on the floor to push herself up.

Taking her by the arms, I help her to her feet. "Can you walk, or would you like me to carry you?"

"Look at you being so chivalrous. Whenever I'm in trouble, you're my knight in shining armor. I didn't think men like you existed."

Anchoring my arm around her waist, we make our way slowly from the restroom. "I was in the right place at the right time."

At the elevator, we step inside. She rests her head on my chest. Holding her in my arms feels right. Like I want to protect her and help her for the rest of my life.

Sighing, she says, "Under your grumpy, cold exterior, you are a decent guy."

I choke back a laugh. "Grumpy and cold?" Of course she'd think that. "I'm sorry I've given you that impression. I've had my reasons, although I'm sorry for how I've made you feel."

The doors of the elevator open and we step out. Even though I can tell she's having no trouble walking on her own, I don't let go. I love having her close to me.

"Harper said you have your reasons."

Without breaking apart, I pull the keycard from my back pocket and swipe it to unlock the door. "She did? What else did she say?"

I finally let her go so we can walk inside the room. "Nothing. Don't worry, your deep, dark secret is safe."

"I don't have secrets. But there are some things I'm not comfortable talking about."

"If you ever need anyone to talk to, I'm a great listener." Her eyes are glassy, and her cheeks are flushed. I need to get her to bed. There's no time for talking.

As we step further into the room, the king-sized bed dominates the small space, making it glaringly obvious there's only one bed. We pause and stare at it.

Alyssa glances around the room. "There's no couch."

I slide my hands in the pockets of my jeans and rock back on my heels. "You're sick. If you're worried we'll do—"

"No, I'm not."

I think she wants to say 'because you keep rejecting me,' and I can understand why she'd think that. After all, it is what I keep doing. She doesn't know how much I want her. *I* am the problem, not Alyssa.

"We can put a pillow between us if you think I'll try to seduce you," she jokes.

I chuckle. "I'll take my chances."

Flopping face-first on the bed, she groans, "I'm so tired."

On the nightstand the hotel staff have left a packet of Tylenol. I pick up the box. "Don't fall asleep yet, you need drugs."

In the bathroom I fill a glass with water and take it back to the room. Alyssa's eyes are closed and she's breathing heavily.

I nudge her shoulder. "Wake up, Twinkle Toes. You need to take this."

Cracking her eyes open, she shuffles into a sitting position where she can take the Tylenol and drink it down with water. I place my palm on her forehead and frown. She's burning up. Hopefully the acetaminophen will bring the fever down.

Taking the glass from her hands, I place it on the nightstand. "I need to take your boots off so you're more comfortable."

She nods and I get to work pulling them off. When they're off, she folds her legs up, presses her hands together and tucks them under her cheek. Closing her eyes, she mumbles drowsily, "Thank you for taking care of me."

I brush a wayward strand of hair from her face that's escaped from her bun. "Anytime, Twinkle Toes." If the fever hasn't reduced in half an hour, I'm calling a doctor.

A few moments later, her deep breathing tells me she's fallen asleep. Kicking off my shoes, I sit on the other side of the bed and lean against the headboard. I turn on the TV and put on a movie with the volume low so I don't wake her.

What feels like only moments later, the sudden jolt of my chin hitting my chest jerks my head up. Blinking groggily, I glance around the dim room and at the clock on the bedside table. It's two hours later. I must have fallen asleep.

I turn to look at Alyssa. She's tucked into a shivering ball. "Shit!" I bound from the bed, run around to her side, and cup her face in my hands. Fuck, she's hotter than before. "Alyssa, wake up." I shake her shoulder.

Her eyes slowly blink open. "I'm so cold. I need a blanket."

"What you need is a doctor."

She shakes her head. "No. I want to get warm and sleep."

Raking my hands through my hair, I blow out a long breath. "We need to get your fever down. If you don't want to see a doctor, then you need a shower."

She frowns. "A shower?"

"A cool one."

Shivers rack through her body. "No, thanks."

"The Tylenol didn't work. It's that or the hospital."

She gives a heavy sigh. "Fine."

Taking her by the hands, I help her to her feet, and we slowly walk into the bathroom. It doesn't go unnoticed that we've been in a similar situation before. That time did not end well. With Alyssa in this condition, there is no way I am tempted to touch her again. This is about getting her better. Nothing more.

I turn on the cold water. "Maybe you should...arhhh...take off your clothes."

She smiles and props a languid hand on her hip. "Hayden Alessi, are you trying to get me naked?"

Heat creeps up my neck. "No... You're sick...this will help."

She laughs. "I'm joking. As gorgeous and tempting as you are, I'm in no condition for a make-out session."

"You think I'm gorgeous?"

She rolls her eyes. "Don't pretend you don't know you are."

I put aside how her comment makes me feel. I've got more important things to focus on. Like getting her temperature down fast.

Leaning into the shower, I adjust the water temperature while she strips out of her cargo pants and t-shirt. When she's down to her bra and panties, she steps into the shower, hissing as the cool water covers her body.

Worried that she's not steady on her feet and might slip, I kick off my shoes and step into the shower fully clothed.

Her eyes widen. "What are you doing? You're getting saturated."

I brush water from my face and slick my hair back out of my eyes. "I don't want you to fall."

Standing under the rain-showerhead, her teeth chatter. "I'm fine. You don't have to do this."

During her nap, and with water in her hair, the bun on top of her head has fallen into a haphazard mess. I find the pins, pluck them out, and drop them onto the floor. Her hair tumbles past her shoulders, and I run my hands through it to untangle it.

"Someone needs to take care of you." And I'm glad it's me.

"Thank you." As soon as the words leave her mouth, her head falls on my chest like she needs support.

I anchor an arm around her waist, another around her shoulder, and draw her in so our bodies are plastered together. Her body trembles, and I rub my hand along her shoulder and arm to comfort her, tucking her head beneath my chin.

This is different from the last shower we took together. Then I was filled with lust and longing and wanted to get my hands on every part of her body. I wanted to taste her. Fuck her. Do everything that plays in my dreams. Now, with her so vulnerable in my arms, I want to comfort her. Protect her. Take away the pain and discomfort she's experiencing. Like she—apart from Lily—is the most special person in the world.

Fuck! What's come over me? How have I gone from not looking at a woman to having one consume my every thought? Alyssa has made me feel things I never thought I would. She's not only woken up my body, but my heart is also beating a different tune.

My life was fine the way it was. But that's all it was—fine. Not great. Not exciting. Not amazing. Just fine. Having spent time with Alyssa, I've realized I need more. Only if I have the guts to take it.

We stand under the spray in silence for about ten minutes until Alyssa tips her face up to me. "You're quiet. You look so serious." I swipe water off her face, noticing that her skin feels cooler. "What are you thinking about?" she asks.

Not ready to say what's in my heart, I focus on what's happening with Alyssa. "Your fever has dropped. That's a good sign. You can get out of the shower now."

Nodding, she pulls away. I turn the water off, and we carefully step out of the shower. I hand her a towel and pat my face dry with another. She wraps the towel around her, and I glance away. She may be sick, but she looks sexy as hell in lace underwear.

"I'll get you something to wear," I say. "I'll be right back."

Scurrying out of the bathroom, I take a deep breath to try to control my racing heart and keep my cock from stirring to life. I need to remind myself that she's sick. What kind of sicko am I to ogle her?

I find what I need, and head back to the bathroom to find her black, lacy underwear flung over the shower door. I swallow hard. That means she's naked under the white, fluffy towel. Holy fuck!

I pass her a t-shirt and boxers. Clearing my throat, I say, "These will be too big, but that's all I have."

She smiles. "Thank you." The color has returned to her face.

"How are you feeling?" I ask.

"Better. The shower helped a lot. Thank you for staying with me. The way I was feeling, I would have face-planted the floor."

"No problem. I'll leave you to get dressed."

Grabbing another towel from the vanity counter, I bring it into the bedroom. I peel off my wet jeans, t-shirt, and underwear and toss them into a corner of the room, then I wipe my body dry.

"Oh, sorry," Alyssa gasps behind me. Spinning around, I see that she has her back toward me. "I should have warned you I was entering the room."

"It's okay." I wrap the towel around my waist. "You can turn around now. I'm decent."

Turning around, her eyes widen. "You said you were decent." She waves a hand up and down the length of my body. "That is *not* decent."

"The main parts are covered. Have you gotten shy, Miss Alyssa?"

Putting her hand on her hip, she gives a jaunty shrug. The neckline of the t-shirt she's wearing slips off her shoulder. Fuck, she's sexy, and she's not even trying. "I'm not shy. If I need to convince you of that...you have a great ass."

I choke on a laugh. "Had a good look, did you? You must be feeling better." Her natural olive complexion is back. I'm relieved that the worst is over.

"I might be sick, but there's nothing wrong with my eyes." She grins.

I shake my head. "I'm about to drop the towel to get dressed." I hold her gaze like I'm challenging her. Will she turn around? Or prove again that she's not shy?

"Are *you* the shy one? You've got nothing I haven't seen before." She tests back.

When I slip my fingers into the knot of the towel, her gaze flicks to my hands. "I'm not shy." I loosen the towel and slowly open it.

What is it about Alyssa that makes me act this way? Like she's sucking all the seriousness out of me and filling me with fun. Who am I? I'm liking this side of myself.

She whips around, giving me her back. I smile with satisfaction. *Not so brave, are you, Miss Alyssa?*

I slip on sweatpants and a t-shirt. Normally I sleep naked, but with Alyssa sharing the bed, clothes are a must. Once dressed, I say, "Okay, now I really am decent."

Turning around, she scans me from head to toe, giving me an appreciative glance. It's hot enough to burn my clothes right off. Why bother getting dressed if she's going to look at me like that?

She moves to the bed and hesitates at the edge. "I'm tired. I should...arhhh..." She hooks a thumb toward the bed. "Go to sleep."

I know what she's thinking, because it's the same as what I'm thinking. We have to share a bed. It will be a long night sleeping next to Alyssa. That's if I can get any sleep with her warm body so close to mine.

"Are you sure you don't want me to put pillows between us to make you more comfortable?" I ask.

"That's okay. I know I'm safe with you." Her smile drops, and a line creases her forehead.

Is she thinking about the times we've been intimate, and I've stopped before it went too far? God, I fucked up. I wish I could tell her how much it killed me to pull away. But now is not the time. Not when she's looking like she's going to pass out.

Alyssa slips into bed. I pull the covers to her shoulders. "Is there anything I can get you? Water...something to eat?"

She screws her nose up. "The thought of food makes me want to throw up."

"You still feel nauseous?" Should I take her to the hospital after all?

"No, just a little queasy. Nothing to worry about. I'm fine." She gives me an assuring, sleepy smile as her eyes blink heavily.

Curling onto her side, she tucks her hands under her chin. Her eyes flutter closed and don't open again. A moment later, I hear the soft sounds of deep breathing. She's asleep.

I stay by the side of the bed and watch her. Her dark brown hair is splayed across the pillow. Her face is soft with sleep. It's so easy to imagine waking up to her every morning. My heart squeezes in my chest like it knows something that I don't.

Chapter Eighteen

—◦—

ALYSSA

My heavy eyelids blink open. The room is dark. Something hot around my waist and over my leg is anchoring me into the mattress. Soft breathing fans my face.

It takes me a second to remember where I am. In Hayden's hotel room. In his bed. With Hayden draped over me! During the night, we've turned to each other. I should slide out from his embrace. Surely, he doesn't know what he's doing. If he did, he'd probably spring from the bed and run out of the room. Isn't that what he does anytime he gets too close?

Instead of moving, I take a moment to soak this in. When will I ever get this chance again? Never. Not with the way he keeps pushing me away.

As much as I would love to stay in this position, I need to pee. I try to lift Hayden's arm off my waist only for him to take a stronger hold, pulling me closer. Again, I try to move his arm, and again, he holds me tight.

"Where are you going?" he mumbles. "You feel so good. Never leave me."

I freeze. Does he understand what he's saying? My eyes have adjusted to the dark, and with the soft glow of the digital clock on the nightstand, I can see his eyes are closed. Is he talking in his sleep?

"Hayden," I whisper so not to startle him awake. "I need to use the bathroom."

"Want you here. Don't go." He rubs our noses together and then plants a soft kiss on my lips. Now I know he must be sleeping.

Nudging his shoulder, I say louder, "Hayden, wake up."

He tucks me under him and rolls over the top, burying his face in my neck. "Don't leave me. Never leave me."

His mouth sucks at my neck, his tongue licking over my racing pulse. Oh, it feels so good having his lips on me. I close my eyes and enjoy the sensation. If he's sleeping, I should try harder to wake him up. And I will...in a second.

Hayden nestles between my thighs. My legs voluntarily open, and I welcome the feel of his erection pressing against my sex. I will wake him...

When his hands float up my torso, under my t-shirt, and cups my breasts, my back arches off the bed. God, this feels so good. But it's so wrong. *Stop, Alyssa. Stop!* Instead, I grip onto his hips, digging my nails into his skin, pressing myself firmer to where our bodies meet. I'm burning up—this time not from a fever. I want more. *Crave* more. Hayden's warm breath fans over my neck, and his hand ghosts down my stomach and slides behind the waistband of my boxers.

"I fucking need you," he groans against my neck. "More than anything."

We agree on the same thing. Yet this is wrong. I need to stop what's about to happen. Before he can slide his fingers into the spot I desperately want him, I shake myself out of the haze of lust I've fallen into. The man isn't lucid. He could be dreaming of someone else.

Is that why he pulls away from me? Because there's another woman? What a stab to the heart that thought is.

Pulling his hand out of my boxers, I shake his shoulder. "Hayden, wake up."

Hayden's head lifts and he stares down at me, confusion lining his features. A second later, understanding shoots from his eyes, and he rolls to the side and springs from the bed to his feet, raking his fingers through his hair. "Fuck. What did I do?"

I sit up and tuck my legs under me. "Not much."

Scrubbing his hands over his face, he says, "I was on top of you."

"It's fine. Nothing happened." *Except for those few moments you made my body burn.*

He links his fingers together and places his hands behind his head, his face screwing up with disgust. "I was about to fuck you."

My body deflates. Why is this happening? Why do I let myself get pulled toward him only for him to reject me? "Am I so repulsive? Does the thought of having sex with me sicken you?"

Dropping his hands by his sides, his eyes widen. "How can you think that? Every time I am near you I can't keep my hands to myself."

I pick up a pillow and hug it to my chest. "That's not how I see it. Every time things get heated between us, you run away like I'm enemy number one."

"You're not my enemy."

"Why are you running away from me then? Why don't you finish what we start?" It's time to lay everything out. Whatever his problem is, it's affecting what's happening between us. If he can't be open and honest, then this is it. No more. No matter how much I'm drawn to him. I can't keep putting myself through this torture.

The bed dips as he sits on the edge. He places his forearms on his thighs and lets his hands dangle between his legs. Staring at the floor, he says, "I'm fucking scared."

Spoken so softly and with his back toward me, I'm not sure I heard right. "What did you say?"

He turns his head over his shoulder to look at me. "I'm scared."

I sit up on my knees on the mattress, tossing the pillow on the bed. "Are you scared of me?"

He shakes his head. "No, not of you. What can happen if we have sex."

The room is too dark for this conversation. I lean over and flick on the lamp sitting on the nightstand. Studying his face in the dim light, his sullen expression tells me he's deadly serious. "What do you mean?"

"If we have sex, there's a chance you'll get pregnant. I'm fucking petrified of another unplanned pregnancy."

Wait... What? He's worried I'll get pregnant?

He bounds from the bed. "As much as I love Lily and could never imagine life without her, I can't raise another baby on my own. I can't look into another child's eyes and try to understand how a parent can abandon her. Lily is asking questions about her mother. How the fuck do I tell her that her mother didn't want her? That she screwed me once then dumped Lily at my feet without looking back." Hayden's head drops to stare at the floor.

When Harper told me Hayden has his reasons for acting the way he does...is this why? He's worried if we sleep together, I'll get pregnant and leave him to raise another baby on his own. Part of me is furious he could think that of me. I'd never be so heartless. Then I take one look at him and my heart breaks for him and for what he's been through.

Getting off the bed, I walk to him and place my hand on his arm. "I would never do that to you or to a baby. Is it only me that scares you? Do you think I'm capable of abandoning a baby?" A stabbing pain pierces my heart. Does he think so low of me? "Are you like this with other women you've slept with?"

Hayden clutches onto my shoulders. "No, I don't think you're cruel. After having Lily, I'm too scared to take that risk…with anyone. I know it sounds ridiculous. I know the chances of it happening again are slim. Yet I can't let myself go there again."

"Wait…are you saying you haven't had sex since Lily was born?" How is that possible? Hayden is gorgeous, caring, sweet with a wicked side to him. Any woman within walking distance would want a piece of him.

"Yes."

"She's eight."

He nods. "At first, I was so busy trying to keep her alive. Between feeding, changing diapers, and washing bottles, I never left the house. When she slept, I took the time to read everything about babies I could put my hands on. I worked from home most days or took her with me into the office. I had no interest in anything else. When she got older and started school, I went back to work full-time, working from home as much as possible."

"You didn't hire a nanny?"

"No. I was raised by one and spent more time with her than my parents. I didn't want that for Lily. She already has no mother. I want to be the one to raise her one-hundred percent of the time."

I take him by the hand and guide him to the bed. Sitting down on the edge, I say, "You have done a wonderful job raising her. She's a great kid."

Pride lights up his face. "She is my life. I can't believe I haven't fucked it up yet."

I laugh. "I'm sure you won't fuck it up."

Pulling a face, he says, "I'm dreading the teenage years."

I scoot back on the bed, leaning my back against the headboard. Hayden follows. "Keep doing what you're doing," I say. "She'll be fine."

Thinking back on my teenage years, I cringe. There were a couple of years where I wanted to forget about my parents' wishes for me to dance every second of the day. So I skipped classes, went to a few drunken parties, sneaked out of the house late at night to hang around boys I had no business being with. Like a special *fuck you* to my parents, I lost my virginity in the dance studio's costume room.

But there's no point sharing that part of my past with Hayden. I don't want to scare him about what could be in Lily's future. My wild side came from wanting to rebel against my parents. I know Lily is loved no matter what she wants to do. Thankfully, my love for dancing and Miss Lucia's guidance got me back on track.

"Why did Lily's mother leave her?" I ask.

I'm not a mother, yet I could never imagine giving my baby away. Leaving my dog with a friend when I moved to New York made me cry for weeks. I still FaceTime Benji weekly.

When Hayden doesn't answer, I say, "I'm sorry. If you don't want to talk about it, I understand." If his past has scared him so much he can't have sex, it must be painful to relive it.

He folds his legs up and rests his wrists on his knees. "No, it's fine. I met Rachel one night in a club back when I partied too hard and didn't care who I fucked. Rachel was hot, eager, and I had her in a hotel room half an hour after meeting her. The next morning, we parted ways.

We didn't exchange numbers. There were no plans to meet. I never expected to see her again."

Hayden gets off the bed and walks to the minibar. Plucking a tiny bottle of whiskey from the fridge, he holds it out, offering it to me. I shake my head. He twists off the lid and chugs it down until it's empty. Like he needs something to help him deal with the past. Tossing it in the trash can under the counter, he comes back to the bed.

"Nine months later, she shows up at my office. I'm no celebrity, but our fashion house is big news. She must have worked out who I was. Anyway, she shows up with Lily in a baby carrier and a diaper bag, dropping the bomb that she's mine. The news floored me. Left me speechless. Her parting words were 'I don't want her. Would have gotten rid of her if I hadn't found out I was pregnant after it was legal to do it. She's all yours.'"

My hand flies to my open mouth. "What the hell? How can she be so evil? This sounds like a Hollywood movie." Who does shit like that?

He scrubs his fingers across his forehead. "More like a nightmare."

"You just accepted the baby as yours and took her from Rachel?"

"She didn't give me much choice. After she handed Lily to me, she ran from the room and out of the building before I could form a sentence. The shock had hit me hard."

"Did you ever look for her? Could she have been dealing with postpartum depression?" I ask before I judge too harshly.

"I hired a private investigator—"

"Now this is really sounding like a Hollywood movie."

He grins at my comment, making my insides tingle down to my toes. "He told me she married a wealthy stockbroker, lived in a mansion, and for the last five months of her pregnancy, vacationed in Italy, or so she told her husband. Instead, she was renting an apartment in

Long Island. After giving birth and giving Lily to me, she went back to her husband like nothing had happened."

"Oh my God, Hayden. I'm so sorry. Did you ever wonder if Rachel was telling the truth?" What if Lily wasn't his? With her sandy-brown hair and brown eyes, she doesn't look like Hayden.

"Absolutely. Until I got the results of the DNA test, I'm ashamed to admit, I wasn't exactly a loving father. I took care of her and made sure she had everything she needed. But I didn't want to get too attached if she wasn't mine. Although, by the time the results came in, she'd wormed her way into my heart. I don't know what I would have done if she wasn't mine." He takes a seat on the bed next to me again.

Loved her anyway. Because that's the kind of man he is.

"Has Rachel ever contacted you again? Even though she had a rich husband and lived a life of luxury, she may have been struggling mentally."

"Because the private investigator followed her for a while, he knew the places she liked to visit. I found her in a coffee shop near her house. Let me tell you, she wasn't pleased to see me. Thought I was trying to give Lily back to her." He shakes his head in disgust. "Not once did she look at the baby or ask how she was doing. She had zero interest in her daughter. Turns out, she kept the pregnancy a secret from her husband. He would have divorced her if he'd learned she had an affair. She chose money and the life of luxury over her flesh and blood."

This story gets worse and worse. "Thank God Lily has a father like you." What would her life have been if she'd stayed with her mother? Probably a miserable one with no love and affection. Hayden is giving her enough love for two parents.

He rests his head on the headboard. "Thank you."

Fiddling with the hem of the t-shirt, I say, "So, raising Lily hasn't given you time for…relationships?" I really want to know how he's lasted eight years without sex. A man like him would have women drooling over him. Me included.

"There's been a couple of women who have made their interest known."

Only a couple? Yeah, right. More like a swarm of women. "And you refused?"

"Yes. They never interested me enough to take the risk. I'm done with one-night stands. Done with casual sex with women I don't know."

I pull my knees to my chest and hug my legs. "Oh, so that's why you're not interested in me. You see me as a one-night stand."

He faces me, looking incredulous. "Not interested in you! You consume my every thought. My body aches to be near you. Every time I look at your lips, I want to kiss them. My hands want to touch every part of you. Being with you is the most excitement I've had in years. I haven't stopped thinking about you since Harper and Finn's wedding. I wanted to rip Kai Hart's arms off for touching you, because you were right, I was jealous. So, not interested? You couldn't be further from the truth."

Wow! The words knock the breath from my lungs. He had all of that hidden behind his serious, standoffish exterior. "If that's true—"

"You bet it is," he says as serious as a heart attack.

I smile. "I've wanted you just as much."

Taking my hand, he links our fingers together. "I picked fights with you to push you away. I've been fighting this attraction and losing. When I think I can take the next step with you, I remember the past and I run scared. I've given you mixed signals. I'm sorry. Sorry for the hurt I've caused."

Seeing the vulnerability on his face and hearing the sorrow in his voice squeezes my heart. Rachel has caused more damage than she will ever know. Not that she'd care. I'd like to slap her for the pain she's caused. Also, a part of me wants to thank her for removing her wickedness from Hayden and Lily's lives.

"There is nothing to be sorry about," I say. "What you went through was difficult. I'm glad I know the truth. I'll stop being snarky with you now." And stop putting him in situations where he feels the urge to cross the line.

"I made you snarky?" he says.

"Yes, you did. It happens when I'm horny and unsatisfied."

He gives a surprised chuckle. "I put you in that condition?"

Shuffling closer, I playfully slap my hand on his shoulder. "You know you did."

His lips tilt into a crooked grin. "How are you feeling now?"

Staring straight into his eyes, I say, "Horny and unsatisfied." Hey, if he's getting things off his chest, so can I.

His smile and all amusement drop from his face. A flair of heat burns from his eyes. "I want to help you with that."

A sudden rush of heat hits between my legs, making me squirm. "I'd be more than happy for your help. Although, I don't want you to think you owe me anything. If you're not ready, I'll understand."

"I promised myself I'll never have a one-night stand again."

My shoulders deflate with disappointment. For a moment, I'd hoped now that things are out in the open, he could get past what's holding him back. I was wrong. I stare at our linked fingers, wishing things could be different.

"I want more than one night with you," he says.

My head jerks up. "What are you saying?" I hold my breath, waiting for the answer.

He rubs his thumb over my wrist. "I've never had a relationship. I don't know what the fuck I'm doing. All I know is that I want you—*need* you in my life. If what I've said has scared the crap out of you and you never want to have anything to do with me again, I get it. But if you want to give me a chance, I'll do everything I can to make you happy."

The vulnerability on his face makes my heart fill with emotion. It's taken a lot for him to let his guard down. It's sweet and sexy. How can I refuse? I've never felt like this about anyone before. I need him too.

When I don't answer, he pulls his hand away. "I shouldn't have said all that. This isn't what you want—"

I straddle his lap, clasp his face in my hands, and kiss him. His body sighs with relief a second before he wraps his arms around my waist. I pull back to say, "I want this. I want you. Not just in bed but out of it too."

His lips pull up into a sexy grin. "You're already in my bed, how about we get started with this first?"

With his erection pressing against my sex, I know physically he is ready. What about mentally? I don't want to rush him. "Are you sure you want to do this? We can wait—"

Slamming his lips on mine, he hooks his arm around my waist and flips me onto my back. "I'm ready. Wait..." Then he stiffens. Oh no, is he getting scared again? As hard as it's going to be, I have to be patient. "You're sick. You need to rest."

My body sags. He's not getting scared. He's worried about my health. "I'm fine. Great. Never felt better." It's true. Whatever bug was in my system has gone.

He searches my face. "Are you sure?"

I blow out a frustrated breath. "Put your hands on me, Hayden Alessi."

"Are you always so bossy, Twinkle Toes?"

I squirm under him. "Are we going to talk or fuck? Because there are parts of your body I want to put my mouth on." I slide my hand between our bodies and hold on to his erection through his sweatpants. He sucks in a breath. "Especially your cock."

His eyes darken. "I love it when you talk dirty."

"At this rate, talking is the only thing we're doing." With my body wound up so tight, I don't want to wait any longer.

Hayden's face screws up like he's in pain right before he drops his head on my shoulder. "Shit! I don't have condoms."

My body screams with frustration. Are we always going to have something stopping us? "I don't have any either." I'm at a freaking dance workshop with children. How was I supposed to know I'd need protection? It's not like I thought I'd be having sex with Hayden. Then a light bulb goes off in my head. "I'm on the pill." I remind him with joy.

Instead of looking relieved and getting busy, Hayden rolls off me and onto his back, throwing his forearm over his eyes. "I can't risk it."

Even though he's telling me he wants a relationship, he's still scared of an unplanned pregnancy. I can't blame him. He's been through a lot and we've only moments ago agreed to be together. It doesn't stop the prickle of disappointment that sex with me without a condom scares him.

"Well...I guess we should go back to sleep. We have a busy day with the kids in the morning." Or maybe I need to go into the bathroom and give myself a little self-care.

Hayden drops his arm and turns his head toward me. "We are not sleeping."

I frown. "We're not?"

"Just because we can't have sex, doesn't mean there aren't plenty of other things we can do." He gives me a sexy-as-fuck grin.

I turn to my side, my heartrate kicking up a beat. "I'm listening."

"We have our hands." He slides his hand between my legs, a fraction away from my sex. "We have our mouths." His gaze drops to my lips. "I want to make good use of your pretty, little mouth."

I swallow hard. Multiple uses with it come to mind. Sliding his hand further up my thigh, his fingers float over my sex. Even through the fabric of my boxers the light brush causes heat to blast through my body.

"I can fuck you with my fingers. Fuck you with my mouth. What do you say?" Holy hell. The words dripping from his lips can cause an orgasm alone.

"I say you talk too much."

When he chuckles, it vibrates low in my gut. This man turns me on like no other man has ever done before.

His thumb presses on my clit then glides over my slit. I groan with pleasure and frustration. There's too much fabric between us. I want to feel every part of his touch on my skin.

As if he's reading my thoughts, he slides his hand behind the waistband of my boxers and pulls them from my legs. With my t-shirt bunched up at my waist and my panties hanging over the shower to dry, I'm giving him full view and access to my pussy. It doesn't take him more than a second to get to work.

Yes! That's where I want him. "More."

I give a throaty moan as his finger glides over my folds. He keeps his touch light. Ghosting over me in circles. Flicking...pinching. Making me desperate for more. He stares intently at me. His tongue darting over his bottom lip makes me want his mouth to replace his fingers. A gush of heat heads south.

"You're so wet. I wish I could pound my cock into your pussy," he says, sliding a finger inside me. "It's killing me not being able to fuck you properly."

"I wish you could too…but this…" I gasp when he adds another finger, stretching me open. "…is pretty damn good."

"If it's only *pretty damn good*, I need to do better. It's been a while, I'm rusty," he says with a teasing grin.

My heart sings with joy because I'm the woman he's broken his sex drought with. That thought is quickly forgotten when he pulls his fingers from me and sucks them into his mouth. My insides melt into molten lava. Something tells me there's nothing *rusty* about Hayden.

Damn having no protection. Note to self: from now on always carry condoms at all times.

Standing from the mattress, he walks around to the foot of the bed and grabs hold of my ankles, spreading my legs apart in a high V-shape. With myself exposed to him, he zeroes in on my pussy and bites his bottom lip. My body trembles with anticipation. Bringing my ankle to his mouth, he presses his lips onto my skin, slowly sliding his tongue up along my calf and over my inner thigh, crawling on the bed as he goes. Just before he reaches the sweet spot, he tilts his head up, giving me the sexiest look I've ever seen.

"Tell me how much you want me to fuck you with my tongue, Twinkle Toes." His warm breath fans over my sex. Goosebumps spread across my skin.

My hips tilt up off the mattress toward his face. "Tell me how much *you* want to fuck *me* with your tongue." I hope he's feeling as wound tight as I am. My body is burning up, and I need him to do something…anything… Now!

Instead of putting his mouth on me, he works his fingers over my bud. Circling and pressing on it until I feel like I'm about to explode.

This is the most turned on I've been in my life, and we've barely touched each other. God, if Hayden is this good with his hands, I can't wait to see what he can do with his mouth.

"I want to fuck you so damn bad with my mouth. I'm so hard just thinking about it."

Propping myself up onto my elbows, I say with a demanding tone, "What are you waiting for?"

"I'm taking in the sight of your beautiful pussy. Lay back and relax. I'm making it mine."

I settle back on the mattress and wave a hand toward my lower body. "Go right ahead."

I don't think I've ever been this playful during sex. It was always about getting our needs met. There was never any dirty talk or banter. I like this. Thank God there are plans to do more. If sex with Hayden is this good, then sign me up for life.

Am I getting ahead of myself? Probably, but I have lust on the brain, and I never want this to end.

Without waiting another moment, his mouth covers me and his tongue flicks over my clit. "Oh God...Oh God..." My back arches off the bed.

He laps me up faster. Circling. Pressing. His lips nibble...suck. Never have I felt this sensitive before. My body jerks with each touch. My hips rock into his mouth.

Digging my fingers into his hair, I moan, "I need more." And he delivers. He inserts two fingers inside me without breaking his mouth away and keeps working me over.

The oversized t-shirt Hayden gave me now feels like it's too tight and suffocating me. Ripping it off my body, I toss it on the floor. His mouth and fingers are in sync, giving me sweet torture.

As the pressure builds, I squeeze my eyes shut, holding his head wedged between my thighs. "Hayden...it's happening...I'm going to..." I pant like I'm running in the New York City Marathon.

He pulls away long enough to say, "Let go, Twinkle Toes. I want you coming in my mouth." Then he dives back in, working his tongue and fingers harder and faster.

Oh Christ, his words set me off. My legs fall open wider. My hips buck off the mattress. "Yes! Yes!" I scream as wave after wave of ecstasy rips through me. Hayden is right there with me, lapping up my orgasm. Quivering until the last spasm subsides, I fall into a languid heap. After catching my breath, I say, "Wow."

Hayden lifts his head and licks his lips. "That's all you've got to say?" He grins, knowing perfectly well he just rocked my freaking world.

I boost myself onto my elbows. Not having enough strength to hold myself up, I drop back onto the bed. "I'd say more but right now I can't think straight. Or move."

Sliding up onto his side next to me, Hayden leans onto his elbow and rests his head on his fist. With his free hand, he circles a finger around my nipple. "I'm not done with you. I'll give you a couple of minutes to recover."

I don't need a couple of minutes to recover. With his light touch, my body is awake. I trail my hand down his torso and over his erection tenting his sweatpants. He's still fully clothed while I'm buck naked. That's a problem I'll happily resolve.

As I rub him over his pants, his eyes flutter closed. "You, Mr. Alessi, are wearing too many clothes." I slide my hand into his pants and clutch my fingers around his hot, throbbing erection.

He hisses as I stroke him. "I want you in the shower. We have unfinished business in there."

Oh yes, he does. I don't hesitate when he reaches out his hand for me to take. Getting off the bed, I follow him into the bathroom.

As he strips out of his clothes, I take a moment to appreciate his gorgeous body. His tanned skin, muscles, and corrugated abs make my mouth water. He is gorgeous.

He turns on the water, and the room fills with steam. It will be nice to have a warm shower with him for a change. Stepping inside, we stand under the spray.

Glancing down, I stare at his huge erection standing at attention. I lick my lips. I want him in my mouth. "You've had a taste of me. Now it's my turn to taste you." I push his back up against the wall and drop to my knees. Looking up at him, I see his eyes are at half-mast and he's biting his bottom lip. I'm getting wet—and I don't mean from the shower.

"Fucking hell, Twinkle Toes. I'll come in a second if you keep looking at me like that," he groans.

"We wouldn't want that now, would we?"

"No, we would not. Now fucking get your mouth on me," he says through gritted teeth.

I love seeing how desperate he is. How much he wants my mouth on him. I'd love to tease him and drag it out, but it's been a long time for him. It's cruel to torture him.

With one finger, I trail the length of him until I reach the tip. Swiping off the pre-cum, I lick it off my finger. His heavy breathing vibrates through the shower stall. His body quivers. The tension in his body is so wired. I love that I'm giving this to him. Love that I'm the woman he's waited for to have this moment with. I ghost my hand over his balls, giving them a gentle squeeze.

Dropping his head back on the ivory-colored tiles, he moans, "You're killing me."

I wrap my hand around his cock, open my mouth wide, and take him in.

"Fuck me," he moans, clutching my hair in his hands as I suck him in deep.

My head bobs up and down, slowly at first. Faster when his hands encourage me to pick up speed. One of his hands stays tangled in my hair and the other hand slaps the tiled wall in front of him like he needs the support.

He stares down at me. "Yes...like that...fuck yes."

I twirl my tongue around the tip then slide my tongue down the length of him before sucking him back in for more, my hand pumping him at the root. With his hand gripping tighter in my hair, he thrusts his hips toward me. He's fucking my mouth so hard, hitting me in the back of the throat.

Hayden gently pulls my hair, tugging me off his dick. It falls from my mouth with a pop. I look up with confusion. Why would he stop when I could feel his body shaking and getting ready for release?

"Hayden?"

"Get on your feet," he demands, helping me up by my shoulders. I like this take-charge side of him. It's sexy as fuck.

When we're facing each other, he cups my face in his hands and kisses me. His tongue swirls inside my mouth. Taking the kiss so deep, it sucks the air from my lungs. When we break away, we stare at each other. Our breathing choppy. Our chests heaving. Water is pelting our heads, but we don't care.

I'm not sure who moves first, but we are clinging to one another. Lips smashing together. Hands touching everything within reach. It's like a dam has opened and we are tumbling and swirling through choppy water only for our heads to break from the surface for a second to catch our breaths and fall under again.

His hands land on my hips and he spins me around, splaying my hands high on the wall. Fingers clutch the base of my skull, and he presses his chest against my back. His lips hover over my ear. "Ever since you were in my shower, I've dreamed about fucking you like this. Whenever I step into it, I instantly get hard. My cock has never gotten such a workout."

His grip on my neck loosens, and he runs his palm down to my lower back. I arch like a cat at his touch. "It's been on the top of my playlist too."

With a firm grip, he grabs my hips and pulls me to his crotch. His cock slides between my legs, the tip of his erection prodding against my clit. My legs turn to jelly. I bite my bottom lip to stop myself from crying out.

Like he knows I'm trying to keep quiet, he moves my hair over one shoulder and tilts my head to the side. Leaning his face closer to mine, he whispers, "I want to hear you scream my name."

My knees shake. My sex throbs. All I can do is nod.

"Good girl," he says, nibbling at my shoulder. "Bring your thighs closer together," he instructs.

Doing as I'm told, I shuffle my feet, sandwiching his erection between my legs. With his hands squeezing my hips, he slowly pumps his cock, hitting my swollen nub with each thrust. Yes, this is how I want him. Hot and pulsing against me. For now, this is as close as I'm going to get from going all the way. I freaking love it. Being so close to fucking yet not able to makes it more thrilling. Forbidden.

He presses harder against me, and I squeeze my thighs as tight as my wobbly legs allow. His cock glides over my folds and presses on my clit over and over again. The more he thrusts against me, the more my body craves.

"Oh...Hayden...Hayden..." My voice gets louder every time I say his name.

"Does it feel good?" he asks with a raspy voice.

"Yes," I pant. "Feels...so...good." I push my ass back against his crotch and wiggle, letting him know with more than words what he's doing to me.

"Oh Jesus. I want to be inside you so bad. You feel so damn good. I can only imagine how you're going to feel when I'm fucking your pussy properly."

He thrusts harder while squeezing my hips. "Almost...there," I gasp. My body tenses. My legs shake.

Hayden reaches around me and pinches my clit. "Come for me, Twinkle Toes," he groans in my ear.

It only takes one more thrust and Hayden's fingers playing with my clit like a harp to send me over the edge. "Hayyydeen!" I cry, my voice echoing off the bathroom walls. Well, he wanted me to scream his name.

"Fuck me!" he moans as he drives harder into me before quickly pulling away. A warm squirt of come splashes on my back.

He collapses forward, bracing himself with one hand on the wall. With the other hand, he spreads his come over me like he's branding me. Oh, that's freaking hot.

Turning me around, he kisses me long and deep. When we pull apart, he gives me the sexiest satisfied grin. "Fuck, that was good."

I giggle. "Two orgasms in one night. I can't complain." They were the best two orgasms I've ever had.

Hayden turns off the water, and we step into the bathroom, wrapping fluffy towels around our bodies. Dropping his hands on my waist, he draws me close. "I'm not finished with you yet. Be prepared for more."

My knees grow weak. Oh boy!

Chapter Nineteen

━━━◆O◆━━━

HAYDEN

Tap. Tap. Tap.

A light, irritating noise breaks through my sleep. After the sex-with-no-sex I had with Alyssa last night, my body is heavy and languid. It takes a moment to realize the tapping sound is someone knocking on the door.

My eyes fly open. Shit! Bright light is breaking through the gaps of the curtains. What time is it? I roll to my side to check the digital clock on the nightstand. 8:42 AM. Fuck! Breakfast with the kids was at eight. The workshops start at nine AM.

I glance over my shoulder at Alyssa. She's spread out naked on the bed. I pull a sheet over her and search for my sweatpants. Tugging them on, I rush to the door and crack it open enough to see out but no one can see in. Pippa from the bus and Lily are standing in the corridor.

"Good morning, Pippa. Hey, Lily Pily. Did you have a good night?" I say, blocking the view into the room.

Pippa's gaze travels over my bare chest then her gaze flicks over my shoulder like she's searching for something—or *someone*.

"It was fun. We stayed up until eleven and ate candy." Lily smiles brightly.

"How is Alyssa feeling?" Pippa asks. Without waiting for a reply, she lifts onto her toes, trying to peek into the room and calls, "Alyssa, are you coming to class?"

"Sshhh," I whisper. "She's asleep. She was up most of the night." I'm not lying. We'd only gotten to sleep two hours ago. Not because she was sick like I want Pippa to believe. Because we couldn't keep our hands off each other.

"Oh, I hope she feels better soon. Do you think she'll make it to the workshops?" Pippa asks.

"I'm not sure. As soon as she wakes, she'll let you know," I assure her.

"There's only one bed, Dad. Did you sleep with Miss Alyssa? You might get sick too," Lily innocently says with concern.

Oh shit. I'd forgotten that Lily had seen the room configuration when we dropped off our bags. Pippa's eyebrows rise like she's interested in my reply.

"There are two beds, sweetie."

Lily shakes her head. "There's only one. Remember you said if I kicked you in my sleep, you'd make me sleep on the floor?" She giggles like she did when I teased her about it.

Scrubbing a hand through my hair, I say, "Hotel beds can separate in two. Someone from the hotel fixed them for us." I love my daughter, but if she doesn't drop the subject, I'll have to gag her. "Are you here for your dance gear?" I say, steering the conversation in another direction.

"Yes. It's ballet today, I'm so excited."

"I'll help her get ready." Pippa steps toward me like she wants to enter the room.

I don't budge. There's no way she's getting inside. One look at that room and she'll know what's going on. "That's not a good idea. I'm not sure if whatever Alyssa has is out of her system. I don't want you two to risk catching anything. If I get her things, do you mind taking Lily back to her room and help her get ready? Or ask Margo if she can do it please?"

"Sure, not a problem," Pippa says, sounding annoyed. I bet it's because I'm not letting her in.

Closing the door—making sure I lock it in case Pippa tries to follows me in—I rush to the corner of the room where Lily's luggage is stowed. Alyssa is sitting up in bed, a sheet dangerously close to slipping past her breasts. The sooner I get Lily's bag ready, the sooner I can get back in bed with Alyssa.

"You made two beds?" She giggles.

I put a finger over my lips. "Shhh. I don't want Pippa hearing you," I whisper.

She makes a gesture of locking her lips with her fingers.

Quickly collecting Lily's clothes, I crack the door open enough to slide my arm and the bag out. "I put your toothbrush in there too."

"Are you coming to the workshop, Dad?"

"Yes, I'll be down as soon as I'm sure Miss Alyssa is okay. I won't be long."

She smiles. "Okay."

I say goodbye to Lily and Pippa, close the door, and lean my back against it, letting out a heavy sigh. I hate lying to Lily. But now is not the right time to tell her about Alyssa. Especially in front of Pippa.

"Is it safe to speak?" Alyssa whispers dramatically.

Pushing away from the door, I walk to the bed and sit on the edge. "It's all clear. Although, if we don't show our faces soon, I'm sure Pippa will barge in here demanding answers."

While I was giving Lily her things, Alyssa slipped on the t-shirt I'd given her to sleep in. The hem of the shirt is barely covering her pussy, and my mouth waters at the sight. My dick twitches to life. How can I want her again so much after everything we did last night? The answer comes quickly. Because I'll never get enough of her. And it doesn't scare the crap out of me.

Taking Alyssa's hand in mine, I link our fingers together. "I'm sorry I didn't tell Lily about us. It wasn't the right time. Not with Pippa around. Can we give it a little time before we tell her? I've never brought a woman home. I need to figure out the best way to go about this."

She gives my hand a squeeze. "This is new and unexpected. I still need to wrap my head around it too. It's too soon to tell Lily. We don't know yet how we are going to work together. We are phenomenal in bed," she says with a cheeky grin, "but we might hate each other in two days. We didn't start off liking each other too much." She laughs.

That's because I was scared of her. Scared of any feelings I had. Thank God I've pushed past my insecurities and have taken what I want. This is not a two-day relationship. I want forever. I keep that to myself in case I frighten her away.

"I'd say after last night, we like each other a lot more." I release her hand and trail my fingers along her inner thigh, sliding them beneath the t-shirt. Floating them over her bare pussy, I gently stroke her folds. On a low, soft moan, her eyes flutter closed.

"We should get ready for the workshops." Her voice is raspy.

I push a finger inside. "They're not expecting us yet."

She drops her head back on the headboard. "They might wonder where we are and start talking."

"You're sick. There's nothing to talk about." My thumb circles her clit.

"I'm feeling better now," she pants.

Adding more pressure to her clit, I say, "Are you sure? You're looking a little flushed." Getting to my knees, I lift her t-shirt up to expose her tits. Her rosy, pink nipples are erect, waiting for my attention. I lick my tongue over one and then over the other. "I think we should make sure you're feeling one-hundred percent before we venture out." I suck a nipple into my mouth.

She threads her fingers through my hair, clasping on tight. "If you insist."

Chapter Twenty

ALYSSA

Two days after the dance workshop, I'm finally spending time with Hayden. We're using Lily's private lesson to sneak some time in. Hopefully we can tell Lily soon and we won't have to hide our relationship anymore.

How will she take the news? Will she be happy? She seems to like me, but that's as a ballet teacher. It might change when she learns I'm her dad's girlfriend. It has always been just the two of them. I'd hate to upset her if this is not what she wants.

God, it's what I want. It's the last thing I thought I needed. My career was my focus. Nothing was getting in the way of that. Yet Hayden is consuming my mind. I'm bursting out of my skin with excitement to see him. After our night at the workshop, I'm floating on air.

Before I head over to his house, I stop at my apartment to freshen up after class. On my way to the bathroom, my phone rings. I glance at the caller ID. My mother. I don't want to talk to her today; she'll only pop my happy bubble I've been living in the past two days. Ignoring the call, I toss the phone on the bed. It stops ringing. A second later, it starts again. I pick the phone up and answer. What if it's important?

"Hey, Mom. What's up?"

"Have you been on any auditions lately?" *Pop*. I crash to the ground.

I pinch the bridge of my nose. Why did I have to answer the call? "I'm fine thanks, Mom. How are you?" Sarcasm drips from the words.

I hear an annoyed scoffing sound. "How are you, Alyssa? How is your ankle?"

Dropping to the edge of the bed, I shake my head. Of course she'd ask about the ankle. That's all she cares about. The injury has put a hold on my career. She doesn't care how I'm doing. Why do I let this still bother me? I should know my career is her number one concern.

"It's better," I say. "There's hardly any pain."

"Excellent. That means you can get back at it."

"Yes, I can. I'm sure The Temple will be happy to have me back," I lie. I haven't heard from them since I called them about the injury. They've no doubt replaced me by now. Their loyalty to their employees isn't the best. You don't work for a couple of nights, and there's always someone who will take your place.

"Alyssa Martinez. When are you going to stop working there? It's beneath you and embarrassing for our family. What if someone we know sees you dancing there?"

"I didn't know you had friends who visited The Temple. People like that are *beneath you*." Why do we always have this conversation? I hear a heavy sigh. Before she can lecture me about my choices in life, I say, "Is there any other reason you're calling, Mom? I need to jump in the shower, I have plans tonight." I'm finally seeing Hayden. My heart flips in my chest every time I think of him.

"Yes, Christina is performing in *Swan Lake* at the American Ballet Theatre. We're flying in from Paris to watch. Your father is expecting you to join us. All our friends are attending. The family must attend to show support. We are extremely proud of her."

I can't think of anything worse. Not because I don't want to see Christina perform. I love watching her dance. I love soaking up the brilliance of the production. Marvel in how graceful Christina moves. She's brilliant. I don't want to go because my father will tell me the same story he does every time we watch her perform.

Christina is a born natural. She danced right out of the womb. Look how graceful and easy she makes it appear. You need to work hard at it and practice every moment you have. No matter how many hours you put into dancing, you'll never be as good as Christina, but you can do something with the talent you have. Follow in her footsteps and you too will achieve success.

Follow in her footsteps and you too will achieve success. That is their mantra. I've heard it for years.

"Tell Dad I'll try my best to be there."

"Oh, you must. It's not an option—"

"Gotta go, Mom. Love you. Bye." I end the call before she can say another word.

The phone rings again. I tilt my head back and stare at the ceiling. Is she going to keep insisting? Looking at the screen, my lungs deflate with relief.

I answer the phone and greet my agent, "Hey, Davey."

"Alyssa, honey, how are you? How's the ankle?"

I'm sick of talking about my damn ankle, but he's my agent, it's important that he knows so he can set up auditions for me. "Getting better every day."

"That's wonderful news. Are you ready for an audition tomorrow?"

"I sure am. What have you got for me?" I twirl my ankle from left to right. Up and down. There's only a slight twinge. I stand on my feet, lifting onto my toes and plie. Another small tug of discomfort. It's nothing I haven't danced through before. In fact, I've danced through a hell of a lot worse.

"They are auditioning the lead roles for *Moulin Rouge*, and you have everything they're looking for."

I've heard that five million times before. *Moulin Rouge* is a dream role. If I can land the lead role, I'll finally make a name for myself. Finally get my parents off my back. Finally make them proud of me. I need this role.

"Send me the details," I say.

"Will your ankle be strong enough? This show is huge. You can't afford to be injured before you start."

"My ankle is fine. I can do this." I send a silent prayer to the heavens for this to be true.

"Excellent. We'll talk soon."

We say goodbye and end the call. I bounce on my feet a few times. My injury is almost gone. It will hold up. It has to. I need to prove to my parents I'm not the failure they believe me to be.

This is my shot.

It's my time.

I'm ready.

⸻ ◆ ⸻

As much as I love spending time with Lily and watching her dance, I'm excited that the lesson is over. Because there is a gorgeous man I want to spend as much time as possible with and he's waiting for me downstairs.

In the kitchen, Hayden has prepared spaghetti in a delicious-smelling tomato sauce, ready for us to eat. During the meal, when Lily isn't looking, he keeps eyeing me, dirty thoughts clear on his face. Anticipation of what's to come is heating my body.

When we finish eating, we rinse the dishes and stack them in the dishwasher. Lily is sent upstairs to shower and go to bed. Hayden brews coffee and pours it into two mugs, sliding one to me as I sit at the breakfast counter.

"I thought it was our bedtime too." I wink so he knows exactly what I mean. How could he not? For two days he's called me late at night, burning me up with explicit details of the many ways he's going to fuck me.

He grins that oh-so-sexy smile of his. "Patience, Twinkle Toes. We'll get there. Once Lily is asleep, we're good to go." Hayden slides onto a stool next to me, cradling his mug in his hands. "You've been quiet tonight. What's on your mind?"

During dinner we chatted about our day and laughed at Lily's antics. I thought I did a great job hiding the way I felt about my mother and my agent's calls. It surprises me he can tell I'm a little preoccupied.

"How do you know I have something on my mind?" I ask.

He shrugs a shoulder. "What you're feeling is written on your face no matter how hard you try to cover them. Good or bad, they show. I've experienced the bad a time or two." He chuckles.

No one has ever saw past the mask I've learned to put on. At first, being compared to Christina and being told I wasn't good enough had me running to my room crying. It didn't take long to learn how to suck back the tears, put a smile on my face, and pretend their words didn't hurt. They believed me. That's how good I was at hiding my feelings. Yet Hayden saw through it.

Letting go of his mug, he puts his hand on top of mine. "Do you want to talk about it? Or you can tell me to mind my damn business."

My lips tilt into a smile. I'm loving this warm, strong hand on top of mine. It's comforting. "Before I arrived here, I had a phone call from my mother. She loves to remind me that my choice of career isn't suitable for the family's reputation and I'm an embarrassment. She also insisted I attend my sister's ballet so I can aspire to be just like her."

Hayden squeezes my hand. "Jesus. She said that to you?" The tone in his voice hardens. "What the hell is wrong with her?"

I give a nonchalant shrug. "I'm used to it. Throughout my life, my parents have compared me to Christina. If I'm not dancing at her level, I'm a failure."

"Have they seen you dance? You're amazing. They should be proud not embarrassed."

"It means a lot that you think I'm amazing." I don't hear it often. Not that I need praise every time I'm on stage. It's just nice to have someone believe in you.

"I don't just think it, I *know* it," he says. "If they can't see how great you are, there's something wrong with them. Not you."

If only my parents thought the same way. I wouldn't be busting my ass trying to please them.

I give a ghost of a smile. "They're highly experienced dancers. Both have performed around the world on all the major stages. They even danced for Queen Elizabeth. They are considered gods in the ballet community. So, they know what they're talking about."

Hayden slaps the palm of his hand on the counter, which makes me jump. I'm surprised by the hard expression on his face. "No one should be treated that way. I don't care how experienced they are. I'm sorry you go through it."

My heart flutters. I love how defensive he is over me. I love having him in my corner.

"If their names are so respected, why don't they help you get your break?" he asks. "If they're embarrassed by where you work, why don't they do something about it?"

I twirl my cup in my hand. "I refuse to use their influence to land jobs."

He cocks an eyebrow. "Why?"

"They would control where and who I dance with. I want to make that decision. I want to make it on my own. How will I ever know if I'm good enough unless I do it myself? I don't even use my surname when I audition. I use a stage name so no one can join the dots."

Hayden stares at me with pride. Something I've never seen on my parents' faces. "You are amazing. They don't know how extraordinary their daughter is."

My cheeks grow warm at the compliment. "Thank you."

"So, you have a stage name?" His lips turn into a crooked grin. "What is it?"

Putting on a faux stern façade, I swivel around on my seat, cross my legs, and fold my arms over my chest. "If you think it's something kinky, you're wrong. It's Alyssa Martin. Not so different from my real name."

"You've popped that fantasy," he jokes.

I giggle.

His face turns serious. "Has performing on Broadway always been your dream?"

"Not always. I thought I'd be a prima ballerina like my mom, like we knew Christina would be. When I came to the realization I wasn't good enough, I turned my love for theatre into my next passion. My agent has an audition lined up for me tomorrow."

Hayden frowns. "Can you dance with your injured ankle?"

"Yes."

His frown deepens. "After Lily's lesson, I saw you massage it."

"I've had worse injuries and danced through it. This is nothing. I can't let the opportunity go."

"Is this what you truly want? Or are you doing this for your family?"

Is it what I want? It's not the first time I've questioned my career choice. Performing is all I know. All I've envisioned. I'm doing this for me and my family. I need to prove to them I can make it. Then when I do, they'll look at me with the same pride as Hayden. If I can do this, maybe one day they'll love me like they do Christina.

"I'm doing this for me," I reply.

Hayden is quiet for a moment as he stares at me. Like he's searching for the truth in my answer. "You're going to smash your audition. You'll get so famous you won't remember us little people." He smiles.

Sliding off the stool, I position myself between Hayden's legs and hook my arms over his shoulders. "Well, you better make tonight a night I'll never forget." Leaning forward, I bring my lips to his ear and whisper, "I bought two boxes of condoms."

He turns his head to whisper in my ear, "I bought three boxes."

Chapter Twenty-One

HAYDEN

I take Alyssa's hand and guide her from the kitchen, up the stairs and into my bedroom. "Let me check on Lily. I'll be right back."

"I'll be waiting," she says with the sexiest smile. Making it hard for me to leave her, even if it's only for a few minutes.

I make my way to Lily's room and peek inside. She's snuggled up with her blue stuffed penguin and breathing heavily. She's out cold. Turning off her nightlight, I give her a kiss on the forehead. Her little, soft, sleeping face makes my heart melt.

I could never imagine treating her the way Alyssa's parents treat her. Comparing her to another person. Telling her she isn't good enough. Not being proud of her achievements. What kind of people are they? Ones Alyssa hasn't taken after, because the way she treats her kids in class, the way she treats Lily, there's no way she's not proud of everything they achieve or *try* to achieve. There's no judgment. No comparison.

This is the woman I want to bring into Lily's life. Someone I know will love Lily like she's her own. But is it too soon? With Alyssa chasing her Broadway dreams, and with her talent, she can go anywhere in the world. My life is here with Lily. Can we make it work? I'd hate for Lily to get too attached to Alyssa only for her to leave our lives.

Maybe I'm thinking too far into the future. This relationship is new. I should enjoy it. Not end it before it's began.

Leaving Lily's room, I close the door behind me and walk back into my bedroom. I stop short in my tracks at the threshold, my tongue rolling out of my mouth. Alyssa is leaning against the headboard, her unbound hair falling like chocolate waves down her shoulders. She's removed her pants, t-shirt, and boots and is lying on my bed in a red, lacy bra and matching panties. Her fingers are working her pussy behind the lace.

With heavy-lidded eyes, she says, "I'm warming myself up for you."

Holy fuck. I'm living in my wildest fantasy.

Kicking off my shoes, I yank my t-shirt over my head, dropping it on the floor. Next, I make quick work of taking off my jeans and underwear.

As I stand by the bed, I look at the mattress and chuckle. Condoms are spread all over the bedspread. I lift an eyebrow. "You are ambitious if you think we're going to use them all." Although, I'll certainly try my damndest.

"I want them within easy reach. I've waited for this moment for two days. I want nothing slowing us down." She smirks.

What isn't slowing down are her fingers. It should be me doing the work, but damn it's hot watching her pleasure herself.

"Are you going to stand there all night and watch, or are you going to take part?" She removes her hand from her panties and crooks her index finger. "I want you inside of me."

Taking her by the ankles, I tug her legs. She squeals as she slides onto her back. Before she can take her next breath, I hover over the top of her on my elbows. "Sshh," I whisper. "I know how much you like to scream, but you'll have to keep it down. We wouldn't want to wake Lily."

She gives me a sultry look. "Well, you'll have to put something in my mouth to stop me."

My arms grow weak. "I'll be happy to put my cock in your mouth."

She giggles. "I was thinking more like your tongue. Although, your cock will work too."

My head drops. "Fuck me." My body is burning for her. I need to touch every inch of her. Make her as hot as I am.

Leaning onto one elbow, I place my hand on her throat. Our eyes connect, our breathing heavy. Her chest is rising and falling, bringing my attention to her breasts. I smooth my palm down her chest to capture a breast in my hand, her nipples pressing against the lacy fabric of her bra. There's a clasp at the front of the bra, and I unhook it with one finger, breaking her gorgeous tits free.

"For someone who hasn't done this for a while, you're good at unhooking a bra." She grins.

"It's like riding a bike. You never forget," I say. I twirl my fingers around one nipple and move over to the other one, giving it equal attention. "I love your tits."

"They're small," she gasps as I pinch and flick.

"They fit perfectly in my hands." I take a breast in my hand, showing her how well they fit, and giving it a light squeeze. Her back arches off the bed. I replace my hand with my mouth and lave my tongue over the nipple. Her fingers tunnel into my hair. I pull away. "And they fit perfectly into my mouth."

Her hand sneaks between our bodies, and she takes hold of my cock. I hiss as she strokes me from root to tip. I'm so ready for her. If she continues, I'll finish in her hand. For two days, I've thought of nothing but fucking her. I've wound myself up so tight that the smallest touch is going to set me off.

"I'm not sure this big thing can fit in me." Her brow creases with concern.

My chest puffs with male ego. "Don't worry, baby, I'll make it fit."

Her eyes burn bright with desire.

"As much as I want to take my time with you, I need to fuck you now," I growl against her chest.

"I need you too. We can take it slow next time."

Yes, next time. Because once will never be enough.

Instead of pulling her panties off, I rip them and toss the flimsy piece of lace on the floor. Alyssa gasps. "I paid good money for that."

"I'll buy you the whole damn lingerie shop. Now spread your legs and bend your knees. I want to see if you're wet for me."

She does as she's told, and I glide my finger over her slit. My finger comes away drenched. Yeah, she's ready.

Shuffling onto my haunches, I rest my hands on her knees and spread her legs wider, getting a good look at her. "I need one little taste first." Leaning forward, I run the flat of my tongue along her folds, then suck on her clit. "You taste so good," I mumble.

"Hayden…" she half-moans, half-cries. "Please… I need…"

"I know what you need, Twinkle Toes." I position myself over her, putting my weight onto my elbows. Before I take what we both want, I gaze down at her flushed face. "God, you're beautiful. This is more than wanting to fuck you. I haven't felt this way about anyone…ever. I've waited eight years for you…only you." I want her to know she is important to me. I cradle her cheek in my hand and place a feather-light kiss on her lips.

"I haven't felt like this before either." Her eyes shimmer up at me, making my heart kick through my ribs. Earlier I was worried Lily would get too attached. If Alyssa leaves to dance all over the world, it's me who will be a wreck.

I deepen the kiss. This woman has buried herself in my heart. She's all I think about. All I want. I fucking think I'm falling for her. Scratch that...I *know* I'm falling for her. Never in my wildest dreams did I think this would happen. I never expected my heart to kick-start in my chest and make me picture a life with someone. But I am. I'm picturing a life with Alyssa.

Our tongues twirl in our mouths. Her hands slide over my shoulders, down my back and up again. Her nails dig into my skin as the kiss turns frantic. Breaking away, we gasp for breath before I kiss her jaw, trail my lips down her neck and over her collarbone, moving on to her breasts. Taking another taste of her peaked nipples as I flick my tongue over them.

"I can't get enough of you," I mumble.

Grabbing a foil packet laying on the bed, I rip it open. With shaky hands, I slide it on my throbbing erection. Fuck, I've never been this hard before. Shifting closer so my cock is at her entrance, I slide inside her slowly, giving her time to get used to my size. She bites her bottom lip, stopping a moan from escaping. I suck in a breath. Holy fuck! She's wet, warm, and tight. This is what I've missed in eight years.

No, this is what I've never had. Because all I've ever had is sex. This is so much more. The feelings I have for Alyssa blows anything else out of the water. My body instinctively thrusts inside her. Slow at first. When she clutches my ass and sucks my neck, I pick up the pace. Diving in deeper and harder.

"You feel so good," she moans against my neck. I swivel my hips. Pump in and out. "Yes...yes...yes!" she cries. I cover her lips with my mouth. As much as I love to hear her scream, we have to keep it quiet.

"That's it, Twinkle Toes, come for me," I encourage.

Her hips buck under me, matching me thrust for thrust. The pleasure is so intense, I'm not sure how much longer I can last.

Slipping my hand between our bodies, I find the sensitive bud that will set her off. When I pluck at it, her eyes roll in the back of her head, and she tosses her head from side to side. "Oh God...oh God...Hayden!"

Hearing my name on her lips is nearly my undoing, but I grit my teeth and hold on. I pound into her so hard and fast, the headboard is bouncing off the wall.

"I'm going to...going to..." She bites her bottom lip again. I lower my head and suck a nipple hard into my mouth. "Yes!" With a stifled cry, her body jerks and bucks as she rides the wave of her orgasm, clenching me so tight, it pulls my release from my body. I come so fiercely, I lose my breath.

When the spasms subside, I collapse onto Alyssa, careful to keep the weight on my elbows. Dropping and rolling onto my side, I gather her into my arms. Her hands caress my back.

I push Alyssa's hair from her face. "That was amazing."

With a lazy grin, she says, "Phenomenal."

Chuckling, I kiss the tip of her nose. "Pretty good for a man who hasn't had sex in eight years."

She tilts her head back to look at me. "Are you blowing your own horn?"

"No, but as soon as I clean up, I'll be *blowing* you."

She gives me a playful slap on the shoulder. A moment later, her expression turns serious. "Did you mean it when you said you've never felt this way about anyone?"

Running my thumb over her lips, I gaze at her with complete seriousness. "Yes."

She drops her head and lightly plucks at my chest hair. "You've never been in a relationship. You've only had sex with women. How do you know if you really lo—have feelings for me?"

Did she stop herself from saying *love*? Do I love her? I know I'm falling for her. Have I hit the ground yet? She's the woman I want. The woman I want to take home to Lily. The woman I see as part of my family. Knowing all that, I don't want to admit my true feelings. Not when I'm not sure where her career is going to take her.

Placing a finger under her chin, I tilt her face up. "I don't need to have had past relationships to know that what I'm feeling is special. That I've never felt as alive as I do when I'm with you." I cup my hand on her cheek and place a kiss on her lips. "Every moment I spend with you gets better and better."

She breathes in a shuddery breath and smiles. "I think you're pretty special too. God, you were such a jerk, and now...you're not." She laughs.

"I'm sorry for being a jerk. You went against everything I thought I wanted. I was trying to protect myself from whatever I was feeling. I must admit, I'm glad you fell into my life one rainy night." How long will she stay in it?

Alyssa reaches out and swipes her finger on my brow. "Why the frown?"

I can either keep my insecurities to myself and let them stew or I can be upfront and know where I stand. "Alyssa, I know how I'm feeling. How I want a relationship with you, but what do you want?"

Pulling a surprised face, she says, "I've told you...I want this. Us."

"Yes, but you also want a career on Broadway. A career that can take you around the world. I would never want to stand in the way of your dreams. You're a few years younger than me. We're at different stages of our lives. My place is here with Lily. You're chasing a career, I'm raising a daughter. How do we make this work?"

Alyssa shuffles up into a sitting position, hugging a pillow to her chest. "We don't even know if I'll have a career on Broadway."

I sit up too. Rolling the condom off, I drop it by the bed. I'll clean it up later. "You said you have an audition."

She makes a scoffing sound. "I always have an audition. It doesn't mean I'll get it."

"It's only a matter of time."

"Can we worry about this if it happens?"

I take her hand and clasp it in mine. "I can't. Not with Lily in the mix. I don't want her getting attached only for you to leave." Another woman can't leave her.

"If my career takes off—"

"*When* it takes off," I correct.

She smiles. "I can perform in the same city for months at a time. I have no intention of leaving New York. The work I want is here. I'm not going anywhere."

Linking our fingers together, I lift them to my mouth and kiss her knuckles. "Are you sure staying in New York is really what you want?"

"Yes," she says firmly. "I want to stay here. Not only to dance but for you too."

"What about Lily? We're a package deal."

The smile she gives me lights up her face. "It's really Lily I'm here for. You're a bonus."

I squeeze her hand. "Is that so?"

With her free hand, she taps the side of her chin. "Unless you can show me again how useful you can be?"

Growling, I flip her on her back and show her *exactly* how useful I am.

Chapter Twenty-Two

ALYSSA

"When will you know if you get the part?" Harper asks as I limp out of the kitchen with a bag of frozen peas.

Dropping onto the couch, I rest my leg on a cushion on the coffee table and place the peas on my ankle. I don't want to look too closely. What if it's swollen? What if I've done more damage? Two days of being on my feet dancing, singing, and acting might have caused a flare-up.

"It can take days. I'm not holding my breath."

Harper cradles Avery onto her chest and pats her back. "It's only a matter of time."

"That's what—" I was about to say *that's what Hayden said*. I haven't told Harper about our relationship yet. It's all so new. I want to keep it to myself and enjoy each other with no outside input. "That's what my agent said," I correct myself.

"He knows what he's talking about. Hang in there."

The sound of the front door opening and closing puts a stop to our conversation. Moments later, Lily, dressed in her ballet outfit, runs into the room. "Aunty Harper!" she calls. "Is Avery awake? Can I hold her?"

"What about saying hello to your aunt first," Hayden says, following behind. At the sight of him, my skin tightens with goosebumps. It's been two days since I've seen him, but it feels like two years.

"Hi Aunty Harper," she sings.

"She wanted to come and see Avery before her dance lesson. I hope that's okay."

Harper pats the seat next to her, and Lily climbs up and sits down. "Happy to have her pop in whenever she wants."

Turning toward me, Hayden smiles, and the gesture shoots through my chest. If my face is looking as goofy as it feels, Harper will know in a second there's something going on between me and Hayden.

"Hello, Miss Alyssa," he says. "I wasn't expecting to see you here." He's being oh so formal. So sexy.

"Lily and I both had the same idea. I wanted to see Avery before dance class too."

Harper scoffs. "Does anyone want to visit me anymore? Is it always going to be about Avery?"

"Yes, it's all about Avery," I joke.

Harper pulls a mock affronted expression, making Lily giggle.

When I look at Hayden, every part of my body buzzes with excitement. He's planning to sneak me into the house after Lily goes to bed tonight. I'm counting down the minutes until I can be in his arms.

Hayden's gaze falls on my legs, and he frowns. "You've hurt yourself again." Rushing toward me, he sits on the coffee table and gently places my ankle on his lap. Taking the peas off and putting them on the table, he smooths his palms along my calf and bends his head to look at my ankle. "Does it hurt?"

Over his shoulder, Harper raises an eyebrow, giving me a knowing grin. Hayden's hands on me is personal.

"Not much. It's fine."

"It doesn't look fine. It's swollen."

Damn it. Not what I wanted to hear.

"Come with me, I'll take you to a physiotherapist."

I shake my head. "One—I'd be lucky to get an appointment this time of day. Two—I have classes to teach soon. And three—are you wearing pink nail polish?"

Hayden holds his hands up, inspecting them like he has stepped from a nail salon. "It's coral," he corrects.

"Oh wow. They look amazing." I giggle. The color is not only on his nails but his skin too.

"I did them," Lily announces.

"You did a fantastic job. Your dad looks good wearing pink—I'm sorry, I mean *coral*."

Lily smiles with pride. "Next time he's letting me do his makeup."

I laugh. "That I would love to see. Make sure you use the brightest colors you have."

"I have gold glitter eyeshadow."

"Perfect," I say at the same time Hayden says, "I love gold."

This softer side of Hayden is beautiful. I've gotten to see the reserved side of him—with part jerk coming out. I've seen the lusty, playful, dirty-talker sex god side. But seeing him with Lily melts my heart. Letting his eight-year-old daughter use him as her real-life doll is ovary exploding.

Kids haven't been in my near future. Nor have I thought about wanting any. My parents had me and my sister in their late thirties after they retired from ballet. I always assumed I'd do the same. Worry about family when I had more time. But seeing Hayden with Lily makes me wonder if I'm making the right decision.

No, I can't doubt myself now. I have my future planned out. Kids are not in the cards. Not until I get the career I'm working my ass off to achieve.

"Lily Pily, give Avery a kiss goodbye. It's time for ballet. Miss Alyssa, can I give you a ride?"

"Sure, I'd love that. Thank you." We give each other a secret smile.

"Can I stay here a little longer. Pleeese?"

Gently putting my sock on, I slip my foot into my boot. "We're learning a new routine. You don't want to miss that, do you?"

Lily bites her bottom lip as she looks at the baby.

Harper taps Lily on the leg. "If it's okay with your dad, why don't you come back after class and maybe we can try another sleepover? You were a lot of help the last time you were here." Harper winks at me. Oh, she is so onto us. She's giving us time alone.

"Can I stay the night, Dad?"

Hayden slides his hands into his pockets. "You have school tomorrow."

"Just bring her school uniform when you pick her up in the morning, and she can get ready here." Harper gleefully offers a solution. I love my best friend.

"Are you sure you want to, Lily? Last time you wanted to come home."

"I'll be okay, I promise." She crosses a finger over her heart.

"You don't need to promise. If at any time you want to come home, call me and I'll come get you."

"Thanks, Dad." She bounds off the couch and throws her arms around Hayden's neck. He buries his face in her neck, making her giggle.

Oh, my ovaries are doing their thing again!

We say goodbye to Harper and Avery, and before I leave the room, I turn back and mouth *thank you*. Thanks to Harper, I don't have to sneak out of his house at the crack of dawn.

She mouths back *you're welcome*. Then out loud, she says, "Have fun!"

I know she's not talking about dance classes.

—◦—

Hayden drops us off at the studio but doesn't come inside, trusting me to walk Lily in safely. Is he getting her used to me being in her life and preparing her for our relationship? Or am I overthinking it and it's just convenient because we're going to the same place?

While warming up the children for their lesson, a woman walks into the waiting room and gives me a little wave. Giving Nikki instructions for the class, I excuse myself and head over to the woman.

"Hello, can I help you?" I don't recognize her as one of my student's parents or guardians.

She smiles. "Hi, yes. I've recently moved to the area, and I want to check out some dance studios for my daughter. She's obsessed with dancing and insists I enroll her into a school by the end of the day." She rolls her eyes and chuckles.

"Well, you've come to a great studio. The teachers are highly qual-ified, great with kids, and have a passion for teaching. What style of dance does your daughter do?"

"Oh...ummm...you know..." She waves her hands around. "Jazz. Tap. That sort of thing. I'd love to be able to watch the class to make sure this is a studio she'd like to attend."

I point to the class as they do leg work at the barre. "This is a ballet class. If you'd like, you can bring her here tomorrow for a trial lesson. We have jazz and tap classes running then."

"Oh, she does ballet too." She chuckles. "She does so many classes it's hard to keep up. Would you mind if I stay and watch?" She looks over my shoulder and into the studio.

"I'm sorry, the studio's policy doesn't allow spectators unless you have a child in the class. If you come back with your daughter, and she does a lesson, you're more than welcome to watch then."

The smile on her face stiffens.

"I can give you a free one-lesson-per-style pass for your daughter to try, that way she can decide if we're a good fit," I offer to soften the situation. I've been around enough dance moms to know they can be a prickly bunch, especially when they don't get what they want for their kids.

"Thank you," she says through stiff lips.

I've pissed this woman off today. Oh well. The safety of my school comes first. *My school.* It really feels like it is. I've grown up here. Most of my best memories are here in this building. It's a shame Miss Lucia wants to sell. I hope that whoever buys it loves it as much as I do.

"Give me a minute and I'll get you the pass." I head to the reception desk and take a card from the drawer.

When I turn back, the woman is gone.

Chapter Twenty-Three

HAYDEN

"It's such a beautiful night, I could stay like this forever," Alyssa says, snuggled under my arm. We're lying on the outdoor lounge, staring at the starry night sky. The sounds of insects and the city come to life. With Lily at Finn and Harper's house, we have the luxury of lying together and enjoying the moment without worrying about Lily busting us together and the questions I'd have to answer.

I know I wanted to take my time telling Lily about our relationship, but right now I'm wondering why. Having Alyssa in my arms is perfect. I can't imagine not having her this way. I want her in my life—in Lily's life.

Trailing my fingers up and down Alyssa's arm, I kiss the side of her head. "I want to tell Lily about us."

Alyssa twists in my arms, tilting her head back to look at me. "You do?"

Brushing her hair from her face, my heart swells as I stare at her. "Yes. I don't want to hide you away or sneak you out of the house before she wakes up anymore. I know you haven't signed up for a kid in your life, but me and Lily are a package. Are you ready for me to tell her about us?" My heart pounds as I wait for the answer. What if it's all too much for her?

With a beaming smile, she says, "Yes, I'm ready to tell Lily. I've told you the reason I'm hanging around you is because of your beautiful daughter."

I poke her in the ribs. "Oh really?"

She squeals and twists in my arms. "She's much cuter than you."

I tickle harder. She squirms and kicks her legs. "Is that so?" I ask.

"Yep. If it wasn't for her, you would never see me. *Ever!*"

Pushing her onto her back, I hover above her. "If you never saw me, you wouldn't get this." I nuzzle my face in her neck and swipe my tongue over her quickening pulse.

"I'd be fine with that." She giggles.

"What about this?" My lips skim down to her collarbone and to her breast. The thin fabric of her oversized t-shirt does nothing to stop her nipples from peeking through. I suck one into my mouth.

"I...can live...without it," she pants.

"Liar," I say right before I devour her mouth.

The kiss is long and deep. Wrapping her arms around my neck, she draws me closer. I pour all my feelings into the kiss, hoping she can feel how much I want her. She's so perfect, she fucking scares me. Yet she's here. With me. Despite of the shit I put her through. She could see past it. Made me believe we're *perfect* together.

Pulling away, I say, "I love you." Words I never thought I'd say to a woman spill from my mouth. It feels amazing to say them. Like something has unlocked in my chest and light is bursting out.

Alyssa's eyes widen. "You love me?"

Giving her a feather-light kiss, I take a deep breath. "Yes, I love you so much."

Her bottom lip quivers. "I love you too."

I blow out a breath I didn't know I was holding and sag with relief. I knew she had feelings for me, but I didn't know if they were as strong as mine.

Wanting to show her how much she means to me, I cup her face and kiss her, opening her mouth with my tongue. The passion in the kiss ignites me, lighting up my core. I need to see her. Touch every inch of her.

I break the kiss long enough to yank the t-shirt off her body. When she arrived at the house wearing nothing but an oversized Def Leppard t-shirt, I almost dropped to my knees. She has legs that go on for days. Legs I want wrapped around me.

Sitting back, I make quick work of my clothes, making sure there is a condom within reach. Positioning myself above her, I nestle between her thighs, covering her with my body.

I never thought I needed a woman in my life. Now I can't imagine Alyssa not in it. There is a reason I was never open to anyone before, and not the one I first thought. It's because I was waiting for Alyssa.

Her fingertips glide up and down my spine. Even in the balmy summer evening, my skin explodes with goosebumps. My mouth trails kisses along her jaw and to her neck, breathing in her floral scent. Moving lower, I take playful nibbles of her shoulder, suck on her breasts, which causes her to dig her fingers in my ass, and trail my tongue from her breastbone to her stomach and back again.

She squirms under me, as impatient for me to be inside her as I am. I kneel back, pick up the condom, and rip open the foil packet. Alyssa's heated gaze follows my hands as I slide it on. Drawing her knees apart, I slide between her legs and again position myself above her.

Looking deep into her eyes, the love I feel for her is shining back at me. God, how could I have ever pushed her away? She's beautiful. She sees things in me I never knew existed.

"I love you." Now that the words are out, I want to tell her every chance I get.

She smiles, and it lights up my soul. "I love you, Hayden."

Sealing our lips tight, I enter her slowly, resisting the urge to pound into her. With our mouths and bodies fused together, I want to savor the moment of love and connection.

When Alyssa squirms under me, I can't hold back any longer. I move in and out of her, picking up speed as she meets me thrust for thrust, whimpering with need.

"Hayden...you feel...so good," she gasps between the words as her body quivers beneath me.

Our mouths are kissing anything within reach. Our hands exploring every inch of each other's bodies as I plunge deeper inside her, making her body tremble.

"I'm there...I can't hold on...any longer," she says.

"I know, baby, I know. Let go. I'm with you." My words spur her on, and she bucks against me.

"Oh God!" she cries as her body spasms. Her orgasm clutches around my cock, drawing out my release.

We lay in each other's arms, breathing heavily, waiting for the trembling to subside. This moment is perfect. Alyssa is perfect. Nothing can ever take this away from me.

⬥

Later that night, snuggled behind Alyssa's warm body, her ass presses against my crotch. How can my cock spring to life again when we've been going at it like animals all night? With the way Alyssa is squirming, I'd say she's not done either.

Leaning over her shoulder, I whisper in her ear, "You want more, Twinkle Toes?"

"Hmm-mmm," she mumbles sleepily.

"Tell me what you want?" I nibble at her shoulder, my hand caressing the curve of her hip.

"I want you to fuck me."

"Haven't you had enough?" My hand glides to her stomach, then I skim my fingers between her legs.

"Never enough," she replies. I love how she wants me so damn much.

I slide a finger inside her. She's already wet, and judging by the way she's pushing against my hand, impatient.

There's no way I'm going to let her wait. Removing my hand, I part her ass cheeks to give me better access to her sweet spot. With one swift thrust, I enter her. She cries out. God, she feels so good. Giving her a moment to adjust with such a forceful entrance, my body coils tight, waiting for her. Thank fuck she moves against me. With no finesse, I squeeze her tits as I pound from behind like a jackhammer. She links her fingers with mine like she needs to touch her tits too. Fuck me! She's sexy as hell.

"Even when I fuck you hard, you're so responsive."

"I love it when you fuck me hard," she gasps.

Holy hell, that pushes me over the edge. I'm clinging on by my fingertips, trying not to come before she does.

I thrust harder and pinch her nibbles. "Yes! Yes!" she cries. Her body is trembling. She's ready. A second later, she spasms and falls apart. "Hayden!"

One thrust...two...and I'm gone.

As soon as I catch my breath, my body stiffens. *Fuck!* What I've done explodes in my head. How could I have been so careless? Wrapped up in the moment, and half-asleep, I wasn't thinking straight. I spring into a sitting position and look down at Alyssa lying on her back with a satisfied smile on her face. Her smile drops as she looks at me.

"What's wrong?" She sits up next to me.

I jump from the bed, pick up my jeans off the floor and shove my legs into them. I don't bother buttoning them up. "I forgot to use a condom."

"I'm on the pill, remember."

"It doesn't always work." I link my fingers behind my neck and pace the room.

Sliding off the bed, she walks over to me. "Neither does a condom, yet we still had sex."

I stop pacing. "It was safer with two forms of contraception."

"It will be okay," she says reassuringly.

Dropping my hands by my side, I shake my head. "How can you be so sure?"

She links her fingers with mine. "The pill is highly successful at preventing pregnancies."

"So are condoms, and look what happened with Rachel," I reply. Alyssa jerks back like I've slapped her. Regretting the words immediately, I say, "I didn't mean—" She steps away. "I shouldn't have said that." I want to pull her into my arms and let her know I'm sorry. But based on her stiff posture and the way she's glaring at me, it's not a great idea.

"A pregnancy is the last thing I want. I have my career to think about. A baby doesn't fit into my schedule." Snatching her t-shirt off the floor, she yanks it on. Next, she grabs her boots and shoves them under her arm.

"Alyssa, I'm sorry." I feel like the biggest jerk reacting the way I did and for what I said to her.

"Yeah, so am I for thinking you wanted more between us." She spins on her heels and marches from the bedroom.

"Please understand where this is coming from," I call out after her.

She stops and turns around. "I do. You had a life-changing experience. Something so difficult it scarred you. The cause was with a woman you met at a nightclub and had a one-night stand with. Tonight, you told me..." Her hand presses against her chest. "You told me you loved me. That you wanted to tell Lily about us."

"I do lo—"

She holds up her hand, stopping me from saying more. "Maybe you should think about what you really want before you tell Lily about us. Because if we continue this relationship, there'll always be the risk of a pregnancy. Protection is not one-hundred percent effective."

"This all came out wrong." God, I have royally fucked this up.

"Really? So, the thought of me getting pregnant doesn't scare the bejesus out of you? You haven't thought, even for a split second, that I might dump a baby on you?"

Dropping my head, I stare at my feet. I'm ashamed to admit that I did.

She sighs. "Maybe I need to think about what I want too. Because at the moment, this isn't it."

Fuck! How did this night turn from being the best of my life to utter shit? When everything was so perfect? Except *I'm* not perfect. In a blink of an eye, I've destroyed everything.

Alyssa hesitates at the threshold of the door like she's waiting for me to say something. Fix what I've fucked up. When I say nothing, she turns to leave.

This time, I don't stop her.

Chapter Twenty-Four

A week later, I'm in the studio getting ready for ballet class. Nikki is still demonstrating most of the dance routines even though my ankle is better. I could probably teach the lesson myself, but after getting a callback from my audition I don't want to risk flaring up the injury.

As students arrive, my heart flutters with nerves. I'm waiting for Hayden and Lily. I haven't seen him since the night he broke my heart. I couldn't even bare going back to give Lily a private lesson. Guilt plagued me at the thought of disappointing her. How can I face Hayden when he told me he loved me one minute, and the next, he took it away? He may not have said the words, but his actions did.

I've spent the past week focusing on teaching and my audition, trying to get Hayden out of my mind. It hasn't worked. He's all I think about. He's the man I love, and he ripped my heart from my chest. How can he tell me he loves me and place me in the same category as Rachel? A woman who would abandon her baby for him to raise alone.

When they arrive, my heart clogs into my throat. Our eyes lock from across the room. My gaze drinks him in like I'm dying of thirst. God, I've missed him.

He walks toward me. "Alyssa." My name on his lips washes over me. I've missed the sound of his voice.

Taking my eyes off him, I turn to Lily. "Sweetheart, run inside and get ready for class. We're doing the routine you like."

"Yes!" She bobs up and down on her toes with excitement before racing into the studio.

Being mindful of the other parents and their curious gazes, I pull Hayden to the side of the waiting room. "Hayden, I—"

"Why haven't you answered my texts?" he interrupts with an annoyed expression on his face.

I glance over my shoulder, checking to make sure that no one can overhear us. "I told you I needed time to think about what I want," I say, keeping my voice low.

"What do you want?" he asks.

For the nightmare to disappear. For me and Hayden to go back to telling each other we loved one another. For a future together. "Trust."

"Alyssa, I do trust you. It's just—" He puts a hand on my shoulder. I go to step away, but he doesn't let me. "Parents will talk," I say.

"I don't give a fuck if they do," he says through thin lips.

"What if it gets back to Lily? Do you want her asking questions about us? Especially when things have changed?" Now that the relationship has died before it got started. My chest raises up and down as tears sting the backs of my eyes.

Hayden drops his hand from my shoulder. "We need to talk. Can we meet after you finish your classes? Once Lily has gone to bed?"

Sadness is etched on his face. The distance between us has been hard on me this week. Has he felt it too?

"I'll be there." I can't keep avoiding this conversation. Although, I'm not sure if there's much to say. If there's no trust, what do we have?

He nods. "See you later."

The next hour drags on. Even though things aren't great between me and Hayden, I still crave to see him. I can't touch him, hold him, but I can look at him. For now, that's all I can have.

The students practice their positions, pirouettes, arabesques, and the dance routine for parent watch week for the end of the term. Finally, Nikki takes the class through their warm-down. I've never been so happy for a class to end. One down, two more to go.

Out in the waiting room I see the woman who had inquired about the studio a few days ago. I hadn't seen her again and assumed she'd chosen a different school for her daughter. Leaving Nikki to finish the class, I make my way over to her. "Hello again. Will your daughter be joining us today?" I glance around the waiting area in case I missed seeing her from the studio. There's no one out here but us.

The smile she gives me is stiff and...smug? There is something about this woman that makes the hairs at the back of my neck stand up. I don't know what it is, but she can take her daughter elsewhere.

"My daughter is already in the class." She looks over my shoulder and into the studio. "I've come to pick her up."

I turn my head to look into the room. The kids have finished their warm-down and are heading out. Had I been so preoccupied with Hayden on my mind that I'd missed a new student? Surely not.

"Who is your daughter?" I ask.

When Lily enters the waiting area, the woman's gaze lands on her, and the woman's face lights up with a huge smile. "She is."

What the hell is she talking about? Is this woman crazy? Then my heart drops to the floor. They have the same eye and hair coloring. The same creamy complexion. Something in the way they both smile looks similar. No...it can't be. Is this Lily's mother?

Over the woman's shoulder, I see Hayden stop at the top of the stairs, all color draining from his face, standing so still he could be mistaken for a statue. The death glare he's throwing at the woman confirms my suspicions.

This is Rachel.

When Hayden breaks free from his shock at seeing Rachel, he storms over and growls low and deep, "What the fuck are you doing here?" The vibration from his body is palpable.

Her eyes widen with mock surprise. "I'm here to pick up my daughter." Rachel is speaking like this is what she does every week.

Before Hayden can say another word, Lily skips over to us.

"Here she is," Rachel says brightly. "How lovely it is to see you after so many years. You've grown into such a beautiful girl." Lily looks at Rachel then to her father with confusion. "And you have the same hair and eye color as me. Isn't that wonderful?"

Hayden's body is visibly trembling with anger. Before he explodes in front of Lily, I squat down next to her so I'm eye level. "Miss Lucia is in the storeroom. Can you please ask her to find the Gisele costume for me?"

Lily nods, a crease of confusion still on her brow. As she walks away, she turns back to look at the woman. Rachel waves. The murderous expression on Hayden's face is one I never want to see again.

"You have two seconds to get the fuck out of here and away from *my* daughter." A vein ticks on the side of his clenched jaw.

Rachel crosses her arms over her chest. "I want to talk with Lily and get to know her."

"Not happening."

The parents who have arrived to pick up their children have sensed the tension and are looking over at us with curious expressions. I smile like all is fine and wave them goodbye.

"I have every right to talk to her. I'm her mother."

Deathly still, Hayden's face darkens. I'm surprised Rachel hasn't burst into flames. "You are the woman who gave birth to her. You will *never* be her mother. The day you dumped her at my feet is the day you gave up all rights to her."

"I've changed my mind. I want to be in her life." She tilts her chin up.

Hayden's hands clench into fists at his sides. I put a hand on his arm to sooth him before he does something he regrets. "Hayden, you and Rachel need to go somewhere private and talk. Lily can't walk out and see this. She can stay with me while I teach the next class."

The fierce expression doesn't leave his face. Without taking his eyes off Rachel, he nods. "Tell Lily I won't be long." To Rachel, he says, "Let's go."

Thankfully she doesn't argue, and she walks down the stairs. When she's out of sight, his body deflates. My heart goes out to him. This is such a shock. How is he going to deal with the situation?

Scrubbing a hand over his face, he turns to me. "Please don't say anything to Lily."

I'm a little taken back that he'd think I would, but he's had a major shock, so I let it slide. "I won't. I'll tell her you had an emergency at work."

"Thank you."

I put a hand on his arm. "Can Rachel see Lily if she wants?"

"Not if I can help it." He blows out a harsh breath. "Why the fuck is she here? I know it really has nothing to do with Lily. She wants something."

"You'd better go after her and find out." Whatever it is, it can't be good. Why now? Has she had a change of heart about giving up her baby? No. She wouldn't turn up out of the blue at her dance class.

"I'll be back as soon as possible," he says.

I nod.

He dashes from the studio. Tonight, we were supposed to talk about our relationship. With Rachel showing up, reminding him of what she did, I pray that her appearance hasn't reenforced Hayden's belief and made this a whole lot worse for us.

Chapter Twenty-Five

⊶◦⊷

HAYDEN

In a nearby coffee shop, I sit across the table from Rachel. She's sipping her mocha latte looking as if she doesn't have a care in the world. Like we're old friends catching up. If she knew the murderous thoughts running rampant in my mind, she wouldn't look so relaxed. My hands ball into fists on my lap.

The sooner I find out what her deal is the sooner I can get back to Lily and protect her from this evil bitch. "Tell me why the fuck you showed up at my daughter's dance lesson. And how the hell did you know where to find her?" That's the scariest part about this. How long has she been stalking Lily?

"You mean *our* daughter," she corrects.

I place my elbows on the timber table and lean forward, getting up into her face. "*My* daughter," I *correct* her.

She rolls her eyes and chuckles like I've told a silly joke. Is this situation some kind of sick joke and I'm missing the punchline?

"If you don't tell me what you're doing here, I'm getting the police involved," I say.

"And tell them what?" She gives a smug expression as if to say *what will calling the police do?*

"You're stalking my daughter."

She makes a disbelieving sound. "I'm her mother. I can see her at dance classes if I want to."

Is this woman insane? "What part of 'you're not her mother' don't you understand?"

"We never had a legal arrangement of me relinquishing my rights as a parent. There's no custody agreement in place. As far as they're concerned, I have every right to see my kid. I miss her. Is that so hard to believe?"

"Yes." The word shoots out faster than a bullet.

"I'm in a better place now. I can take care of her." She rapidly blinks her eyelids. Is she trying to make herself cry?

"How does your husband feel about this? I can't imagine he'd be happy to learn your five-month vacation eight years ago was really time away to birth a child. You hid a pregnancy with another man."

She shuffles in her seat and spins her cup around. "He...arhhh...doesn't know."

Leaning back in my seat, I take a closer look at her. For someone who lives a multimillion-dollar lifestyle she's not looking like someone dressed head to toe in designer clothes. She's looking rough around the edges. She doesn't scream *money* like the private investigator led me to believe.

Then it hits me. "Your husband left you, didn't he?" Things are making sense. If she's lost her money source, where can she get more? Fat chance getting it from me.

She taps her fingers on the wooden table. Her silence and the agitation on her face tells me I'm on target.

"Tell me why you're really here," I say. "And it's not because you want Lily."

"The bastard divorced me when he learned I had a kid while we were married. He left me with nothing. Nothing! How am I supposed to support myself?"

"Get a fucking job like everyone else does." For a moment, I'm curious to know how her husband found out about Lily. I shake the thought away. I really don't care. All I want is for Rachel to go the fuck away.

"I have had to get a job at a diner. Do I look like someone who should serve people food? And look what I have to wear—clothes from Walmart!" She shivers as if she's said a dirty word. "Don't get me started on the flea-infested apartment I have to share with two other women."

She's gotten what she deserves. "So, what you're really saying is you want money." My shoulders sag with a mix of relief and disappointment. Relief because this problem is fixable. She's only here for money not Lily. Disappointment because Lily deserves so much better. She deserves a mother who loves her, cherishes her, and wants to spend every moment watching her grow into the incredible kid that she is.

Scratching the side of her neck like she's brought the fleas with her, she says, "You have lots of money. I only want fifty thousand dollars to get me back on my feet."

And prepare herself for her next sugar daddy victim. Behind her disheveled state, she's still a beautiful-looking woman, so she could probably do it. Too bad her heart is rotten.

"Not going to happen," I reply. Giving her money won't make her go away permanently. When she's blown through it, she'll only come back for more.

She points a finger in my face. "I can take Lily from you if you don't give me what I want."

Hooking my arm over the back of my chair, I give off a relaxed demeanor. Inside, my blood is boiling. "You can threaten to take Lily until you're blue in the face. It will never happen. Nor am I giving you any money. If you know what is good for you, you'll leave New York City and stay as far away from me and *my* daughter as possible."

"I'll go to the media and tell them you took her from me and haven't let me see her. Who will they believe? You or a crying, depressed mother?" she gloats like she's won the battle.

"Do you think I care if you go to the media? You still won't get money from me."

"Your reputation will be ruined," she points out.

I shrug. "I don't care. Tell them your story. Let's see what happens when I give them the information I have on you. Who do you think will come out smelling like roses or shit?"

A flush of red stains her cheeks. "I need money!"

"Find yourself another sucker to get if from." I stand, pull out my wallet from my pocket. Taking a ten-dollar bill out, I toss it on the table. "To cover your coffee. That's all you'll ever get from me."

Turning my back on her, I leave the coffee shop with heaviness weighing on my shoulders. How can that monster be the mother of my sweet, sensitive, gorgeous little girl? For a moment I was petrified she'd really come for Lily. That Lily's world would be turned upside down. I can't let that happen. I won't let that happen. This is why I kept our lives simple. Just the two of us. So nothing or no one could ever come between us.

Walking up the stairs to the studio, my body is quivering with rage. Before I enter the room, I pause to pull in several deep, fortifying breaths. I should have taken a few minutes to calm down before picking up Lily. All I want is to see my daughter, wrap my arms around her, and protect her. When my racing heart simmers down, I walk into the waiting area.

Through the studio's window, I see Lily at the front of the room with Alyssa and the student teacher demonstrating dance moves for the students in the class who are twice her age. I watch her little face beam with happiness. The way she smiles fills my heart with love. She is my life.

No one in class notices me watching; they're focused on the lesson. My gaze drifts to Alyssa. She's holding Lily's hand and instructing her to do something. Lily gets on her toes, folds up one leg, and Alyssa spins her around like she's standing in a music box. Lily's giggles float in the air to me. Alyssa is giggling alongside Lily. Cheering her on with every spin.

When Lily stops, she wobbles dizzily on her feet. Alyssa puts her hands on Lily's shoulders and hugs her to her chest. After a moment, she pulls away and gives Lily a high-five. A lump lodges in my throat. I swallow hard to push it down. There's no doubt Alyssa genuinely cares for Lily. It's easy to see that the feeling is mutual. After every class, all I hear is Miss Alyssa this...Miss Alyssa that. Alyssa would have fit easily into our little family. The way I reacted when I forgot to use a condom and seeing Rachel has sent my mind whirling. I'm not sure if I'm ready like I thought I was.

A few seconds later, Alyssa's gaze locks with mine. Her smile drops. From this distance, I can read the concern on her face. She says something to Nikki then takes Lily's hand and walks her out to me.

"Hey, Lily Pily." I force a smile. "I see you've been promoted to dance teacher."

She giggles. "I was helping Miss Alyssa teach the class."

Alyssa runs a hand along Lily's shoulders. Another gesture of affection that comes so naturally. "Pretty soon she'll have my job," she jokes, although I can see tension on her face. "Did the meeting you got called away for go well?"

"Yes, it did. Thank you. I won't be having any more trouble from the supplier."

Her shoulders visibly sag with relief. "I'm so glad to hear that."

"Thank you for watching Lily."

"No problem."

Picking up Lily's bag, I fling it over my shoulder. "See you next week."

Lines furrow between her brows. I know we planned to talk about our relationship later tonight. With my head in such a mess, if we talk now, I'm worried I'll screw things up even more.

God, I hate doing this to her. She deserves better. I always knew I wasn't good enough for her.

Chapter Twenty-Six

HAYDEN

"Dad, who was that woman at ballet?" Lily's question hits me like a boulder to the head. She's tucked in bed, and thankfully, my back is turned toward her while I put her clothes away in the closet. I'm sure there is fear plastered across my face.

"What woman?" I'm stalling because I don't know what the fuck to say to her.

"The woman who has the same hair as me."

"You don't have the same hair," I say with a little too much force. Shit, I don't want her to think I'm angry with her. Hanging the last dress, I turn to face her with a smile on my face. "She's no one." If I had the choice, that's exactly who she would be.

Lily tucks the stuffed penguin under her chin. "She said I've grown up. Has she seen me before?"

"Once when you were a baby."

How much longer can I keep the truth from her? Lily is too young to know what happened. It could mess up her life like it fucked up mine. Rachel won't be back. Not if there's no money. I don't need to put Lily through the trauma of knowing she means nothing to the woman who birthed her.

Before Lily can ask any more questions, I bend to give her a kiss on the forehead. "It's time for sleep. I'll see you in the morning. I love you."

She snuggles down into the blankets. "Love you too."

Leaving her room, I close the door behind me. As I make my way downstairs there's a knock at the door. Immediately I think of Alyssa. Even though I told her without saying the words that I'd changed my mind about her coming over, I'm glad she didn't listen.

With enthusiastic strides, I reach the door and open it. My shoulders slump. Finn and Lucas are standing on the porch. "Oh, it's only you."

My brothers look at each other with amusement. "Wow, what a heartfelt greeting," Lucas says with sarcasm.

"I hope he doesn't pop from excitement," Finn teases.

I roll my eyes. "Whatever you're here for, I'm not in the mood." The last thing I want is company.

"Too bad." Lucas pushes past me. Holding a six-pack, he heads into the kitchen.

Finn follows him into the house. "We thought you could use a drink. We heard you had a run-in with Rachel."

I cock an eyebrow. "News travels fast."

Finn shrugs. "The girls talk. How did Lily's mother find her?"

My body tenses. "Rachel is not Lily's mother."

Holding up his hands, Finn backs up a step. "Sorry. I can see this has upset you. How are you doing?"

I scrub the back of my neck. "I've been better."

We meet Lucas in the kitchen, he's removed the caps off the bottles and has them placed on the counter. Finn and Lucas take a seat on the stools. I'm too agitated to sit.

"How did Rachel find Lily?" Finn asks again. This time remembering to not call the woman 'mother.'

Placing my palms on the counter, I shake my head. "I don't know. She knows where I work. She probably followed me."

My gut twists in a knot. How long was she stalking us? Where else had she followed Lily? Our home? Her school? I'll be making an appointment with the principal to make sure there is no way Rachel can contact Lily. I'll stick a fucking bodyguard on her 24/7 if I have to.

"That's fucked up." Lucas frowns and takes a swig from the bottle.

"Yeah, it is. *She* is fucked up." I tell them about her demands and her attempt at blackmailing me.

"She obviously doesn't know you well. You'll guard Lily with your life and let no one get between you," Finn says.

"Did I let my guard slip? I've been so focused on Alyssa, sneaking around with her and keeping our relationship a secret. I should have seen Rachel coming. Taken notice of what was going on around me. If my head wasn't so far up in the clouds, maybe this never would have happened." This is my fault. I'm supposed to protect Lily. I haven't done my job well enough. I'd die if anything were to happen to my daughter.

Finn and Lucas freeze with stunned expressions on their faces. Their eyelids blinking rapidly are the only parts of them moving. Then Finn shakes himself out of his trance. "What did you say?"

Oh crap! I'd forgotten that I haven't told my brothers I've been seeing Alyssa. Because I hadn't told Lily, I wasn't ready to tell anyone. Now I've said more than I wanted. Especially with our relationship already on rocky ground. I saw the hurt expression on Alyssa's face when I told her I'd see her next week. Does she think we're over? Are we over? How can we continue when I'm still fucked up? How can I live my life without her?

"How the hell did I not know you were seeing Alyssa?" Finn says with exasperation.

"I'm surprised Harper said nothing to you. She's onto us."

He shakes his head. "She never mentioned a thing. Girl code is tight."

"You and Alyssa are seeing each other? That's great." Lucas raises his beer. "It's about time."

My legs don't have the strength to hold me anymore. I pull out a stool and deflate onto the seat and stare at the bottle in my hand. "I've been spending time with Alyssa. Trying to fight the attraction was pointless. I couldn't keep away from her. Things moved quicker than I thought possible and we...well...have taken the next step."

"The next step?" Lucas raises an eyebrow.

I clear my throat. "We slept together."

Both Lucas and Finn's eyes grow round.

"You're riding again? Congratulations!" Lucas raises his hand to give me a high-five. I glare at him. With a sheepish grin, he drops his arm.

"This is huge," Finn says. "Things must be serious. Otherwise, you'd never sleep with her."

Propping my elbows on the counter, I scrub my hands over my face. "It was serious, then so much has happened and now my brain is fucked up. I can't think straight."

"Is this about Rachel?" Finn asks. "Will she try something else? Like somehow get between you and Alyssa?"

"I won't see Rachel again." I pull back on my beer. I need to wash away the foul taste in my mouth whenever I mention that bitch's name.

Finn nudges my shoulder. "If it's not Rachel, what's fucked up your brain?"

"I had unprotected sex." Christ, I still can't believe I was so careless. There's something about Alyssa that can make me get so lost in her that I forget about the real world.

Finn blows out a breath. Lucas lets out a long whistle. They both know how huge this is for me.

"Is she pregnant?" Lucas asks.

"It's too soon to tell. She's on the pill and told me not to stress." I shrug. "I'm stressed."

"Is this because you can't see a future with Alyssa? Is she just someone you want to blow off steam with?" Finn asks.

I glare at Finn. He gives a hard stare back. This is his wife's best friend. He'll tie my balls in a knot if I'm only messing around.

"It was more than that. Then we had unprotected sex, and I'm back to being terrified. I thought I'd come to terms with what happened to me—to Lily. I finally could let myself fall in love with someone. But one careless action has changed everything."

"Whoa! Did you say you fell in love?" Lucas claps. "This story keeps getting better and better. Well, maybe not the part where Alyssa might be pregnant. Although, I can't see the problem since you love her."

I rub my fingers up and down my forehead. A headache is brewing. What Lucas said is true—it shouldn't be a problem. Yet I can think of many reasons it is. "Alyssa has a career that can take her anywhere around the world. A baby will get in the way."

"Do you think she'll leave you with a baby like Rachel did?" Finn asks.

"No...yes...I don't know." I'm so confused. I know I'm letting my experience with Rachel muddy my feelings for Alyssa.

Concern lines Finn's face. "You said you fell in love. Do you know how Alyssa feels?"

Hearing Alyssa tell me she loved me was one of the best moments of my life. My cold heart that had been lying dormant for so long began beating again with new energy. So much love poured from me, making me dizzy. "She loves me too."

Finn lifts his palms up. "What's the problem then? You love her. She loves you. If she's pregnant, you'll get through it together."

I wish my brain could process it that way. "It's not that simple."

"Sure it is. You're making it complicated with all these *what ifs*. What if she's pregnant? What if she moves away for work? What if she leaves me with a baby?" Finn holds up his hand and counts with his fingers. "One—she's on the pill. The likelihood of her getting pregnant is low. Two—she hasn't made it on Broadway yet. When she does, who said she's moving from New York City. Three—she would never dump a baby on you."

I drop my head. "I'm being stupid, aren't I?"

"No, not stupid. You're cautious. Scared. It's understandable. Alyssa is not Rachel. If you think for a moment that she would do to you what Rachel did, then you don't deserve her. You're pushing away someone you say you love for something she hasn't done. For something *someone else* has done."

My gut twists into a knot. That's exactly what I'm doing. If I can't sort my shit out and continue with a relationship with Alyssa, I'll end up hurting her.

Hurting her is the last thing I want to do.

Chapter
Twenty-Seven

❖

ALYSSA

Sitting in the theatre, the buzz of excitement for *Swan Lake* soon to start stirs through the room. The lights dim, the orchestra comes to life, and the stage fills with color and beauty. Ballet dancers, looking like they're floating on air and can leap into the sky, grace the stage, and the performance begins.

I hold my breath, watching Christina in her first principal role as Princess Odette. The angles of her body, her strength, and sheer beauty is unlike anything I've seen before. I've watched old videos of my parents dancing, and I think my sister blows them out of the water. It won't be long until she is the talk of the ballet world. She deserves this time in the spotlight. The hard work and dedication are paying off. Her talent is as natural as breathing.

There was a time the green-eyed monster reared its head inside of me. Especially when our parents compared us. It made me rebel and not put in the time. What was the point when I wasn't as good as Christina?

Now, as I watch her perform to a sold-out theatre, I'm so proud of her. The ballet scene is her world. It's not mine. I love the variety of dance styles too much to stick to just one. That's why Broadway is more suitable for me. After the call I'd gotten from my agent today, I'm finally going to live my dream.

After the final bow my parents and I head backstage to join Christina and the other dancers. The room is filled with excitement after their brilliant performance. When my sister spots us, she prances over. My parents, one at a time, air-kiss her cheeks like they're acquaintances instead of family. I engulf her in a huge hug.

"Great job, sis," I congratulate. "You smashed it."

She brims with pride. "I can't believe I did it. I was so nervous I thought I was going to puke or stumble and fall on my ass." She giggles.

"Darling, you were superb. You hid your nerves well. That is the sign of a true professional. You've done us proud. You will be talked about for months." My mother beams.

Dad nods in agreement. "Truly wonderful."

My mother looks at me and says, "What your sister has done is magnificent! This is what you must strive for. Then you too will know how it feels to have such accolades thrown your way. What are you waiting for?"

"Mom." Christina pulls a face at my mother, indicating that she wants her to stop talking. "Alyssa is doing great."

"I don't see working at a strip club as doing great." My father screws up his nose.

Why do we always have this conversation whenever I talk with my parents? It's come to the point where I'd rather avoid them.

"Let's go for a drink. There's a cute bar two minutes up the street I've heard good things about." Christina, obviously picking up on the tension, tries to distract us.

"Another time. I have an early appointment in the morning. Before I go, you might be interested to know I've landed a principal role in the musical *Moulin Rouge*."

My parents' eyes widen with shock.

Christina beams with pride. "Lyssi, that's amazing! Congratulations." She throws her arms around my neck. "I can't wait to watch you."

My parents' shocked expressions dissolve into relief. "Finally." My mother sighs dramatically with her hand on her chest. "We thought this day would never come."

Oh...wow...okay. So much for having any faith in me. Did they ever believe I had talent? Or did they push me only because a career on stage was the only option for their daughter?

"Don't sound so excited," I say with sarcasm.

My mother rolls her eyes. "Of course we're excited. Now you finally have a respectable job. I'm proud of you, darling." She gives my cheeks air-kisses.

My father pats me on the back. "Well done. This is good news."

After years of wanting them to be proud of me, I've finally heard the words. Why don't they fill me with happiness? This is the most affection I've received from them, and it's because I'm on Broadway. *Dance somewhere respectable and we will love you. Land a leading role and we will love you.* Just be me with an ordinary job...not acceptable.

Leaving the theatre, I should be feeling exhilarated after giving my parents my news. I should be beaming with pride because I've made them happy. Instead, I walk heavy-legged to the subway. My heart knows what I'm too afraid to say out loud. My parents' love comes with conditions.

The next morning, after ending a call with my agent, I stare blankly at the phone in my hand. If Davey had hit me over the head with a brick, I'd be less shocked. One detail about our conversation I had to ask him to repeat five times before I understood what he was saying. How could I have not known that the musical I'd auditioned for is showing in London? Davey said he'd mentioned it when he sent me for the audition. Did he?

It's freaking London! How would I have missed that information? Maybe because I've been so stressed with auditions, an injured ankle, my parents on my back, and the mess with Hayden, that it got lost in translation.

Holy shit! London. Can I do it? Can I move to the other side of the world to chase my dreams when everyone I know and love is here? My friends... Hayden.

I fold my legs up onto the couch. Would he care if I go? He hasn't contacted me in over a week. Not to talk. Not for Lily's private lesson. When he drops her off for class, he gives me a ghost of a smile then leaves. It's the same when he picks her up. I don't even know what happened with Rachel.

Our relationship sizzled before it began. Maybe I can scratch him from the list of people I'd be leaving. Tucking my knees to my chest, I wrap my arms around my legs. How can he tell me he loves me then walk away like I mean nothing?

Anger percolates in my gut. How can he be so heartless? Playing with my feelings is not okay. If you love someone, no matter what happens, you should be able to work through it together. Not push them away. Not act like nothing has happened.

I pick up the phone and dial his number. The call goes straight to voicemail. I hold out the phone and look at it with disgust. Is he ignoring me? I bring it back to my ear and wait until his I'm-not-available message finishes. When it's time to speak, I stand. With my hand on my hip, I pace the room.

"Hayden, it's Alyssa. Or *Twinkle Toes* as you like to call me. Remember me? The woman you've slept with. The woman you told you loved. The woman you're now ghosting. Well, I'm calling to tell you I don't like being ignored. You are with me or you're not. From the way you're behaving, I'm guessing you're not. Since you won't speak to me face to face, I'm calling to tell you I have news—big news. But since you won't answer my call, you'll never know what it is. It's been fun for all of two seconds. See you around. Or not." I disconnect the call so hard I'm surprised I don't shatter the phone screen.

The screen isn't the only thing that's at risk of shattering. My heart isn't too stable. At any moment, it's going to crumble into a million tiny pieces.

I continue to pace the room until the adrenaline from the call wears off. My legs shake, and I sink onto the couch. Resting my elbows on my knees, I drop my head into my hands and take deep, shuddery breaths.

Crap! What did I do? Why did I have to call Hayden and spill my guts? Groaning, I wish I had a rewind button so I could go back in time and never make that call. I sit up straight. Maybe I can ask Harper to sneak into his office, steal his phone, and delete the message. I sag into the cushions of the couch. This isn't a Hollywood movie. Damn it.

Anxiety over what I did buzzes through me, and I can't keep still, so I decide to scrub the apartment. An hour later, when I haven't received a reply, I relax slightly. Hopefully he doesn't listen to his messages and will never hear it. Or he has listened, deemed me crazy, and is relieved that he doesn't have to have anything to do with me again.

I'm so wound up with thoughts in my head it takes me a moment to notice someone knocking at the door. I freeze with the sponge in my hand I'm using to scrub the coffee table. Could it be Hayden? Surely not, he wouldn't leave work to come and talk to me, would he? I'm not up to seeing anyone, so I ignore it. If it were Harper, she would have called first. Now that she has Avery, she likes to know I'm home before she packs up everything she needs plus the baby for a visit.

The knocking gets louder. "Alyssa, open the door."

My heart drops to my feet. It's Hayden. He listened to the message. Why else would he be banging on my door? If I'm quiet, he'll think I'm not home and go away.

"Alyssa!" he calls.

I need to get into my bedroom. The walls and doors are paper thin, and I'm worried he'll hear my panicked, heavy breathing. Tiptoeing around the coffee table, I don't see the basket of cleaning products I left on the floor. I trip over it and stumble, smacking the side of my body into the wall. For a dancer, sometimes I feel like I have two left feet.

"Alyssa! I know you're inside. Open up." He pounds harder.

After making construction-site noises in my living room, there's no way I can pretend I'm not home. Oh well, it's better to get this conversation over with. Taking a deep breath, I walk to the door and open it. Before I can say a word, Hayden barrels into the apartment. Closing the door behind us, I wait for what he has to say.

"You said you have news," he says.

"Yes, I do."

"Are you pregnant?" He scans my stomach like he has x-ray vision, a look of panic in his eyes.

His question spears through my chest, cracking every rib with it. We haven't spoken in days, and this is what he says to me. How could he ever had said he loved me? Is he another person in my life putting conditions on their love? I deserve better.

"It's too early to tell," I say without emotion, feeling numb inside.

He blows out a long breath. "When will you know for sure?"

"Not for a couple of weeks."

He rakes his fingers through his hair.

"I know an unplanned pregnancy is not what you want. It's not what I want either, yet I'm not acting like the world is collapsing around me." Only my heart.

He puts his hands on my shoulders. For days I've longed for his touch, but this feels stiff and unfeeling. "I'm sorry. With Rachel coming back...I haven't been myself."

I pull away from his grasp, and his arms fall to his sides. The distance between us started before Rachel's visit to the studio. "What happened with Rachel?" I ask.

I thought he'd call to let me know how it went. Although, if we're not in a relationship—and by the way things are looking, we are not—why would he? The way he has been acting he's still not ready for a commitment. A sharp pain slices through me, and I sit on the arm of the couch.

He pushes his hands into his pockets. "She tried blackmailing me for money. She didn't really want Lily."

"Did you give it to her?" What kind of sick person is she?

"Not a dime."

"Do you think she'll stop trying?"

He shrugs. "If she doesn't, she'll be met by the same response. She doesn't love Lily. Doesn't want her in her life. Money is what she desires. Nothing more."

The pain etched on his face makes me want to pull him in my arms and comfort him. Instead, I stay seated. "For your sake and Lily's, I hope she never comes back."

He rubs the back of his neck. "I can't believe she got so close to Lily."

"Are you ever going to tell Lily about Rachel?"

Tipping his head back to stare at the ceiling, he squeezes his eyes shut for a second. This situation is beating him up, and here I am sending stupid voice messages and acting like I should be the center of his universe.

"At the moment, she's too young to know the truth," he says. "I'll tell her more when she's older."

It can't be easy having to live with this turmoil. I can't stay seated a moment longer. Hayden is suffering. Rising from the couch, I go to him and wrap my arms around his waist and rest my head on his chest. Holding my breath, I wait for him to pull away.

When he holds me tighter in the embrace, my breath releases in a relieved gush of air. With me standing in his arms, the reality of our relationship ending hits me hard. This may be the last time he holds me this way.

Hayden smooths his hand up and down my back. "Tell me about your news. Is it good?"

Pulling away, I step back and immediately miss his warmth. Any other time, I'd want to shout my news from the rooftops. Finally, I've gotten what I've dreamed of. With so much happening, the excitement hasn't hit me yet.

"From the look on your face, it's not good news. What is it? What's wrong?" he asks with concern.

Plastering a smile on my face, I force cheer into my voice. "Nothing is wrong. It's actually great. I've been cast as the lead in the musical *Moulin Rouge*."

Hayden's eyes light up. "That's amazing. Congratulations."

"It's in London."

His shoulders slump. "Oh... Are you taking it?"

"This is what I've worked so hard for." And yet, I didn't confirm with Davey I was taking the part. There is so much to consider. But what is keeping me here? I'd be a fool not to take it.

He nods, nibbling on his bottom lip. There's a part of me that wants him to beg me not to take it. To tell me he loves me too damn much to let me go. Promise he'll move heaven and earth so we can be together. As the seconds pass by, he doesn't say any of those things.

"When do you leave?" he asks.

My heart drops to my feet. He isn't going to fight for me. Why would he? His life and family are here.

"It won't be for a few months."

"I'm happy for you. You deserve this. I know you're going to smash it." The somber tone doesn't match his encouraging words. "What if you're..." His gaze lands on my stomach. "...pregnant?"

Would I still be able to perform? How could I if I have a growing stomach? The costumes aren't going to hide anything. I'm getting ahead of myself. "I'm not."

"You said you won't know for a couple of weeks."

"It's just a feeling." Surely there'd be some signs by now. Harper complained about tender breasts and hated certain smells early into her pregnancy.

Hayden doesn't look convinced. "Let me know as soon as you find out."

Is this the man who once showered me with love and affection? The man who wanted to share his life with me? I blink back tears that sting the backs of my eyes. I won't let him see how his words are shattering my heart.

"I will," I reply.

He rocks on his heels like he's unsure what to do or say next. Then he says, "I better go."

It feels like he's punched a fist in my chest and ripped out my heart. How is he so cold? He turns to leave. "Hayden," I call.

He stops and turns around.

"What are you doing?"

He cocks an eyebrow. "What am I doing?"

I'm swallowing my pride and making him tell me what's going on. I can't live with the unknown. "To us. What are you doing to us? You told me you loved me. We were planning to tell Lily about our relationship. We make one mistake, and you can't look at me anymore."

Hayden's head drops, and he scrubs his hands over his face. When he looks back at me, I see pain etched on his features. "With you going off to London, how will it work? I can't follow you with Lily. Our place is in New York City."

A dagger digs into my chest. "You pulling away from me started before my news about London. This is because we had unprotected sex. Does having a baby with me scare you so much?" If he loved me like he said he did, it shouldn't be that way. This isn't love.

"If you're pregnant, what then? Do you hand it over to me while you're working so far away?"

The dagger is getting buried deeper and deeper into my chest. My legs give out and I stumble back, dropping onto the couch. "You think I would do that?"

He digs his thumbs into his eye sockets. "I don't know."

"How can you think that of me? Especially after you told me you loved me?" I say, my voice trembling.

"I do love you."

I shake my head. "This is not love. Not when it comes with conditions."

"Conditions?" He frowns.

A burst of annoyance thrums through my body, and I get the feeling back in my legs. I rise on my feet as high as I can to look him in the eyes. "My parents only show me love when I'm dancing in things they approve of. You only show me love if you think I'm not pregnant. Their love for me should be unconditional. *Your* love should be unconditional. Is it?"

"Of course it is."

"Why do I feel like it comes with a bunch of strings tied up into a messy knot?"

"My life is complicated."

I cross my arms around my waist. "*You* have made your life complicated. It doesn't have to be."

Hayden lifts his palms into the air. "What do you want from me?"

"You shouldn't have to ask." A tear I've been struggling to hold back slips down my cheek.

"Alyssa..." He reaches for me.

I step back. If he touches me, I'm not sure if I can stay strong and not fall into his arms, taking whatever he can give me. I steel my spine. I'm tired of trying to prove I can be loved for just me. To my parents and now with Hayden.

"You should go," I tell him. "I'll let you know in two weeks if anything changes."

Looking like he wants to say something, he hesitates for a beat. Whatever it was, he's keeping it to himself. He turns, opens the door, and walks away.

And out of my life forever.

Chapter Twenty-Eight

HAYDEN

Three days later, I'm sitting in my kitchen, staring sightlessly into my coffee cup. I've looked at it for so long when I take a sip it's stone cold. Pouring it down the sink, I place my hands on the counter and drop my head.

I can't remember the last time I felt so miserable. I can't eat or sleep. I'm fucking things up at work, and I've snapped at Lily for no reason, which, of course, makes me feel even worse. Without Alyssa in my life, I'm an unhappy bastard.

I have to remind myself that with time things will get better. This is best for both of us. I only wish I hadn't hurt Alyssa. She can live out her dream career in London with no ties keeping her here, and I can continue on with my life. Soon I'll be a distant memory to her. But my future looks bleak without her in it.

At the sound of someone knocking at the front door, I glance at the clock on the microwave. This is the time Lily usually has her private lesson. Since I canceled them all—in a text; I'm such a coward—I'm not expecting anyone. When I told Lily there will be no more private lessons with Alyssa, she'd cried, stormed into her room, and slammed the door. She hasn't talked to me in two days. I hate I had to do that to her. Hopefully, I can find another teacher she'll love just as much.

As I leave the kitchen, Lily comes bounding down the stairs, dressed in her ballet costume.

"I'll get it!" she sings.

"What are you doing dressed like that?" I ask. She doesn't answer and opens the door.

My heart skyrockets to my throat. Alyssa is standing in the doorway, dressed all in black. Instead of looking depressing in the color, she's like a ray of sunshine brightening up the room. God, she's beautiful. I've missed her so much.

"What are you doing here?" The words come out harsher than I meant them to.

Her eyes widen at my tone. "You texted me asking for a lesson. If it's not a good time, I can leave." She turns away.

"No, wait! I'm surprised, that's all. I never sent you a text."

Turning back, she frowns. "You didn't?" She pulls a phone from her pocket and looks at the screen. "It came through an hour ago."

Next to me, Lily shuffles her feet. "I sent it."

"That explains the smiling emoji." Alyssa grins.

That smile is enough to make me want to drop to my knees. Pulling my attention away from her mouth, I focus on Lily. "Why did you do that? I told you we needed to cancel them." I avoid looking at Alyssa because I'm such an asshole.

Lily tilts her chin. "I wanted my lesson."

"You can't take my phone and do whatever you want without asking me. I said no more private lessons."

"You never said why," she complains.

I can't tell her the real reason, so I improvise. "Because you don't need them anymore. You've caught up with the rest of the class." I glance at Alyssa for confirmation, hoping it's the truth. I hate canceling something Lily loves, but Alyssa being in my house every week when I can't have her will kill me.

Alyssa nods her head. "You have improved so much, Lily. You should be proud of yourself."

"I really can't have any more private lessons?" Lily stares up at me with those wide, deep brown eyes that tug at my heart.

"Since Miss Alyssa is here, and if she doesn't mind, you can have one more."

A small smile lifts Alyssa's lips. "I don't mind."

Is she missing me like I'm missing her? Is she as miserable as I am? Our eyes lock. It's there—the longing, and the hurt I've caused. Damn it, why couldn't things be different?

"I'll let you two get to your lesson. I'll be in the living room if you need me."

⚬

While Lily and Alyssa are upstairs, I pace the room, then I make my way upstairs only to stop halfway and come back down—twice. I brew coffee, only to leave it to cool on the coffee table, and pick up a book to read. The book could have been upside down and in German, and I wouldn't have noticed; I don't read a single word.

When the music stops, I toss the book aside and pick up the remote control and turn the TV on and pretend to watch whatever program is showing. Soft footsteps come down the stairs, and a moment later Alyssa and Lily enter the living room.

"We're finished," Alyssa says.

I flick my gaze to her then stare back at the TV. If I look at her longer, I might beg her not to leave. What good would that do? I can't give her what she needs.

"Thanks for giving Lily the lesson."

"No problem. I'll see myself out."

Shit. Whenever I push her away, I turn into the biggest asshole. "I'll walk you to the door."

She waves her hand to stop me. "That's okay. I wouldn't want to interrupt you watching the mating habits of lions."

My head swivels toward the TV. On the screen are two lions getting it on. I dive for the remote and turn the TV off. There are only so many questions I can take from Lily. I'm not ready to explain about reproduction.

A ghost of a smile plays on Alyssa's lips.

"Miss Alyssa, can you come to my open classroom at school on Thursday?" Lily asks, snapping my attention away from Alyssa's mouth.

"Lily, that's for parents," I remind her.

"Daphne's nanny is coming. Why can't Miss Alyssa?"

Good argument. One I have to put a stop to. "Because Daphne's nanny takes care of her like a parent." Fuck...what a lame excuse.

"But I made a diorama of my ballet studio. We had to make one of something that makes us happy. Dancing makes me happy. I put Miss Alyssa in it too. I want her to see it." She looks at Alyssa with pleading eyes. "Can you please come?"

Alyssa looks over Lily's head at me. I can see the indecision on her face. She doesn't want to let Lily down yet is unsure what to say.

Just because I'm finding it hard to be around Alyssa doesn't mean I should take the joy away from Lily. She obviously loves Alyssa. She's become an important person in her life. Why else would Lily include

Alyssa in a school project? If I'm worried Lily's getting attached, well, I think it's already happened. If I can keep their relationship in the dance studio, there shouldn't be a problem. I'll let Lily have this one more thing, then it's dancing only.

"It starts at ten AM. If you have time, we would love for you to join us."

Alyssa's eyes widen like she wasn't expecting the invitation from me. "I'd love to see your classroom, especially your work," she says to Lily.

"Yes!" Lily beams with excitement.

"Would you like me to pick you up?" I ask.

"That's okay. I'll find my own way."

"I'll message you the school's address and Lily's classroom."

She nods. "Well, I'll see you Thursday, Lily."

"Bye," Lily says and runs from the room and up the stairs.

I follow Alyssa to the front door. "Thanks for doing this for Lily. You've made her happy."

"It's my pleasure. She's a great kid." She hesitates for a moment then says, "I'll see you at the school."

I open the door. "See you then." God, we're standing at the doorway talking to each other like strangers.

She walks out of the house. For a moment, I watch her as she makes her way up the driveway. As I stare at her retreating back, I wonder if letting her go is the biggest mistake of my life.

Chapter Twenty-Nine

ALYSSA

Walking into Lily's school, I'm surprised I'm here. What was I thinking? I'm supposed to be breaking away from Hayden, not getting involved in his daughter's schoolwork. All it took for me to agree was her pleading, puppy dog eyes that pulled at my heartstrings and the way Hayden said 'we would love for you to join us' in his oh-so-sexy voice. Even though he said *we* and not *I*, it still tipped me over the edge. I couldn't refuse.

Splaying my hand over my stomach, I take a deep breath. All morning I've been a jittery mess; not knowing what to expect is making me nauseous. Following the signs to Lily's classroom, I find it at the top of a set of stairs. Kids and parents are gathered in front of the room. Standing taller than any other parent is Hayden. My stomach flips at the sight of him. Will that ever go away? I doubt it.

Like he feels my presence, his head turns toward me. Our eyes lock, and a smile tugs at his lips. The man is beautiful. Everything inside me is drawing me toward him. Instead, I stand still on the spot, wishing that his love for me was unconditional.

When Lily sees me, she comes running over. "You came!"

"I said I would."

"Dad told me you might be busy."

My head snaps up to look at Hayden. He dips his head with a sheepish expression. This is a strange situation to be in, so I don't blame him for thinking I might cancel. "I'm excited to see your diorama."

Hayden's gaze travels the length of my body. Not in a I-want-to-strip-your-clothes-off kind of way, but one of surprise. "What are you wearing?"

Self-consciously, I glance down at my clothes. "Is this not okay?"

I had to make a mad dash to Harper's house to borrow a dress and shoes. All my clothes are black and look like they belong in a biker club. I couldn't show up at Lily's classroom looking like I've stepped off a Harley. The soft pink fabric of the flowy dress keeps getting stuck between my legs when I walk, and the sandals—which are a size too big—keep slipping around on my feet. How people wear stuff like this is a joke.

"You look great. It's just...different. I'm not used to seeing you wearing color." He gives me an appraising gaze.

"Can we go inside now?" Lily grabs onto my hand and tugs at my arm.

"Let's see your amazing schoolwork, Lily Pily," Hayden says. He holds his arm out and gestures for Lily to lead the way.

In the room, I'm met with an explosion of color. Painted pictures are hanging from string strung across the room. Art is pinned to the walls. Desks scattered with colored paper, pencils, and crayons are lined neatly in the middle of the room. Written on the whiteboard is

Welcome to our class. The room is so fun and inviting. All the kids are buzzing to show their loved ones their work.

With Lily's hand still clasped in mine, she pulls me to the side of the room where the dioramas are displayed. I can feel Hayden following close behind. So close I know if I take one step back, we'd touch.

"Here it is!" Lily points excitedly at her work.

I lean over to take a closer look. Hayden does the same. Now his chest is pressed against my back as he glances at the diorama over my shoulder. I freeze. Too scared to move in case he pulls away. God, I miss his touch, the scent of his citrusy cologne, and the heat of his body. For a beat, I close my eyes and take a deep breath.

"Do you like it?" Lily asks.

I stand and Hayden moves away.

"This is you." She points at a small figurine dressed in a black leotard and tights standing in front of mirrors made from aluminum foil. She's added ballet bars, arched cellophane windows, lots of figurines for students, and a stereo system made with tiny boxes.

"This looks exactly like the dance studio. Great job, Lily."

A bright, proud smile lights up her face.

Hayden puts a hand on Lily's shoulder. "Is that you?" He touches a figurine dressed in pink standing next to my figurine.

She nods shyly. "This is the day I helped Miss Alyssa teach a class."

The afternoon Rachel showed up at the studio and Hayden asked me to watch Lily while he dealt with her. The day that pulled Hayden permanently away from me. Hayden gazes at me like he knows what I'm thinking. Sadness and regret cross his features.

To stop myself from thinking about it, I say, "You did such a great job helping me."

She smiles with pride.

For the next half hour, Lily guides me and Hayden around the room, showing us paintings, artwork, and schoolbooks. As we're admiring her work her teacher strolls over to us.

With a warm smile, she says, "Hello, Mr. Alessi. I'm glad you could make our open day."

"I wouldn't miss it." Hayden smiles back. When the teacher turns her attention to me, he introduces us. "Mrs. Fredrick, this is Alyssa Martinez."

"It's lovely to meet you, Alyssa. Lily has told us so much about you. She's excited for the wedding and can't wait for you to officially be her mother."

The blood drains from my body. What the hell?

Hayden steps closer to the teacher and lowers his voice, I assume so no one close by can hear. "Mrs. Fredrick, I don't know what you're talking about. There is no wedding. Alyssa is Lily's ballet teacher. Nothing more."

When I think my heart can't break any more, Hayden says something to prove me wrong and the pain lances through me all over again. After all we've been through, I'm only her ballet teacher. *Nothing more.*

She raises her hand and fiddles with the pearls around her neck. "Oh...I'm sorry. She mentioned a wedding."

Lily stares up at us with tears shining in her eyes. Her face flushed red.

"Lily, why would you make up a story like that?" Hayden asks.

Dropping her head, she shuffles her feet and shrugs.

"We are going to talk about this when we get home." To the teacher, he says, "I'm sorry, Mrs. Fredrick, she doesn't normally make up stories."

Mrs. Fredrick gives Hayden a sympathetic smile. "Don't be too hard on her. It's difficult for little girls to grow up without their mothers. She obviously loves Ms. Martinez and can see her fill that role."

The thought of filling the role of Lily's mother gives me more joy than receiving my Broadway news. As far as I'm concerned, no role is more important than the one of a mother. I would happily accept and love her as my own.

But Hayden doesn't want me. It's time to move on. It's a good thing I've decided to move to London. Hopefully distance and being busy with the show will make me forget about what I've lost in New York City and eventually heal my heart. At the moment, with my heart so torn apart, I can't imagine it ever sealing back together.

Tears sting my eyes, and I blink rapidly to hold them back. I can't stay a moment longer or I'll crumble into a teary heap. Squatting down to look Lily in the eye, I cup her face in my hands and kiss her cheek. Her mouth is turned down, her lip quivering. *I know how you feel, sweetheart. I'm not getting what I want either.*

"Thank you for inviting me to your class. I've had a wonderful time, and your schoolwork is beautiful." I pull her into a hug, and her little arms wrap around my neck. I swallow hard. This little girl will always have a special place in my heart. This is my goodbye. I probably won't see her again.

The tears I'm trying to hold back spill down my cheeks. Oh God! I swipe them away, but they keep falling. Getting to my feet, I dash from the room.

"Alyssa!" Hayden calls after me.

I don't stop. This is all too much. I should never have come. Being here has only solidified how much I want Hayden and Lily in my life and how I'll never have it.

"Wait up!" he calls, but I keep running.

When I get to the stairs, I take them two at a time. The too-big shoes slip around my feet, causing me to wobble and stumble. Reaching for the support of the railing, my hands flay about, and I don't get a grip. I grasp onto nothing but air. My legs lift from under me, and I roll down the stairs. When I hit the ground, the breath is knocked out of me. My chest is crushing the air from my lungs. The pounding in my head is causing black dots to swirl in front of my eyes.

The last thing I see before darkness takes over is Hayden's face white with fear. Then the lights go out.

Chapter Thirty

HAYDEN

At the hospital, I stare anxiously at the privacy curtain around Alyssa's bed. Because I'm not family, the doctor asked me to step outside. I haven't left her side since the ambulance admitted her. It's killing me that I can't be with her now.

The fall was the scariest thing I have ever witnessed in my life. When she fumbled for the railing, it was like the world had gone into slow motion and my feet were sinking in quicksand. I couldn't get to her fast enough. When she went tumbling down the stairs, my heart froze in my chest, shattering when I heard the sickening thud on the concrete below.

The seconds it took to reach her were the longest moments of my life. With her sprawled on the ground, her eyes fluttering closed, I thought I'd lost her. It's a scene I will never get out of my head.

It's all my fault. If I hadn't chased her from the classroom, she wouldn't be lying injured in a hospital bed.

Not able to sit any longer, I pace the corridor in front of her room, waiting for the doctor to finish examining her. He's taking too long. There must be something wrong. I don't care if I'm not family, I need to be with Alyssa and make sure she is okay. Dashing into the room,

I whip open the curtain. The doctor and Alyssa's heads turn toward me with surprised expressions on their faces.

"I'm sorry, sir, I'm not done examining Ms. Martinez. Please wait outside," Dr. Hofstein says with a disgruntled tone.

Ignoring him, I make my way to Alyssa's side and hold on to her hand. "I'm not going anywhere."

The doctor looks to Alyssa for consent.

"It's okay. He can stay." She gives the doctor a weak smile.

I breathe a sigh of relief. After everything I've put her through, I wouldn't be shocked if she tosses me out of the room. "How is she?" I ask.

Not for the first time, my gaze scans over her, looking for visible signs of injury. My stomach rolls seeing a bruise and graze on the side of her face. I shudder to think if there is any internal damage.

"She has a concussion and will need plenty of rest. That means no physical activities for at least ten to twelve days. If you need anything for the headache, take ibuprofen, but don't hesitate to come back to the ER if things aren't improving. Other than a swollen ankle and a few scrapes and bruises, you are one lucky lady. The fall could have been much worse."

"Thank you, doctor. When can I leave?" Her voice is weak.

"As soon as the paperwork is done, someone will discharge you." He nods and starts to leave.

"Shouldn't she stay overnight for observation? What if you're missing something?" I want her to have the best care and make sure they are one-hundred percent positive she is fit to leave.

"Her scans are clear. There's nothing to be worried about. Like I said, if things don't improve or get worse, come straight back."

He turns to leave again. Once more, I stop him. "Doctor, before you go, I'm concerned about something."

A white, bushy eyebrow raises above his left eye. "What might that be?"

"There's a chance Alyssa might be pregnant. Could the fall have caused harm to the baby?"

The doctor whips his gaze toward Alyssa. "You never mentioned a possible pregnancy. How far along might you be?"

Alyssa rolls her eyes at me. "If I am, it's early. But I'm not." She places a hand on her belly. Is she subconsciously sensing something? I wait for the fear to grip me. When it doesn't, I'm left wondering why it doesn't scare the crap out of me like it normally does.

"Just to be sure, I'll send a nurse in to take your blood." He goes on to ask her questions about her last period, the date of conception, and any symptoms she might be having. I'm shocked to hear her say that the past two days she has had tender boobs and nausea—which she assumed was due to nerves.

"Could the fall have harmed the baby?" I ask again. It's bad enough that Alyssa is hurt, I'll never forgive myself if I caused her to lose the baby.

"If Ms. Martinez is pregnant, it's very early. At the moment, there is only a tiny ball made up of cells. Chances of any harm from the fall is low to none." To Alyssa, he says, "If you feel any cramping or have blood loss, again, come straight back to the ER."

"How long does it take to get the results?" I ask.

"You'll get news in a day or two," he informs me. "In the meantime, Ms. Martinez, you need to rest."

"Thank you, Dr. Hofstein," she says.

When the doctor leaves the room, I turn to her. "Your boobs are tender, and you feel sick? Why didn't you mention this to me?"

She crosses her arms over her chest. "There's nothing to tell. Tender boobs can be because I'm almost due for my period. Meeting you and

Lily at her school made me nervous enough I felt queasy. That's all it is. You don't have to look so scared. I'm not pregnant. In two days' time you'll have proof. Then you can go on with your life like nothing has happened."

Go on with my life like nothing has happened? How the fuck do I do that? When she consumes my every thought. My body craves to be near her. My heart beats only for her.

Before I can say anything, a nurse bustles in with a silver cart and equipment to take blood. After she collects the sample, she pushes the cart out of the room. As soon as the nurse leaves, Harper races into the room.

"I came as soon as I could." She props herself on the edge of the bed. "Are you okay?"

"I'm fine."

"Did Lily get home from school okay?" I ask. I hate that I had to rush away from her. Her white face seeing Alyssa on the ground tore through at my heart. I had to reassure Lily that Alyssa was okay even though I didn't know if it was true.

"Yes, Finn picked her up, and she's at our house helping him with Avery." Looking at Alyssa, she asks, "What did the doctor say?"

"I have a concussion."

"Oh no! That's terrible."

Alyssa shrugs. "It's no big deal."

I scoff. "A concussion *is* a big deal."

"You poor thing. Are they keeping you overnight?" Harper asks.

"No, they're getting ready to discharge me."

"Then you're coming home with me so I can keep an eye on you," Harper says. "You can stay in our guest bedroom."

"That's unnecessary. You have Avery to care for. You don't need me to burden you."

Harper taps Alyssa on the hand. "You are not a burden. We'd love for you to stay. We can pretend it's the old days when we shared an apartment."

"I hope you have thicker walls. Man, I remember some nights when Finn stayed over. You really gave the headboard a workout." She giggles then screws her face up and places her hands on the side of her head.

I move to the other side of the bed. "Are you in pain? Should I call the doctor?" I take a step toward the door to find someone. She claps onto my hand, stopping me.

"I'm fine. I have a headache, and laughing feels like my brain is bouncing around in my skull."

"You're coming home with me," I say.

Alyssa pulls a who-are-you-to-demand-where-I-stay look, but I don't give a fuck.

"I promise I won't make her laugh," Harper says.

"That won't be a problem, because she's coming home with me."

Alyssa gives me a hard stare. "I know for sure you'll give me nothing to laugh about. But if I need a babysitter, I'd rather go with Harper."

I cross my arms over my chest. "It's not up for discussion. Harper has enough on her plate with a baby and my needy brother. You're coming with me."

"If I'm too much trouble for Harper, I'll go home."

"You are not going home," I say through gritted teeth. Boy, she can be stubborn.

She blows out a breath. "You can't tell me what to do."

Harper slides off the bed. "Ummm, let me interrupt before this disagreement turns into a war. Alyssa, you can't stay home alone. Something might happen." Alyssa opens her mouth to speak, but Harper raises her hand like a stop sign. Wow, she's only been a mom a couple of months, yet she's already got the hand gestures down pat. "Avery wakes up crying two times a night to be nursed. I'd hate for her to disturb you. You need rest. I think the best place is with Hayden."

I puff out my chest like I've won a prize. Alyssa narrows her eyes at me like a sore loser, but she doesn't argue.

She tilts her head back on the pillow and sighs. "Fine. I'll go to Hayden's house. Does that make everyone happy?"

"Yes," Harper says at the same time I say, "Absolutely."

"There better be a guest room for me to sleep in, because there's no way I'm sharing a bed with you."

"We'll work out the sleeping arrangements when we get home."

This is not the time to remind her that the guest bedroom is now Lily's dance studio.

⚬

"Absolutely not." Standing in my bedroom with her hands on her hips, Alyssa stares at the king-sized bed in the middle of the space. "I am not sleeping in your room. With *you*."

I drop her luggage bag by the door. After she was released from the hospital, we made a quick stop at her apartment to collect her clothes and other items she'll need for her stay. On our way home, we stopped to pick Lily up from Finn's house. I can tell the time out of bed has exhausted Alyssa; she is in no condition to stand around and complain.

During the car ride, I could have told her multiple times about the sleeping arrangements. I kept them to myself because I'm sure, had she known, out of stubbornness, she'd refuse to stay at my house. I'm to blame for the fall. Taking care of her is my responsibility. And deep down, I'm holding onto her for every second I have left before she leaves the country.

Lily jumps onto the bed and bounces on the mattress. "Miss Alyssa can sleep in my bed with me."

"She is not sleeping in your room. You kick about in your sleep. She already has a concussion, I don't need you breaking any of her bones."

Lily giggles, dangling her legs over the edge of the bed. "If Miss Alyssa is sleeping in your bed, where will you sleep, Dad?"

"I'll make a bed on the floor. That way if Miss Alyssa needs something, I'm not far away." I still need to talk to Lily about the story she told her teacher about Alyssa and I getting married. But after the fall and trip to the hospital, there hasn't been time. I'll have a chat with Lily when things settle down.

"Can I sleep on the floor too? We can have a slumber party."

I shake my head. "Miss Alyssa needs rest. Go wash up for dinner. I've ordered pizza."

"Yummmy!" she cheers and races from the room.

Alyssa looks worn-out on her feet, so I guide her to the bed and nudge her shoulders to sit down.

She makes an impatient sound. "I'm not an invalid, you know."

"Do you want to keep standing until you fall? Make yourself comfortable and relax."

She pulls a face like she doesn't like being told what to do but sits on the bed. She shuffles up along the mattress and leans against the headboard. "Are you really going to sleep on the floor?"

"No."

"You're not sleeping with me."

"I'm staying close in case you need me."

She slides down onto her back, propping her head on the pillows. "I don't need you." Why does it feel like she's not talking about this moment but in her life?

"I won't try anything if that's what you're worried about. What kind of sick person would that make me?"

She closes her eyes. "You might."

"Are you saying I'd take advantage of you with a concussion?" I shake my head. "I'm not an animal. Unless it's *you* who can't control *yourself*?"

She cracks open one eyelid. "Puh-lease. You're safe." Her eye closes again.

"Okaay," I say like I don't believe her.

"It's true."

"I think I'll put pillows between us just in case."

She huffs and opens her eyes. "Not necessary."

"Your hands wander in your sleep." I grin.

She rolls her eyes before closing them again. "Whatever. Now let me sleep."

I sit on the edge of the bed. "I'll wake you in a few hours to check on you."

With a soft, sleepy voice, she says, "Wake me when the pizza arrives." I guess the concussion hasn't affected her appetite even after she vomited three times at the hospital. "I hope you ordered...pepperoni," her voice trails away.

Pulling a blanket from the end of the bed, I drape it over her. Alyssa's head tilts to the side with her lips slightly parted. Soft breathing indicates that she's fallen asleep. Her hair has fallen across her face, and I brush it back, my fingers touching her soft cheek.

Turning her head, she nestles her face into my palm. "Don't leave me," she mumbles.

Her words shoot into my chest and explode with a burst of regret. *Don't leave her?* She's the one leaving me! But what reason have I given her to stay? Over and over again, I've pushed her away. What was she supposed to do?

Like she said, love shouldn't have conditions. I've given her a condition so fucking unreasonable all because my head's a wreck. I've let a woman who means nothing to me destroy any trust I have in someone so wonderful. Letting her ruin a life I could build with someone I love.

Just watching Alyssa following Lily around the classroom, genuinely interested in her artwork and schoolwork, is proof she's nothing like Rachel. She didn't have to come to the classroom's open day. There were a million excuses she could have used to stay away. Yet she didn't want to let Lily down no matter how tense things were between us.

Alyssa has showed Lily so much love and affection that's gone beyond a teacher and student relationship, and she's not even Lily's mother. What would she be like with her own children? Fucking amazing. Lily could see it. She even made up a story that we were getting married, and Alyssa was going to be her new mother. I had blinders on.

This is a woman who would never abandon her child, no matter where she is or what she's doing.

I'm the man who has royally fucked things up.

Chapter Thirty-One

ALYSSA

Two days later, propped up with pillows in Hayden's bed, I aimlessly flick through the channels of the TV hung on the wall. I'm so bored with inactivity I want to scream with frustration. Every time I suggest getting out of bed, Hayden reminds me I need to rest and heal.

The headaches have subsided, although the fall caused my body to ache like I've been hit by a truck. Whenever Hayden leaves the bedroom, I pace around the small room, trying to stretch the kinks away. I can't stay on my feet too long because my ankle has flared-up again. Will my freaking ankle ever get back to normal? This is not what I need when I'm about to leave for London to start rehearsals. I decided to take the role, but I haven't told my agent about my injuries yet. He might have a heart attack.

I can't say it's been all bad in Hayden's bed. Two days waking up in his arms has given me a moment to dream of what our life could be like if he wasn't so scared to let go of past hurts. That is until his eyes flutter open and the realization of how we are sleeping hits him and he pulls away. I know I said he was the one who can't keep his hands to himself, but in the middle of the night, it was me who snuggled closer. It's where I want to be.

Swinging my legs off the bed, I get ready for my daily stroll around the room. Before I get onto my feet, my stomach churns. For a second, I think I need to run to the bathroom and throw up. I take deep breaths through my nose until the nausea subsides. This is probably the aftereffects of the concussion. There's a prickle of a thought in the back of my mind and I quickly shut it down. I'm not pregnant. I can't be.

On my feet, the room spins, and I hold my head in my hands until it stops. Once the world has righted itself, I head toward the door. I need to see more than these four walls I'm stuck in. Before I can get far, Hayden strolls in with a tray of food in his hands.

"Why are you out of bed?" He frowns.

"I'm bored. There's nothing to watch on TV, and I need fresh air," I complain.

"Open a window," he suggests.

I sigh. "It's not the same."

He places the tray on the edge of the bed. "You look pale. I don't think moving around is a good idea. The doctor said—"

"Yeah, yeah. He said I need to rest. I've rested so much I'm getting bedsores."

He chuckles, and the sound is oh-so-freaking-sexy. "It's only been two days. You are not getting bedsores."

"How do you know? You haven't seen my ass."

When his gaze dips down to zero in on my bottom half, I regret the words. Because the way he's looking at me now isn't to determine the color and health of my skin. More like determining how he can peel my clothes off to give me a full-body examination. One of the good kinds. As much as I'd like for him to do just that, there's something in the air making my stomach roll.

"What's that smell?" I screw my nose up.

Hayden sniffs. "Your lunch?"

I turn to look at the tray of food on the bed. Sitting on a plate is a steak surrounded by vegetables. At the sight of the lump of meat, my stomach pitches and I cover my mouth. Darting as fast as I can on an injured ankle and aching body to the adjoining bathroom, I make it in time to throw up this morning's breakfast.

While emptying my stomach in the toilet bowl, I hear Hayden run the faucet. A few seconds later, something cold is pressed against my neck and his hand is rubbing soothing circles on my back.

When my body expels as much as it can, I flush the toilet, sit back on my feet, and rub my mouth with toilet paper. "I wish you didn't see that." As I get to my feet, Hayden holds me by the elbow to help me.

"Are you okay?"

I nod my head, turn on the faucet, fill my mouth with water, swish it around, and spit it into the sink. I brush my teeth, avoiding any eye contact with Hayden. I know he's worried about me. He'll probably send me back to bed, call the doctor, and demand I don't leave the room for the next two months. I dab my mouth with a hand towel, put it back on the vanity counter, and walk into the bedroom. Hayden is close behind.

When I see the food still sitting on the bed, I pause. "Can you take that away please?"

Hayden rushes to the bed, removes the tray, and disappears from the room. A few seconds later, he's back with eyes filled with worry. "Alyssa, I think I should take you back to the hospital."

"I'm fine. Throwing up is normal after a concussion," I say to appease him. I won't tell him it was the smell of lunch that triggered it. If he suspected nothing else, I'm not filling his head with other ideas. Sitting on the bed, I rest against the headboard.

"What if something is wrong? What if—" He stops midsentence. Color drains from his face. "What if you're pregnant?" The words are strained, like he's having difficulty saying them. It didn't take him long to come to a different conclusion.

What will he do if I tell him I now believe it's a possibility? With the fear straining his features, I suspect he wouldn't take the news well. I don't want to scare him even more until I know for sure. "I'm not pregnant."

A flash of relief crosses his face. Disappointment at his reaction slices through my heart. Why am I disappointed? I've always known he doesn't want a baby.

"Has the doctor called with the blood test results?" he asks.

"No, not yet."

"Should you call the hospital and rush them along?"

God, can he cripple my heart more? An unplanned pregnancy is too much for him. What about me? I've just landed my dream job. If I'm pregnant, this can ruin everything I've worked my ass off to get. But am I sitting here looking like I'm about to go on the scariest roller coaster in the world? No. Because having a baby with the man I love feels natural and right.

"I'm not calling the hospital. They said it can take a couple of days. If I hear nothing by tomorrow, then I'll check. Okay?"

"Alyssa, I didn't mean to sound—"

My phone rings.

"Is that the hospital?" he asks, not hiding the hope in his voice.

I reach over, pluck the phone from the nightstand, and glance at the screen. "It's Harper."

His shoulders deflate. Does he want to know the results that badly? By the frustration on his face, I'd say yes, he does.

"Hey, Harper. What's up?"

"Are you up for visitors?" she asks.

God yes. Someone besides Hayden's dreary face would be lovely. "Only if you bring Avery with you," I joke.

"Will you ever want to spend time with only me ever again?" she asks with a faux annoyed tone.

"Nope. Avery is the light of my life now."

"Our friendship was nice while it lasted. I'll see you soon."

Hanging up, I toss the phone on the bed. "Harper is on her way."

I shuffle off the bed and rise to my feet. I brush past Hayden to go to the bathroom—I don't need to go, I just need to get away from him for a moment. Placing a hand on my shoulder, he stops me. "Alyssa, we need to talk."

I step away and his hand drops. What more can he say? I know how he feels. This time when I walk away, he doesn't stop me.

In the bathroom, I close the door and lock it behind me. Leaning my head back, tears trickle down my cheeks. A few weeks ago, I knew exactly what I wanted for my life. It took one fall on a stormy night to change everything, making me question if I'm on the right path. One that includes raising a baby. If I take this new direction, will I be travelling on this path alone?

"I didn't think Hayden was going to let you leave the house," Harper says.

I roll my eyes. "He's watching over me like a mother elephant. If I move, he thinks I'm going to break."

"That's sweet. He's making sure you're resting." Harper adjusts the muslin wrap covering the baby stroller from the afternoon sun as we wander around the park. My ankle is protesting slightly, but I'm not giving up this time away from the house for anything.

"I'm so sick of that bedroom. Sick of sleeping. Sick of feeling like an invalid." Spotting a park bench, I walk to it and sit down. My ankle isn't as strong as I'd hoped. "I'm staying here and never going back," I say like an insolent child.

"If you're not home in an hour, he's going to send a search-and-rescue team out to find you and drag you back."

I shrug. "He can try." I'll kick and scream before I let that happen.

"What's going on with the two of you? I know you said things weren't working out, but when I see you both together, it feels like your relationship is something that doesn't want to end. Can you work things out?"

I can't believe I haven't filled Harper in on everything. I've been so caught up in my misery I kept to myself. "He told me he loved me."

Her eyes widen. "Why do you look sad about it? Isn't that a good thing?"

I pick some chipping paint off the bench. "He took it back."

Harper's eyebrows disappear into her hairline. "He took it back? What do you mean?"

I rub my palms along my thighs. "He didn't actually say the words. Something happened and he retreated into a hole and hasn't come back out."

Harper taps her fingers on her forehead. "Wait...wait...You need to explain this."

I tell her about the most exciting night of my life. The night the man I love told me he loved me too. It was magical. I could see my life with him. It was perfect. Until it wasn't.

"The walls around him had fallen. Then we have unprotected sex and they snapped back up higher than they were before. I told you about Rachel's visit to the studio, and things got worse. I can't see the man I love anymore."

"Oh, Alyssa." Harper rubs her hand on the back of my shoulders. "He's in shock. That's all. After what he's been through, it was a reflex reaction. He'll come around, and I know he'll feel like crap for treating you this way."

I shake my head. "No. It's over. He's only concerned about the blood test results."

"Is there any chance you might be pregnant?" Harper asks as she gently rocks the stroller when Avery makes little squawking noises.

Deep down I know the answer. It's like a little current of electricity is buzzing through me, igniting everything it touches. I don't want to say it out loud, because I don't know how I'm going to deal with it if it's true.

My phone rings, stopping me from answering. It's probably Hayden wondering how much longer I'm going to be. Pulling the phone from my pocket, I glance at the screen. It's not a number I recognize. Could this be the hospital?

"Hello," I answer on a shaky breath.

"This is Dr. Hofstein. Am I speaking with Ms. Martinez?"

My hand trembles like the phone weighs a ton. Oh God. This is it. This call will determine my life. "Yes, speaking."

"How are you feeling?"

"Good, thank you."

"Any headaches or nausea?"

"Getting better every day." Except for the trip to the toilet bowl this morning.

"And you're resting?"

"Yes." *Please get to the point of the call already!*

"That's good to hear. Now, I have your blood test results, and they have come back positive. Congratulations, you're pregnant," he announces, confirming my suspicions. "You should make an appointment with an OB/GYN to discuss prenatal care."

The doctor keeps speaking, but all I can hear is a buzzing sound in my ears. I'm pregnant! *Oh God! Oh God! Oh God!* Even though I suspected it, having it confirmed has turned my world spinning.

When he asks if I have any questions, I snap back to attention. I tell him I don't and say goodbye. Ending the call, I drop the phone onto my lap and stare sightlessly at the ground. *What am I going to do?*

"Was that the hospital?" Harper asks with concern.

I nod. My head is heavy, feeling like it might roll off my shoulders.

"Is everything okay? Oh my God! Are you pregnant?"

I turn to look at her. Tears well in my eyes. I nod again. It's like I've lost the ability to speak.

"Oh, Alyssa. I'm not sure what to say. This should be wonderful news. But judging by the shell-shocked expression on your face, I'm not sure if you think so."

I swallow past the lump in my throat. "I'm not sure it is either."

Harper puts an arm over my shoulder, pulling me in for a side hug. "What are you going to do?"

"Sit here forever." The sun is shining. It's a beautiful day. The shade of the nearby tree is keeping me cool. This is a nice spot to live.

"Then after that, what will you do?"

"Did you miss the part where I said forever? I'm not moving!"

"I'm sure it will be comfortable living, giving birth, and raising a baby on a park bench."

"It will be character building." I know I'm talking shit. I can't think about the reality of my life just yet.

"Seriously, what are you going to do? When will you tell Hayden?"

I sigh heavily, lean forward, rest my elbows on my knees, and drop my chin on my hands. "I don't know. If I tell him about the pregnancy, how will he will react? He doesn't want this. Hearing him say it to my face will destroy me."

"Maybe he'll react better than you think."

I scrub my hands over my face. "He knows I'm going to London. He'll only think I'm leaving him with a baby."

"Not if you reassure him that won't happen."

I toss up my hands. "I shouldn't have to reassure him. If he knew anything about me, really *loved* me, he'd know that."

Harper pulls a sympathetic face. "Talk to him."

"I need time to think things over."

"That's understandable. We can sit here until you're ready to go back," she suggests.

I pull my shoulders back. "I'm not going to Hayden's house."

"What do you mean? Hayden will have a heart attack if I don't return you. Actually, I'm surprised he hasn't called already to check on you."

My phone rings in my lap. Hayden's name flashes on the screen. "Speak of the devil." It's like we've conjured him up. I can't speak to him now. Not when the world is pressing on my shoulders. I hit the decline button.

"Why did you hang up on him?" Harper asks.

"I don't want to talk to him."

Harper taps my thigh. "Go home. Tell him. Together you can work this out."

My phone rings again. I again decline the call.

"If you don't answer, you'll make him worry."

I shrug. "He'll get over it."

A moment later, Harper's phone chimes with a call. I don't need to guess who it is.

"Don't answer," I tell her.

Harper bites her bottom lip with indecision. "He'll worry."

"I don't care."

She ignores my plea and answers the call. "Hey, Hayden. What's up?" she says overly bright.

"Where the hell is Alyssa? Why isn't she answering my calls?" I can hear his voice raging through the speaker.

Harper's gaze flicks to me. "We're sitting at the park. Her phone must be on silent," she lies. I give her a thumbs-up signal for her quick thinking. She rolls her eyes and shakes her head, not looking impressed at being stuck between Hayden and me.

"Put her on the phone," he demands.

I wave my arms in a big cross and mouth the word *no*.

"Umm...she...she's taken Avery to the swings." Harper slaps her head.

My shoulders sag and I drop my head. Avery is too small for swings.

"Avery can't hold her head up, how is she on a swing?" He's onto us.

Harper widens her eyes like she's trying to think of what to say. "It's some new baby capsule thingy... Anyway, I'll have her call you when she gets back."

"She shouldn't be on her leg for too long," he says.

"Don't worry, she's not far. We'll see you soon. Bye." She hangs up before Hayden can say anything else.

I blow out a relieved breath.

Harper narrows her eyes. "I lied for you."

Giving her a ghost of a smile, I nudge her shoulder. "Thank you. I owe you one."

"Yes, you do," she says with mock sternness to her voice. "You can babysit Avery so Finn and I can have a date night."

"No problem. I'm going to need all the practice I can get."

Harper's expression turns serious. "Does this mean you're going through with it?"

I scrub my hands over my face. "There's no other option for me."

"What about London?"

I toss my hands in the air and wail, "I don't know! Why is this happening now? *How* did this happen? I'm on the pill."

"It's never one-hundred percent effective. And weren't you sick when you went on that dance workshop weekend? If you were throwing up, there's a chance that the pill didn't absorb in your body the way it should."

Shit! I never thought about that. "Here I was telling Hayden not to worry, I'm on birth control." I scoff. "I should have known better."

"What's done is done. No point dwelling on what you can't change. You need to decide what you're going to do next."

The next thing I need to do is go home. And not to Hayden's house. Not with the news hanging around my neck. I need time to think. "Can you take me to my apartment please?"

Harper cocks an eyebrow. "You're not going back to Hayden's house? You know he'll freak out, right?"

I can't worry about how he'll react. I need to focus on what lays ahead for me. I place a hand on my stomach. *For us.* "I don't care. I need time alone."

Harper stares at me with concern. "Are you sure? You shouldn't be alone. Stay at my house if you need time away from Hayden."

"Thanks for the offer, but I'm fine. It's been two days, and I'm feeling better," I say, but Harper looks unconvinced. "I'm *fine*. Promise. If I need anything, or if things change, I'll call you."

Harper twists her mouth to the side like she's trying to determine if I'm telling the truth. "I don't like this, but if this is what you want, I'll take you home. If Hayden blows up at me, you'll babysit Avery every weekend for the next month...no, make that two months."

I giggle. "I might be in London."

"I don't care. You'll fly home to do it."

With all seriousness, I say, "Please don't say anything to Hayden about the baby."

"I won't." She clasps my hand. "He eventually needs to know."

We leave the park, and Harper gives me a ride home. After letting myself in with Harper's spare key, I drop onto the couch with exhaustion. Just when I thought my life was taking off, it comes crashing down in a ball of flames.

◆

For the next half hour, Hayden is blowing up my phone with calls and text messages. I don't have the energy to talk to him. Eventually, the phone goes silent, and I lay on the couch, flicking through photos on my phone.

I smile as I look at the ones I'd taken at the dance workshop weekend. I love seeing the children's smiling faces and their excitement for learning different dance styles and routines. I'm going to miss teaching and watching my students grow. Out of everything I've done in my life, teaching dance has been the most rewarding so far.

God, I'm acting like I'm not pregnant and still moving to London. I'd love to see how a corset looks with a swollen belly

My phone beeps with a message.

Harper: You better answer your phone. Hayden is out of his mind with worry! I had to tell him I took you home. So be prepared for a visit from a raging bull. Good luck with that xx

Damn it. I was hoping for more time alone. After the way he's been hovering over me the last two days, I should have expected he wouldn't sit at home and let me leave. If I text him and tell him I'm okay before he arrives, maybe he'll stay away. *Yeah, right.* What are the chances?

Me: Hey, Hayden. Sorry I forgot to call you and made you worry. I'm fine. Feeling great. Harper took me home because I'm more comfortable here. Thanks for looking after me.

I stare at the screen, waiting for a response. Nothing comes through. But two seconds later a knock pounds on my door. I freeze. Did Hayden fly here? I'm not ready to face him. Not with news that will change our lives.

"Alyssa, open up now!" He pounds harder on the door.

Before he breaks the door off its hinges, I trudge over and open it. Hayden has his arm raised and resting on the doorframe. His hair is disheveled, like he's run his fingers through it a thousand times. His face is dark with fury.

"Why the hell are you at your apartment?" he demands to know.

"I live here?" I shrug.

He narrows his eyes. "You should be home with me. What if something happens to you? *You're alone.*"

I'm going to have to get used to it. Well, only for another nine months, and then I'll never be alone. Excitement flutters in my heart. I never pictured my life with a baby. Not in the near future anyway. Now that it's happening, I can't think of anything I want more. I only wish the man my heart aches for felt the same.

This isn't a conversation we should have at my door. I move aside and gesture for him to come inside. He takes a seat in the armchair. I sink onto the couch opposite him. Picking up a cushion, I hug it tight against me. Like I'm using it to shield myself from Hayden and any negativity.

"Did you and Harper plan your day out so you could sneak home?" he asks with a little hurt shining from his eyes.

"No, it wasn't planned. While we were at the park, I wanted to come home, because being surrounded by my own things makes me more comfortable." *And because staying so close to you is tearing me apart.*

He stands like he's too agitated to sit. "I can take more of your stuff back to my place if you'd like."

"I don't want to be a bother." Why can't he drop it and leave? It's like he's sucking up the oxygen in the room and I'm gasping for breath. Being near him and not having him in my arms is too much.

His jaw clenches. "It's no bother."

"You look like it is. If you frown any harder, your face will crack." If I make him mad at me, maybe he'll leave in a huff. Then I can curl up in a ball and decide where I go from here. I'm not ready yet to tell him about the baby. It's still such a shock to me.

His shoulders rise and fall on a deep breath. "I'm frowning because you went behind my back and made a run for it! Was I not taking care of you well enough? You could have told me if you needed anything. I would give you anything."

Except unconditional love.

"I'm sorry if you feel like it was a secret get-me-away-from-Hayden mission. It wasn't. You've been wonderful. You've done so much for me. It's time for me to come home." *If I had my way, I'd live with you forever. I've never felt more at home than with you.*

"Come back with me. You're not well enough to be on your own." *If he said come back with me and we will face whatever the world throws at us—baby or not—because I love you, then I'd run into his arms.* He's not offering anything more than to take care of me while I'm injured.

"While I was at the park, I spoke to Dr. Hofstein. He said if I'm feeling better, he has no concerns with me coming back home on my own." *That's not what he said...or he could have, I might have blocked the conversation out after he told me I was pregnant.*

Hayden's body tenses. "Why didn't you tell me the doctor called? What else did he say?"

Once again, I see fear spreading over Hayden's face. How could he ever have told me he loved me? Love is growing as a couple. Accepting things that come unexpectedly and dealing with them together. Supporting each other when times are hard. He looks like he'd rather swallow razor blades than learn he's going to be a father.

"I told you. He said I can come back—"

He shakes his head. "About the blood test results."

"I'm not pregnant." The words spill from my mouth. I had no intention of lying. It was a reflex reaction. My way of protecting myself from Hayden's disappointment.

Hayden's body visibly sags, and he sinks onto the arm of the couch. Ice stabs through my heart. He doesn't want to be a father again. It's written clear as day over his face. Why did I hold a tiny bit of hope that he would be disappointed?

"Alyssa—"

I jump to my feet, ignoring the twinge of discomfort in my ankle. That pain is nothing compared to how my heart feels. "So, you've seen I'm okay and you know I'm not pregnant. I don't want to keep you here any longer than necessary. I'm sure you have things to catch up on since babysitting me." I need him out of the apartment—fast! Or I might break down.

"Can we talk?"

I hug my arms around my waist. "There's nothing left to talk about." There's nothing left between us.

As he gets to his feet, his gaze lands onto the magazines on the coffee table. On top of the pile is a travel brochure for London.

"When are you leaving? Surely you can't travel with a concussion."

That's not what I want to hear. Tell me not to go. Fight for me. Fight for us. Tell me you're disappointed I'm not pregnant. I want to yell at him. He stares at me expressionless, not saying any of those things.

"As soon as I'm cleared by the doctor, I'll make arrangements with my agent." I swallow hard. I don't know what I'm doing now or in the future. All I know is that I need Hayden to leave. Being near him is causing me so much pain I can barely stand.

He digs his hands into the pockets of his jeans. "Lily will miss you. You're her favorite teacher."

That little girl has nestled into my heart, filling it with love. It's hard leaving her too. Will she ever get the chance to meet her baby brother or sister? Will it be one more person from her family she'll never get to know? Can I do that to her?

"I'll miss her too," I say. *And what about you, Hayden? Will you miss me?*

Hayden blows out a breath, takes two steps toward me, and clasps his hands on my shoulders. "This is bullshit. We're talking to each other like we're strangers."

"Whose fault is that?" I shrug his hands off me and step away. "You let me believe there was something between us. I believed you when you told me you loved me." I bite my bottom lip, stopping it from quivering.

"There was something—*is* something between us. I do love you. Let's work on this." A yearning look flashes over his face.

Pressing a palm to my chest, I say, "We've had this conversation before. There's nothing to work on if you put conditions on our love. Besides, I'm moving to London. It will never work." This is it. The end of something I thought was going to be beautiful. Nothing in my life has ever felt so soul-destroying. "Goodbye, Hayden." I can't have him in my apartment a second longer.

Hayden gives me a long, sad stare before he nods, turns his back, and walks out of my apartment.

God, what have I done?

Chapter Thirty-Two

◆○◆

HAYDEN

It's been a week since I walked out of Alyssa's life. A week without seeing her face, hearing her laugh, watching her smile. A week without her love. There's an emptiness in my life—in my heart. No matter what I do, how hard I work or spend time with Lily, there's nothing that's filling it. Only Alyssa can do it. And I let her go. *God, will I ever get over this?* I rub my hand over my heart. How can I get over someone so amazing? So full of life. Someone who has brought *me* back to life.

She's leaving for London soon, living her dream, while I'm living my normal day-to-day life like I always have. In the past it made me content. I never wanted anything more until I met Alyssa. Now, apart from Lily, nothing gives me joy. Nothing is the same without Alyssa. I miss her.

Sitting in Lily's school hall, the lights dim, and the chatting parents go quiet for the school play to begin. I draw my attention to the stage and wait for Lily's grand entrance. She'd been so excited to have a solo dance and wanted to invite Alyssa to watch. I hated seeing the disappointment on Lily's face when I told her that Alyssa had other plans and couldn't make it.

I never wanted Lily to get attached to Alyssa, but it happened anyway. Enough for her to tell her teacher we were getting married. That was a teary conversation. It broke my heart listening to her tell me the reason she lied. She wanted to be like the other kids who had a mother and a father. And she had set her sights on Alyssa.

I yank my thoughts away from Alyssa and watch the children act and sing—giggling behind their hands when someone messes up their lines and pulling out chuckles from the audience. Some kids are dressed as trees, one is holding up the sun, and others are dressed as birds, flapping their arms in the air like they're flying.

Ten minutes later, Lily, wearing a white, flowy dress with large, colorful flowers stitched onto the skirt, skips onto the stage. From somewhere behind me, a spotlight shines on her. Spinning and leaping, she's dancing like she's on a major stage. Her face is bright with joy.

My baby girl is a star! The love I have for her bursts from my chest. How could I ever have thought raising her on my own was too hard? Yes, it came with challenges but nothing I couldn't overcome. I'd do it all over again, because she is fucking awesome.

I let my insecurities and warped beliefs of abandonment make me doubt how I truly feel. Yes, I wanted no more children, because I didn't want a relationship. Then Alyssa stumbled into my life and turned my world upside down, making me want more. When she told me she wasn't pregnant, I thought I'd experience a sense of relief. Instead, looking back, it was disappointment. Something had tugged at my gut to do something, *say* something, but with my fucked-up emotions I missed my chance. I'll never forget the sadness on Alyssa's face when I didn't tell her what she needed to hear.

Fuck! I'm such an idiot. I've messed up big time. So big, I don't know if I can make it right. Alyssa is the best thing to happen in mine and Lily's life. How could I have been so blind? Because of my stupidity, I've broken the heart of the only woman I've ever loved.

Lily's dance number finishes, and the audience claps. I stand and clap the loudest. *That's my girl!* I'm a proud father. With a smile on her face, she spots me and gives me a little wave before twirling off the stage. I've always said I wanted to give Lily everything I possibly can. And I'm going to continue to do so.

Suddenly the weight I've been carrying for eight years has lifted from my shoulders. What once freaked me out has no place in my heart anymore. Not when I could spend my life with Alyssa.

It's time to tell her what I've always known but was too scared to admit. My love is unconditional.

Chapter Thirty-Three

⸺◆⸺

ALYSSA

Standing in my apartment, I spin around and gaze at the luggage and boxes scattered throughout the room. Nerves, excitement, fright are all playing tug-of-war in my gut.

"This is really happening!" I draw in several deep, calming breaths. "I can't believe I'm doing this while pregnant." A big elephant of doubt creeps in and stomps on my excitement. "Oh God, what if I screw up? What if I'm no good?"

Harper places a hand on my arm. "You will be amazing. You're made for this. I know you will shine."

"How can you be so sure? You're my best friend. You have to say that."

Harper giggles. "If I thought you were crap, I'd tell you. You're not. You're an exceptional dancer, and I can't think of a role more suited for you." Harper frowns. "Are you changing your mind? It will be difficult with a baby on the way. I'm not sure how you're going to do it with a big, pregnant belly. Will you have someone to fill in?"

I'm not sure how I'm going to do it either. I've decided to do it anyway. It's too late to turn back now. I've signed contracts, accommodation is arranged, all I need is for the movers to collect my things. The buzz of excitement stirs again.

"I'm not changing my mind," I say, "I'll have plenty of stand-ins. This is exactly what I want."

Harper looks around the room. "This apartment will not be the same without you. We had some great memories here."

"It was never the same after you left." I sniff.

Giving me a kiss on the cheek and a hug, Harper pulls away and swipes a tear from her eye. My throat clogs up with emotion. "I can't wait to see you take on your new adventure."

I give a watery smile. "Thank you. You've been so amazing through all of this. I can't imagine doing this without your help. I love having you in my life."

Harper waves a hand. "Stop! You'll make me cry."

Laughing, I say, "You're already crying."

"There's something in my eye," she jokes.

I lean over the baby carrier sitting on the couch and look at Avery. Her eyes are blinking heavily with sleep. Rubbing a finger on her soft cheek, I blow her a kiss. "See you soon, sweetie."

"Well, I better go," Harper says. "Let me know when you're settled. I'll visit as soon as I can."

"I will."

After we say goodbye and she leaves, I stare at my apartment. I've had great times here. I've had sad times too. Nights thinking about and yearning for Hayden are some of the most difficult of my life.

I shake myself out of my melodrama. I've cried enough tears for that man. I don't have time to wallow in the past. I have my future to think about. It starts now. Picking up the luggage bag I need for now, I turn the lights off and lock the door behind me.

Time for a new life.

Time to forget the old one.

Two steps into my new life and the old one knocks the air from my lungs. From the bottom of the stairs, Hayden is staring up at me. My heart gallops in my chest. Will I ever get over him? I can tell myself it's only a matter of time, but everything in my body is telling me I'm lying to myself. He's forever stuck in my memories.

"What are you doing here?" I ask in a low, shaky voice.

His gaze flicks to the luggage in my hand. He doesn't answer, instead asks, "Are you leaving for London?"

I place the bag on the floor. I'm not telling him where I'm going until he answers my question. "What are you doing here?"

"I needed to see you—talk to you before you leave." There's a note of desperation to his voice.

"There's nothing left to say." I can't keep hashing out all the reasons we can't be together. It's too painful. Standing here looking at him hurts enough. I can't listen to him reject me again.

He drops his head, and when he looks back at me, there's sadness filling his eyes. "Please, Alyssa. There's so much I need to say. Things I should have said weeks ago. Can we go inside?"

How can I refuse when he's looking so vulnerable? I nod for him to come up. With my keys in my hand, I turn around and unlock the door. He takes the steps two at a time and follows me into the apartment. As he brushes past me, his citrusy scent surrounds me, making me want to bury my nose in his neck and breathe him in.

Placing my luggage bag at my feet, I stay next to the door in case the conversation gets too intense and I need a quick getaway. Steeling myself, I clasp my hands in front of me and ask, "What do you want to talk about?"

Hayden glances around the room filled with boxes. "You really are leaving?"

I nod. "Hayden, please tell me why you're here? I have a lot to do." And I'm about to fall apart. This is too much. I can't be in the same room with him anymore.

He rubs the back of his neck. "I fucked up. Badly."

Yeah, you broke my freaking heart.

He takes two steps toward me then stops, like he's unsure if he should get closer. Slipping his hands into the pockets of his jeans, he says, "I screwed things up between us. Made you believe that my love for you came with conditions. What I should have realized, what my *gut* was telling me was to hold onto you and never let go. Because you're my everything. My heartbeat. My breath. My soul. I've never wanted to open my heart to anyone until you literally fell at my feet, filling my life with so much love. Like a fool, I didn't trust myself with it. Thought you deserved better. With you in my life, I'm a better man."

My heart trembles, my legs shake, and I lock my knees to stay standing. "What are you saying?"

Anguish is etched on Hayden's face. "You opened up your heart, not only to me but for Lily, who adores you. My life is with you. I can't breathe when we're not together. Twinkle Toes, I love you."

I drop my head and take a deep breath, willing back the tears threatening to spill. *He can't say things like that to me. Not when he can't accept what life has thrown at us.*

When I've calmed down slightly, I lift my face. "You have told me you loved me before. It wasn't enough. When we had the pregnancy scare you freaked out. Pulled away from me. *Ended* us." The torment at remembering him retreating wells up inside me. "You were so relieved when I told you I wasn't pregnant. I can't live like that. Love is experiencing the good things as well as the unexpected." I'm never going to say the pregnancy is bad, because it's a blessing I never thought I needed.

Raking his fingers through his hair, he blows out a breath. "I'd been living my life with so much fear, that was the reaction I thought I was supposed to have. After what happened with Rachel, it was a reflex reaction. Then, as I looked at my daughter, dove deep into my feelings—dusted the bad shit off the good ones—I realized I wasn't relieved you weren't pregnant. I was *disappointed*."

My heart stops beating for a second. "I don't believe you." How can I when he was so adamant he didn't want children? I don't want to hope for something he's not ready to give.

He takes my hands and holds them in his. They're shaking...or is that mine? "Believe it. I won't lie, it took time to work through my shit. I want to kick my own ass for letting you down. I'm sorry I made you believe I never wanted a baby with you. God, if you forgive me, I want to fill you with as many babies as possible. Can you forgive me?" His eyes shimmer with unshed tears. Oh, I want to pull him into my arms.

His words fill me with so much joy...hope for our future. If only I hadn't lied to him. How will he react? "It's not that simple."

He lifts my hands and places them on his chest. His heart pounds against my palms. "It can be. Stay with me. Don't go to London. No...fuck that. Performing is your dream. Go and me and Lily will follow you. There's nothing keeping me here."

I'm breathless. "You'd do that? Pack up and move your life to be with me in London?"

Staring fiercely into my eyes, he says with conviction, "In a heart-beat."

This man is giving me everything I want. His love, his child, his life. But I can't accept it. Not until I tell him the truth.

I've never been so scared in my life.

With hesitation, I step away from him. My heart is thumping wildly in my chest. "Hayden, there's something I need to tell you."

His brows furrow. "You can tell me anything."

Rubbing my hand up and down my arm, I take a deep breath. "You may not want to be with me after what I'm about to tell you."

"Alyssa, what's going on?" he asks with concern.

Nibbling my bottom lip, I avert my eyes. "When I told you I wasn't pregnant, I lied." A gust of air expels from my lungs.

His gaze flicks to my stomach, and he narrows his eyes. "Are you saying you're *pregnant*?"

I nod. "I'm sorry I lied. The day I went for a walk in the park with Harper and the doctor called with the results, I was so con-fused—scared. Unsure of what my future looked like. And then you asked me about the results with what looked like pure fear on your face, I panicked, and the lie slipped from my mouth. When you looked so relieved, I didn't know how to tell you the truth."

Hayden rubs the back of his neck and slowly paces the room. "You're moving to London. Were you not going to tell me?"

Tears well behind my eyes. "At first, that was the plan."

He raises an eyebrow. "At first?"

"I knew I couldn't keep this from you. I needed time to build up the courage to tell you. It was a mistake. It wasn't fair to you. If I could change things, I would." Will he forgive me? Will he change his mind about wanting a life with me?

Hayden stops pacing. "I wouldn't."

Jerking my head back with surprise, I say, "You wouldn't?"

He shakes his head, walks toward me, and gathers me into his arms, enveloping me in his warmth. "If you had told me the truth, it might have taken me longer to realize what an idiot I've been. How stupid I was for letting you go. You have nothing to be sorry about. This is on me. I acted like a fool. You are my world, Twinkle Toes. I can't let you go."

My head drops onto his chest. This time the tears flow down my cheeks. "Are you sure this is what you want?" I couldn't bare it if he pushed me away again.

Tilting my face up, he brushes the tears off my cheeks with his thumbs. I stare into his eyes filled with love. "I've never been surer of anything in my life. You are it for me. Whether or not there's a baby. Wherever you go, I go. Tell me you feel the same. Tell me you want me too. Because I love you so fucking much, I feel like my heart is about to explode."

That's exactly how my heart feels. "I love you, Hayden. You are it for me too."

Cupping my cheeks in his hands, his lips crash against mine. We pour everything we have into the kiss. All our love, hopes, and dreams. When we finally pull apart, our chests are heaving and we're gasping for breath.

He gives me the most beautiful stop-my-heart smile. "London, here we come!"

"Umm, about that. I have something to tell you."

He pulls back slightly, but his arms wrap firmly around my waist, like he never wants to let me go. I hope it stays that way. "What is it?" he asks.

I pick at a button on his shirt. "I'm not going to London."

He cocks an eyebrow and glances around the room. "But...your luggage. Your things are packed."

I dip my head with a sheepish smile. "I turned down the role. Being pregnant won't work, not if I can't commit one-hundred percent to it."

Hayden rubs his hands from my shoulders down my arms and back again. "After the baby is born, you can always get stuck into it again. You'll get another part."

Smiling at his confidence in me, I say, "I'm not auditioning anymore. I'm done with Broadway."

"It's your dream. Don't let a baby stop you. We can do this together."

God, I love this man. My man. We are in this life together, and I've never been happier.

"I thought it was my dream," I say. "Then I realized it was a dream I'd created for my parents, to make them happy. All my life they made me believe that performing on a grand stage is what I needed to strive for. Nothing less was good enough. I kept pushing myself. Not for me—for them. If I was as good at something as Christina, then they would be proud of me. And when I told them about London, for a moment they were. Until I told them my plans had changed. The disappointment they showed when I told them I was pregnant dripped off in waves. How could I be so irresponsible they said. What an embarrassment I've been to the family." I walked away from that conversation with my held head high. Finally believing this is my life. I'm living it the way I want to. Never again will I let someone else create my dreams. "I realized it was teaching kids at Miss Lucia's dance studio that made me happy. Seeing the smiles on my students' faces when they dance gives me more joy than anything I can do on Broadway. Teaching is my new career." Pride pumps out my chest.

"You're staying on as a teacher?" he asks.

"I'm buying the dance studio from Miss Lucia and moving into the apartment upstairs." With a baby, I thought it would be easier to live as close to the studio as possible. "That's why I'm packing."

"That's fantastic. You're an amazing teacher, and the kids love you. You're going to kill it! I'm so proud of you." He pauses for a moment, then says, "There's one problem."

"Oh, what is it?" God, I thought we laid everything out. There can't be any more surprises.

"You can't live in the apartment above the dance studio," he says with a serious tone, yet the corners of his mouth twitch.

"It's a great space. Plenty of room for a baby. We'll be comfortable," I say, playing along. I have a feeling I know what he's going to suggest.

He shakes his head. "You're moving in with me. In my house. In my bed. You, my beautiful Twinkle Toes, are not leaving my side."

"Maybe I want to live on my own," I tease.

He buries his nose in my neck. His warm breath spreads over my skin, making my insides quiver. "Not with what I have planned for you...every...single...day. You'll be begging to move in with me."

Oh yes. My head tilts to the side. I can get used to this.

Hayden abruptly jerks his head back. With wide eyes, he pulls away. "There's something I need to do." Getting onto his knees, he presses his lips against my belly. The sweet gesture melts my insides. On a soft whisper, he says, "I can't wait to meet you."

I can't contain the happy tears rolling down my face. How has my life turned out so perfect?

Back on his feet, an expression of awe lights his face. "We're having a baby," he says like it's only now hitting him. A huge grin spreads across his face. "We're having a baby!" he whoops. Wrapping his arms around my waist, he hugs me tight. "You have made me the happiest man in the world. I can't wait to grow our little family. Lily is going to be so excited. Thank you for choosing me to love." Oh God, my heart is expanding with each word.

"Our lives will change in a huge way. Are you ready?"

He kisses the tip of my nose, my cheeks, then my lips. "I've never been more ready for anything in my life." His voice fills with emotion. "Twinkle Toes, bring it on."

Epilogue

ALYSSA

Six months later

Standing in the wings of the stage, I look over my team of young dancers. Some bright with excitement. Some jittery with nerves. The studio's showcase is a buzz of activity backstage.

As the audience takes their seats and the lights dim, I gather the dancers together. "Have fun tonight. I can't wait to see how amazing you all are."

Dance after dance, my heart fills with pride watching them. They have learned so much over the past few months. All their hard work and dedication is showing.

One dancer has my eyes welling with tears. Lily is so beautiful and graceful, and the sweetest girl I've ever met. And I get to call her mine. I glance at the sparkling ring on my finger. After the baby is born, I'm marrying the love of my life. Hayden insisted we should do it sooner, but I want both our girls present when we commit our lives to one another.

When the recital comes to a close, I walk on stage and take a final bow with the performers. It doesn't take long to spot Hayden in the audience watching on with pride. Next to him are my parents. It took them weeks to get over the shock of me quitting Broadway. They still can't understand why I want to throw away a dance career for the studio. But somehow, surprisingly, they've come around. I have a sneaking suspicion Hayden had something to do with it. Christina is in Paris performing, but she remembered to send me a text to wish me luck.

My heart is full. I sometimes need to pinch myself because I think I'm dreaming. Out of all the dreams I thought I wanted, nothing compares to the one I'm living. I wouldn't trade this for the world.

When the curtain closes, I head backstage to congratulate my students. They're smiling, laughing, and cheering at a job well done.

From behind, warm arms wrap around my very pregnant belly. "Congratulations, Twinkle Toes."

I turn in Hayden's embrace and rest my hands on his shoulders. "The kids were amazing. I'm so proud of them."

"You're amazing. You put together a fantastic show."

"There were moments when I thought it was going to fall apart and we'd have no show." I chuckle. "I'm glad it's over."

"Are you happy? Do you regret giving up on Broadway?"

"I'm so happy. I haven't given Broadway a second thought. You and Lily are everything to me." I drop my head to glance at my growing stomach. "I can't wait for our baby." My throat clogs with emotion and tears well in my eyes. Damn these hormones. I cry over nothing these days. But this isn't nothing. This is my life. My family. "I love you, Hayden."

"I'll never tire of hearing those words. I love you too, Twinkle Toes." Hayden places a soft kiss on my lips.

A cheerful chorus of "Whoooo!" explodes behind us. We break apart and laugh. Turning toward the kids, I see that some of them are pulling kissy faces while some are making gagging actions. One girl who catches my eye and heart has the biggest smile on her face. Lily breaks away from her friends and runs toward us. Wrapping her in my arms, I feel so blessed to be a part of her life.

"Your solo was beautiful," I tell her.

"Thanks, Mom." She beams a smile at me.

God, when Lily calls me mom, my heart swells with love. How did I get so lucky?

Hayden brushes his hand over Lily's head. "Hey, Lily Pily, do you want to sleep at Uncle Finn and Aunt Harper's house tonight? You can tell them all about how wonderful your recital was."

Oh, I'm onto him. Hayden has something on his mind, and if it's what I'm thinking, I'm all in.

Lily tilts her head back. "Can I really?"

He looks over her head and gives me a sexy wink. "Absolutely."

After all the parents have picked up their children, Hayden takes me by the hand. Lily has rushed to the entrance of the stage to wait for us.

"Are you ready for what I have planned for you when we get home?" he asks.

"What do you have in mind?" I can hardly wait.

"First, I'll rub your feet. Then I'll get you comfortable while I massage lotion all over your body. We'll finish up with a warm bubble bath where I'll wash you from head to toe."

"Oh, that sounds like heaven." At eight months pregnant, this is a man who knows what I need. "I love you, Hayden."

He brushes a thumb across my cheek. "I love you too." He glances to where Lily is waiting, then at my belly and back at me. "I'm one lucky man."

Don't want Unconditional to end? Join my newsletter to see what Hayden and Alyssa are up to. Also, get a sneak peek at Lucas and Penny's story, Unbreakable coming soon!

Get it here: Unbreakable. The extended epilogue.

Acknowledgements

Firstly, I want to thank my loving family Tom, Jaime, Ryan and Leah. They continually show me love and support and are my number one fans. A huge thank you to TL Swan and the Cygnet Inkers. The ladies in the group are amazing and always have an answer to my many questions. To my wonderful beta readers Jillian, Michelle and Ashleigh thank you for taking the time to read Unconditional. Your feedback and praise was heartwarming.

Finally to my wonderful readers. You make me keep doing this. I'm so grateful you read my books. Thank you from the bottom of my heart! xx

About Sonia Stanizzo

Sonia Stanizzo is a contemporary romance author living in the beautiful south coast of New South Wales, Australia with her husband and three children. When she's not dreaming up stories about couples and their road to finding love, sometimes bumpy but always a lot of fun, she can be found taking pole dancing lessons, reading and writing.

Thank you so much for reading Unconditional. I hope you enjoyed meeting Hayden and Alyssa and loved them as much as I loved writing them.

Say Hello!

Want to follow me on social media? Follow me here:

Facebook: facebook.com/soniastanizzowriter

Instagram: instagram.com/soniastanizzowriter

Tiktok: ticktok.com/@soniastanizzowriter

Sonia's Website: soniastanizzo

Sonia's email: soniastanizzo@gmail.com

Join my newsletter for free books, new releases and giveaways:

Newsletter

More Titles By Sonia Stanizzo

Trouble in Love Series

The Trouble with Mr. Pretty

Chasing Trouble

Trouble in Disguise
Acting on Love Series

Risk Taker

Rule Breaker

Matchmaker
Alessi Brother Series

Unforgettable

Unconditional

Unbreakable